George Stewart

Curiosities of Glasgow Citizenship

As exhibited chiefly in the business career of its old commercial aristocracy

George Stewart

Curiosities of Glasgow Citizenship
As exhibited chiefly in the business career of its old commercial aristocracy

ISBN/EAN: 9783337423148

Printed in Europe, USA, Canada, Australia, Japan

Cover: Foto ©Andreas Hilbeck / pixelio.de

More available books at **www.hansebooks.com**

CURIOSITIES

OF

GLASGOW CITIZENSHIP,

AS EXHIBITED CHIEFLY IN THE BUSINESS CAREER

OF ITS

OLD COMMERCIAL ARISTOCRACY.

BY GEORGE STEWART,

Librarian of the Chamber of Commerce and Manufactures in Glasgow.

" *Forsameikle as the publict offices of this realme ar the principall nervis and synnowis quhilk joynis the haill body*
" *and retenis and kepis the same in ordour, quhilk being confoundit and out of frame, the haill consequently mon dissolue*
" *and cum to nocht. It is fund thairfoir meit and convenient that sic men be placeit in the saids offices as ar vpricht,*
" *of gude iugement, and ar apt and meit to brouke the qualitie of the posisoun,   *   *   *   sua that all thingis may gang*
" *fordwart vniformelie, quietnes may be kepit, and the pure subiectis easit thairby.*"—*Earl of Mar's Appointment to the
Regency, in Appendix to Scott's Acts, 1571.*

GLASGOW:

JAMES MACLEHOSE, ST. VINCENT STREET,

Publisher to the University.

1881.

TO

THE PRESIDENT, DIRECTORS, AND MEMBERS

OF THE

CHAMBER OF COMMERCE AND MANUFACTURES

IN THE CITY OF GLASGOW,

These Fragmentary Memorials

OF

THE FOUNDERS OF THE CHAMBER

ARE RESPECTFULLY INSCRIBED.

CONTENTS.

PREFACE.

Some time ago the Directors of the Chamber of Commerce suggested the preparation of a few notes descriptive of the circumstances that gave rise to the Chamber, and of the transactions which, at its formation, formed the chief subject of deliberation and discussion at its meetings. I readily acted upon the suggestion, and found the study one of great interest. It, however, occurred to me, that those curious and complicated details might be rendered much more attractive and interesting if, instead of being presented in a dry historical or statistical form, they could in some way be associated with the lives and labours of the most notable of those men who were the early Directors and Members of the Chamber, and to whom, it is no exaggeration to say, modern Glasgow owes a debt of honour and gratitude she can never pay.

With the view, chiefly, of still further enhancing and perpetuating the memory of the Old Glasgow Commercial Aristocracy, who guided the town through times of great difficulty and depression, these Sketches have been undertaken. I have been very careful to verify the accuracy of the incidents which are woven up with the narratives. If, however, through inadvertence or insufficient information, any mistakes have crept in, I trust this will not lessen the interest of the work, or detract from whatever value it may possess.

I am indebted to various friends for help with the "SHORT
BIOGRAPHICAL NOTICES" at the end of the volume, especially with
the following :—

<table>
<tr><td>HUMPHREY BARBOUR.</td><td>ALEXANDER M'CAUL.</td></tr>
<tr><td>JAMES BLACK.</td><td>WALTER EWING MACLAE.</td></tr>
<tr><td>ALEXANDER BROWN.</td><td>MATHEW PERSTON.</td></tr>
<tr><td>JAMES BROWN.</td><td>THOMAS SHEDDEN.</td></tr>
<tr><td>JOHN BUCHANAN.</td><td>WILLIAM SHORTRIDGE.</td></tr>
<tr><td>ROBERT, GEORGE, AND ANDREW
BUCHANAN.</td><td>ARCHIBALD SMITH.</td></tr>
<tr><td>ROBERT COWAN.</td><td>WALTER STIRLING.</td></tr>
<tr><td>ROBERT EUING.</td><td>JOHN TENNENT.</td></tr>
<tr><td>WALTER EWING.</td><td>DAVID TODD.</td></tr>
<tr><td>JAMES FINLAY.</td><td>WILLIAM WARDLAW.</td></tr>
<tr><td>KIRKMAN FINLAY.</td><td>DAVID WATSON.</td></tr>
<tr><td>JOHN FREELAND.</td><td>WILLIAM WHYT.</td></tr>
<tr><td>GEORGE SCOTT FREELAND.</td><td>JOHN YOUNG.</td></tr>
<tr><td>ARCHIBALD HENDERSON.</td><td>MAGISTRATES AND MERCHANTS OF
GREENOCK.</td></tr>
<tr><td>ANDREW HOUSTON.</td><td>MAGISTRATES AND MERCHANTS OF
PAISLEY.</td></tr>
<tr><td>ROBERT HOUSTON OR HOUSTON-RAE.</td><td></td></tr>
</table>

I have also to acknowledge my obligations to Mr. W. BOYD
ANDERSON for the article on "GLASGOW AT THE UNION," as well as
for his labours in preparing the Index and in revising the proofs
as the work passed through the press.

GEORGE STEWART.

CHAMBER OF COMMERCE,
GLASGOW, *October*, 1881.

GLASGOW

AT THE

UNION OF THE PARLIAMENTS,

1 7 0 7.

THE busy inhabitant of the city in the present day can find nowhere a stronger contrast to the din of its hammers, the hum of its machinery, and its commercial hurry, than the quiet town of Glasgow, as it stood in the beginning of last century. The town was little more than a village, lying between the Cathedral and the River, along the line of High Street, Saltmarket, and Bridgegate, with the cross streets of Rottenrow and Drygate at the north, and Trongate and Gallowgate towards the south. So limited was the circuit, that when threatened by the Highlanders at the Earl of Mar's rebellion in 1715, the inhabitants and militiamen dug a trench round it for protection. The town at the Union did not extend further east than St. Mungo's Lane in Gallowgate, or further west than Stockwell Street. Even these modest boundaries were not fully occupied, there being still numerous vacant spaces, while many of the houses in High Street could boast of gardens and orchards behind, and looked out upon green fields and open country. Hutcheson's Hospital, then in High Street, possessed well-kept gardens, much resorted to by the public. Indeed, the city, consisting of little else than one long street, could easily afford room for gardens behind the houses.

Though thus primitive in arrangement, the town possessed many buildings of considerable grandeur. Writing of Glasgow in 1693, Captain John Slezer of the Artillery Company, and Surveyor of Stores and Magazines in Scotland, remarks in his *Theatrum Scotiæ* :—" If we respect the largeness of the city, the number and " stateliness of its public and private buildings, its commerce with ". foreign nations, and the opulency of its inhabitants, it is the chief " of all the cities of the kingdom next to Edinburgh." Captain Slezer's statement may be taken as authoritative, for he visited and sketched views of most of the burghs in Scotland.

But with all this, the town to modern eyes could not have been very inviting, for the streets were narrow, almost if not entirely devoid of pavement and causeway, and totally unlighted at night. There was little attention paid to cleanliness out of doors, and but for the small size of the town, and ready access of fresh air, the effluvia from household refuse must have seriously impaired the health of the inhabitants.

In fact, Glasgow then was a small town hardly emerged from the customs of the middle ages. It retained quite as much of feudal custom and manner as it had acquired of modern thought and development. The town was governed, as now, by the Lord Provost, Bailies, and Council, but their mode of appointment was vastly different. Glasgow was a "close corporation," and elected the Town Council in the following manner. The Lord Provost was elected annually by the retiring Provost and three Bailies ;

three new Bailies were next elected by the new and retiring Provosts and the three retiring Bailies ; and then followed the election of the ordinary members of the Town Council, in like manner, by the old and new Provosts and Bailies, consisting of thirteen members from the merchant rank, and twelve from the trades rank. The Dean of Guild and Deacon Convener, both members of Council, were also elected by the Town Council. They were chosen respectively from three members of each of the Merchants' House and Trades' House, presented to the Town Council by these bodies. The Council administered the affairs of the burgh in rather a primitive fashion, taking a closer oversight of the private doings of the inhabitants than is thought either prudent or necessary now-a-days, and being above all things keenly alive to their own dignity. But more of this afterwards. A visitor of the Maltmen was appointed, whose duties were to visit the taverns and test the quality of the liquor; and in the same way a visitor of the Gardeners was chosen.

Police did not exist; the people, under charge of the Bailies or their own chosen captains, doing the necessary watching- and warding. In 1706 a petition was presented to the Town Council, which shows how police duty was performed. Each master of a family was required to attend in turn, or send a sufficient substitute, to do guard duty. The guard was divided into companies, under a captain, each company being summoned by drum at two o'clock P.M., and kept on duty from three till the same hour next day. As the burgh was unlighted at night, the duties of the guard were occasionally pretty onerous, for the inhabitants were not so well behaved at all times as they are now. In order to keep the peace, all women, boys, young men, and servants were prohibited from being upon the streets "after cloud of night" above a certain number; but it would have conduced more to quietness had other members of the community been restrained instead. The names of all strangers in the town, whether staying in public or private houses, were handed in to the captain of the guard by ten o'clock.

The means of communication with other districts were very limited. Of roads, such as we know them, there were none. There were tracks called roads between the different towns, but these were traversed only by horses. Merchandise was carried on pack horses, necessarily in small quantities, and slowly. Herring and other merchandise were taken in this way as far as Irvine for shipment, and a portion of the foreign produce arriving at Port-Glasgow was conveyed by the same means to Glasgow, the remainder coming up in small boats by the river. In 1709 the first horse post was established between Glasgow and Edinburgh, correspondence formerly being carried by foot postmen. News was scanty, and was conveyed to the city chiefly in a news-letter from a person in Edinburgh appointed by the Council. The communication was written in the shape of a letter to the Council at stated intervals, and contained all information of importance or interest. This was called the " Newsletter." General information was limited, and often of the most shadowy kind.

Scotland did not then possess the wealth of which it can now boast, and Glasgow was no exception; but the rites of hospitality were not neglected. In 1720 the Lord Provost was allowed £40 sterling annually, because the " Chiefe Magistrat, whiles in that " station, is oblig't to keep up a port suitable thereto, and cannot " but be at considerable charge in furnishing his house with wines, " for the entertainment of gentlemen who may have occasion to " wait on him at his house."

Presents were occasionally given instead of money for services to the town, and these often took the shape of herrings. At one time the treasurer was ordered to have a warrant ready "for the "sum of four hundreth four scoir twa punds ten shilling Scots, "deburst be him for herring given to the tounes advocates, and "vthirs the tounes pensioners, this last year; and for carriage of "the said herring to Edinburgh, and for their said advocats their "fialls and pensionne." There are other instances of similar presents of the "Glasgow Magistrate," and also of a free burgess ticket, and even tobacco, being given. The expenses of journeys to Edinburgh show the style of living, which was open-handed and convivial. In 1703, when the Deacon-Convener attended the "ryding of the Parliament" in Edinburgh, with others, his expenses were £263 18s. Scots, of which £188 6s. was spent at some treats and entertainments given by the Provost.

The town, apparently, did not despise secret service, or, at least, did not care always to engross in their minutes the cause of every donation, for one item of the treasurer's accounts is 51s. for four pounds of tobacco given "to ane of the tounes friends att "Edinburgh"; and another is £120 Scots "to ane friend for doing "of ane good turne to the toune."

Glasgow sent only one representative to the Parliament of Great Britain at the Union, jointly with the burghs of Renfrew, Rutherglen, and Dumbarton. Each burgh elected a commissioner, and these commissioners chose the Member of Parliament, the presiding commissioner—the office being occupied in rotation— having a casting as well as a deliberative vote in case of equality. The only burgh which attained the dignity of one member to itself was Edinburgh.

Glasgow was the second city in the country, Edinburgh first.

In 1695 the assessment upon the land rent for six months' supply was imposed as follows :—

> City of Edinburgh, - - £3183 8s. Scots per month.
> City of Glasgow, - - £1800 do. do.

This proportion was observed up till 1704. After that date Glasgow fell in assessible value, while Edinburgh increased, and the cess or land tax was imposed in the same proportions as in 1690, viz.:—

> City of Edinburgh, - - £4000 Scots monthly.
> City of Glasgow, - - £1440 do. do.

This proportion was continued till the Union. At that period there was no return of the rental of the burgh, but a few years later it was carefully valued at £7840 2s. 6d. sterling.

Towards the close of the century the town suffered severely from commercial depression—more than either before or since. From the earliest times the town had steadily increased in wealth, importance, and population ; but now we find the population had decreased in numbers. At the restoration of Charles the Second in 1660 it stood at 14,678 ; and at the Revolution, 28 years later, it had fallen to 11,948. Fifty years passed before the population attained the former figure. In 1708 it was only 12,766. So serious was this "decay in trade," as the Magistrates called it, that nearly 500 houses were untenanted, and the rents of the rest had fallen nearly one-third. The highest rent then paid for a house was £100 Scots, or £8 6s. 8d. sterling. A few years later rents had but little advanced. The highest rent paid for a shop, at the first valuation in 1712, was £5 sterling, and the lowest 12s. The average rent for the 202 shops in the town was £623 15*s.* 4*d.* sterling, being considerably less than what is now paid for one large shop in any of our busiest quarters. But we do not care to be further statistical.

At such a time we must expect to find the manners and social condition of the people primitive and unrefined. Thomas Tucker, reporting to the Commissioners for Appeals for England in 1656, with a view to place the Customs and Excise on a better footing, gives us no very flattering picture of the now fashionable Highlands. He says that the western part of Scotland and the islands are inhabited by the old Scots or wild Irish, who speak their language, and "live by feeding cattle up and down the hills, or else "fishing and fowleing, and formerly (till they have of late been "restrayned) by plaine downeright robbing and stealeing." The plain downright robbing and stealing was resumed, we know, at a much later period.

Although this is not applied to Glasgow, we cannot expect much refinement in a town which was the chief mart for a district whose inhabitants—except, perhaps, a few of the wealthiest and best educated—could hold but the scantiest communication with further advanced parts of the kingdom. We catch a glimpse now and again of the people in every-day life from the records of the time. The people were strong in their likes and dislikes. About the end of the sixteenth century, the Rev. Mr. Montgomerie of Stirling was presented to the Cathedral as Bishop. The Provost and several of the leading Burgesses proceeded to the church on a Sunday to have him inducted, and found the pulpit already occupied by Mr. Howie of Cambuslang, who declined to vacate in favour of the Bishop. A scuffle ensued in church, where some blood was shed; the reverend gentleman was dragged from the pulpit, and shamefully maltreated, his beard being torn, and several of his teeth knocked out.

A century later, the same uncompromising spirit led the Covenanters of Glasgow and the west into the field ; and at the time of the Union we find the Presbyterians very little modified. After an anti-Union sermon in the Tron Church in 1706, the congregation rushed in a body to the Cross and publicly burned the proposed Articles of Union. But in face of all this, the Sunday was but irreverently observed. Taverns and several shops were open, and people, in some cases, carried on their usual business, while others devoted the day to pleasure. This was formally prohibited, but with little ultimate success, for the prohibition was renewed within twelve years, and heavier penalties for infringement imposed, and was followed in 1744—fully forty years after—by a third Act, containing "rules for suppressing profaneness" at great length. But these enactments were not altogether allowed to remain a dead letter, for profanity and Sabbath breaking were punished, and at times severely, although it must have been only in more flagrant cases.

Nothing was more vigorously resented than any defiance of constituted authority, and Magistrates insisted upon due honour being shown to their dignity on all occasions. Expressed contempt of the Magistrates was sometimes visited with both fine and imprisonment ; and even the failure to lift the bonnet to a passing Bailie was considered worthy of punishment, the delinquent requiring to go bare-headed and bare-footed to the Cross to ask pardon of God and the Bailie for his contumely. Open contempt of religion and profanity were punished in the same way.

The people lived in an unostentatious and economical manner. There were very few self-contained houses, even the more wealthy and prominent citizens contenting themselves with a flat in a tenement. Thus, in 1712, we find three ladies of title—among them Lady Glencairn—occupying, along with seven others, houses in "Spreull's Land" in Trongate, the highest rent being only £10 3s. 4d. sterling. These separate dwellings were approached by a common stair leading from the street, often kept in a very untidy condition. The single houses were the property of only the most wealthy. Many of them had considerable claims to architectural beauty, but others were erected with more regard to internal comfort than outward appearance. It would seem as if some of the proprietors thought the town had attained its utmost extension, for they built houses with gardens in places which before this present century were absorbed in the city itself, while the vast majority are now entirely obliterated, and their sites and grounds occupied by four-storey tenements. But the houses of the lower classes were miserable enough. A most disastrous fire occurred in 1652, destroying about one-third of the city; and a second in 1677 was scarcely less severe. The cause of this extensive destruction of property lay in the construction of the houses. They were built almost entirely of wood; and so narrow were the streets the wonder is that nearly the whole town was not burned down. The Magistrates attributed the fires to Divine wrath for the town's iniquities, and prayed that they might be spared a similar visitation. They were, however, sufficiently worldly-wise to see that wooden houses would burn without a special Providence thereto assisting, so their instructions to the Burgesses did not logically follow their statement of the cause of the fire, unless they meant their instructions in defiance. They ordained that, in future, all houses in High Street to be rebuilt or repaired should be built of stone, both for the security of the inhabitants and the adornment of the town.   By the summary clearing away by fires of so many houses, the Magistrates also wisely took the opportunity, we are informed, of having several of the streets widened.   But they were not willing, or perhaps not able, to enforce in full these new regulations; for out of a fund raised to relieve the distress occasioned by the second fire, payments were made to enable proprietors to rebuild, and those who used wood for a portion of the houses were helped as well as those who used stone, although not to so great an extent. It is comparatively recently that the last of these wooden houses have been removed, and poor enough places they were.

The customs and ideas of the people were primitive.   The belief in witches was still strongly held by all but the most advanced; and several poor women were imprisoned for having too intimate an acquaintance with the evil one and his black arts. Very little evidence was required to prove the character of a " witch," and a great deal to rebut the suspicion.   In 1697 some witches were imprisoned in the Tolbooth for several months.

Justice was administered often in the Oriental fashion.   The Magistrates, instead of going to "the gate of the city," stood at the Cross to hear the complaints of the people.

The rule of the Magistrates, while both judicial and executive, was sometimes exercised in rather too paternal a fashion. The remembrance of the dancing school is very pleasant to most of us, for we had no lessons to learn at home, and plenty of sweethearts.   But at this period learning to dance was quite a solemn affair, and opening a dancing school was not to be done without special permission.   With greater care for the sober and moral upbringing of the young than the objects of this care thought necessary, an application to keep a dancing school was granted upon such conditions as would speedily extinguish these institutions now-a-days. The master was bound to behave himself soberly, and teach at seasonable hours, which meant at hours thought suitable by the Magistrates and not by him. But, further, he was not allowed to hold any balls, and had so to arrange his classes that there should be no promiscuous dancing of young men and young women. So strict was this last condition that one class was ordered to be out of the house before another came in. The punishment for infringement was expulsion from the burgh.

But the Magistrates also looked after the creature comforts of the people as well as their calisthenics. In 1675 they admitted Michael Leiper a burgess gratis, and let him sit rent free, on condition of his taking a good house and serving the lieges as "ane "commoune coock." The same privilege of burgess-ship was accorded to Mrs. Hamilton several years later, but she had to pay 50 merks for the privilege of the "cookrie." The advantages of good cooking were fully realised; and to bring them within range of the people, a grant of £10 sterling per annum was made to a Mr. Lochhead—some years after the Union—to defray the loss of the articles made in teaching and remaining unsold.

The town, also, had some regard for music. In 1691 a gentleman, Mr. Lewis de France, agreed to teach music for certain fees, and some of the poor gratis, in consideration of £100 Scots paid annually by the town. To secure him as many pupils as possible he was granted a monopoly, no public schools being allowed to teach music.

There was then no poor law; but the unfortunate were not left wholly to take care of themselves. Besides the institutions for private benevolence—such as Hutcheson's Hospital, the Merchants' and Trades' Houses, which helped their poorer brethren—there were even then several public charities and hospitals—such as

St. Ninian's or the Leper's Hospital, founded by Lady Lochow; St. Nicholas' Hospital, and the Town's Hospital, capable of holding upwards of 150 inmates. M'Ure, writing in 1736, says of the Town's Hospital, that "the building is of modern fashion, and "exceeds that of any kind in Europe, and admired by strangers," who say that "anything of that kind at Rome or Venice comes not "up to the magnificence of this building, when it is finished, "resembling more like a palace than a habitation for necessitous "old people and children." Besides this, special cases of misfortune received attention, and numerous payments were made to those in reduced circumstances. For instance, there was a payment of £5 Scots "for curing John Phillips' child of a broken leg."

There is an old regulation of the Merchants' and Trades' Houses regarding apprentices, "to move them to take their "master's daughter in marriage before any other, which will be a "great comfort and support to freemen;" of which regulation, no doubt, apprentices were willing enough to avail themselves. As if the charms of the lady were not sufficient inducement, the lucky apprentice son-in-law was admitted burgess at a reduced rate.

The College had then acquired considerable importance. The students in 1702 numbered 402, and were even more noisy and turbulent than those of our own day. There was a meeting of the whole body of students with the Principal and Professors once a week, on Saturdays, to hear a Latin oration by the elder students, and to discuss matters of discipline. Despite this the students were irrepressible, and sometimes made their presence felt in a disagreeable manner. In one row they invaded the house of a citizen, destroyed his door, and broke several articles in the house. We have known of similar accidents since that time, *et quorum magna pars fui.*

There is no more common subject of conversation in Glasgow than the rapid rise of the city during this century, and people often take credit to themselves or their fathers for the whole of it. But it is unjust to the memory of those in the beginning of the eighteenth century, and even earlier, to deny them the honour of laying the foundation of our prosperity.

The commencement of the trade of the city dates from a period long anterior to the Union of the Parliaments, or even the Union of the Crowns. It is not within the scope of this sketch to deal with the earliest history of our trade; and we, accordingly, confine our remarks on this as on other subjects to the periods shortly before and after 1707. We merely notice that our first foreign commerce was apparently in fish—the export of salmon and herrings to France, Holland, Norway, England, and Ireland—and the import of the produce of these countries in return. So early as 1605, when the Merchants' House was incorporated, the Letter of Guildry requires that the Dean of Guild shall be always a merchant and a merchant sailor and merchant venturer. Tucker, reporting in 1656, says the trade of Scotland is insignificant, and only on the coast, in consequence of "the barrenesse of the countrey, poverty "of the people, generally affected with slothe, and a lazy vagrancy " of attending and followeing their heards up and downe in their "pastorage, rather than any dextrous improvement of theyr time." Referring to Glasgow, he says the inhabitants are all traders and dealers, some to Ireland, others to France, Norway, and the Isles and western parts.

In the middle of the seventeenth century Glasgow could boast of twelve vessels, of which four were the largest in Scotland at the time, three being 150 tons and one 140. Towards the end of the century commerce was increasing, and merchants owned fifteen vessels solely, and some of them were part owners in other four not belonging to this port. The largest was 200, one 160, and four 150 tons. At the same time, the value of the foreign export and import trade was a little over £17,000 sterling. The imports consisted in a good part of French wines and brandy.

A spirit of commerce was raised in Glasgow about 1660, chiefly owing to the exertions of Sir George Mackenzie, Lord Advocate. Commerce was established, and flourished; and although the total amount of business done would not now be considered great, the following list of businesses carried on at and before the Union shows the enterprise of the people :—

1. The Whale Fishing Company—established in the reign of Charles II. It was soon wound up, owing to losses. They had two ships, built at Belfast, of 700 and 400 tons. The company comprised nine partners, with a united capital of £13,500 sterling.

2. Rope spinning—begun in the same reign. The company was granted a license to import hemp, duty free. This company was begun for the encouragement of shipbuilding—a trade which did not then exist, nor till some years after the Union.

3. Sugar boiling—begun about 1667, when the first sugar house was erected. The sugar or molasses seems to have been imported from Bristol. There were at least two sugar houses in Glasgow before 1707.

4. Paper making—established about or after 1669.

5. The Royal Fishing Company—fostered about 1662 by Sir George Mackenzie, Lord Advocate. It enjoyed the monopoly of taking herrings from the Clyde up till the 20th of September, when the fishing became free. This company retained its monopoly till 1684.

6. Cooperage—begun to supply the fishing company and fish merchants with barrels.

7. Soap manufactory—first begun in 1667.

There were, also, the fourteen incorporated trades of Glasgow, whose business, however, was local. Glasgow was interested deeply in the Scotch scheme for colonising the Isthmus of Darien, a project which speedily and lamentably failed, and cost many brave lives, through the jealousy of England, and the almost criminal apathy of William III.

The range of trade was very wide, comprising the countries of Western Europe, the continent of Africa, the Canary Islands, and the American colonies, but much the larger portion was to the continent. The size of the vessels was small, but it is astonishing how successfully they were navigated. The losses, however, were at times severe, the merchants having lost by war, capture, and storms, in less than 50 years, upwards of one hundred vessels. In 1665 Letters of Marque were granted in favour of the owners of the frigate "George," of Glasgow, to capture vessels belonging to Holland, with which country we were then at war. The "George" was only 60 tons burden, and had a crew of 60 men all told. She had five pieces of ordnance, 32 muskets, 30 swords, and other equipment, and was provisioned for six months. She was successful in bringing in several prizes to the Clyde.

The river was then in a state of nature. Nothing had been done to deepen or straighten the channel save the removal of a ford or two, and the shipping was very poorly accommodated. Our Magistrates have always been alive to the importance of encouraging trade; and with this view, in 1668, they bought about sixteen imperial acres of ground at Newark, on which they built a town, and called it New Glasgow, or Port-Glasgow. Here they built a harbour and warehouses, with accommodation for seamen, carpenters, and others. They had the district erected into a parish, and maintained a church and school. The goods landed at Port-

Glasgow were taken up to the city in small boats or by horses. The harbour dues at the Broomielaw brought in, in 1701, only a trifle over £21 sterling, while the rental of the Port-Glasgow lands at the same time was over £200 sterling.

Notwithstanding these admirable efforts to increase the trade of the burgh, some merchants, to escape the dues, brought their vessels to other convenient and natural landing places on the Clyde. This was against the law, for all vessels were then bound to load and unload at Royal Burghs or their seaports. The Mer-, chants' House, accordingly, in 1705 passed a regulation ordaining, under severe penalties, all vessels bound for the Clyde to lie at Port-Glasgow harbour, except in case of necessity.

Business must have been small or capital abundant, for a branch of the Bank of Scotland was opened here in 1696, and withdrawn next year, as it was found it was not required. A second attempt, in 1731, resulted in a second failure in 1733, and from the same cause. The more wealthy merchants then acted as bankers. Shortly after the Union trade progressed very rapidly, and in a few years numerous new branches of industry had sprung up in the city. Within about twenty years the following, among others, were carried on :—Tanning and the cognate trades of shoemaking and saddlery, earthen and stoneware manufacture, glass manufacture, thread spinning (first about 1722, and shortly afterwards at Paisley, still the chief seat of this business), tobacco importing, plaid manu- facturing, and brewing. A company trading with the American colonies numbered, about 1730, over one hundred partners. The extensive mineral fields of Lanarkshire were apparently worked then only for the coal and iron, to supply local wants. Trade was especially increased by the importation of tobacco from the American colonies, and to such an extent did this grow that in 1717 the Bristol merchants, driven by jealousy and a fear of losing their own trade, objected to the Commissioners of Customs at London that the Glasgow trade could not be honestly carried on. These objections were triumphantly repelled, but were again urged in 1721 and 1722. In the latter year the Bristol people were so far successful as to have the Glasgow trade placed under such severe restrictions of Custom surveillance, and otherwise, that it languished for some years. It again revived, and tobacco importing to the Clyde became greater than ever, and continued to flourish up to the revolt and independence of the American colonies in 1776, when the trade was almost extinguished. In 1716 the first vessel was built on the Clyde for the American trade. It was only 60 tons. In 1735 there were 67 vessels belonging to the Clyde of all classes, 47 square-rigged and 20 coasters.

In 1740 the first real attempt to deepen the river was made by the Magistrates; but it must have had little if any permanent result, as the implements were rude, and the total cost was £100 sterling. Subsequent efforts were made at various times long after the period of this notice.

Such was the civic, social, and commercial position of Glasgow about the time of the Union of the Parliaments in 1707. It only remains to notice the position taken up by the citizens with reference to that important event. Every one now admits the lasting advantages of the Union to both countries, but it was most violently opposed in Glasgow at the time. Yet if we consider the circumstances and the people, and also the practical changes proposed, this opposition does not seem entirely unreasonable, and we can at least understand it. Except the leading classes, who were numerically small, the people were ignorant, and little acquainted with English manners, laws, and everything else. Their knowledge was derived from traditions of the wars, and practically from the prohibitive legislation regarding trade. English methods of reckoning were to be introduced of which Scotland knew nothing, and which she then did not need. English coinage and money, and the same weights and measures, were to be used throughout the United Kingdom. The laws concerning regulation of trade, customs, and excises, were also to be similar in both countries. All this entered into the every-day life of the people, and met them as an annoyance at every turn. The number of Peers and Commissioners from Scotland to the United Parliament was to be reduced from what had constituted the estates of the Scottish Parliament. What things remained unchanged chiefly related to the administration of justice, such as the constitution of the Court of Session and other Courts, privileges of Royal Burghs, heritable offices, heritable jurisdictions, &c. These affected the people in a less direct manner than the proposed changes, and stirred up much bitter feeling. The subject was treated in the pulpit. The General Assembly of the Church of Scotland appointed a day of fasting and humiliation to implore Divine assistance from the impending calamity, and a sermon on the subject was accordingly preached in Glasgow by the Rev. Mr. Clark in the Tron Church. At its close the clergyman exclaimed,—"Wherefore up and be valiant for the city of our God," when the congregation rose in a body, and, headed by him, proceeded to the Cross, and burned the proposed Articles of Union. This feeling did not subside till several years after the Union, when the increasing prosperity of the country irresistibly convinced the people of the advantages of the step. It is impossible to uphold the manner in which the treaty was introduced and passed by the Scottish Parliament. It was hurried through the various stages in a way to which no such important legislation should be subject. The result has justified the proceeding, and however we may criticise the mode of accomplishing the Union, we cannot but rejoice at the effect.

And to quote Mr. M'Ure's conclusion to his View of the City in 1736 :—" Now I conclude, in taking this matter in hand for my " own exercise and pastime. And having handled the same " according to my intent, but not with that diligence I ought, " craving pardon of my fellow-citizens in what I have done amiss, " wishing all happiness to my good neighbours, and that the city " may flourish in prosperity while sun and moon endures."

THE HOUSE OF BUCHANAN,

THE GLASGOW VIRGINIA MERCHANTS.

THERE are few, we believe, who know anything at all about the feuds of the ancient Highland Clans, who cannot relate something about that famous one, the fighting BUCHANANS of LENY. They were the Ishmaelites of their own days, brave to recklessness, and vain of their prowess. As they were surrounded by tribes as lawless and warlike as themselves—the famed Macgregors on the one hand, and the sturdy Maclaurins on the other—they had abundant opportunity for warlike achievement, of which privilege they were never slow to take advantage. The following tale is gravely related by a Highland historian as an illustration of the old clan feud, which we present to the candid reader to show upon what slight foundations peace and good-will rested in those troublous times. We may premise, too, that the tale long formed a "bone of contention" between the respective clans, being as honestly believed by the one as it was indignantly repudiated by the other.[1]

---

[1] "The Gaelic language is very ancient. The ancient Scythians who spoke the Celtic "language, of which the Gaelic is a dialect, were a great and warlike people long before Rome was "built or its founders born ; and the language has, in its constitution, a much nearer affinity to "languages which are acknowledged to be more ancient than Greek or Latin, than to any other "language of a modern date."—*Rev. James Robertson, of Callander.*

"Long since in Eden's Garden,
When Eve appeared in view,
The words that Adam said to her
Were 'Cum erraugh in juc?'"
Glasgow Rhyme.

Long ago a great country Fair was held in a small town with an unpronounceable name in the territory of the Buchanans.   It happened that among the crowds who flocked to see the show a poor half-witted "innocent" of the rival clan Maclaurin somehow got mixed.   This was resented as an unwarrantable intrusion, but as the poor lad was unworthy of having the dirk or skean dhu drawn against him, some one struck him across the face with a new caught salmon.   Of course the "innocent" expended his stock of Gaelic vituperation upon his assailant and his whole clan, and having invited a repetition of the discourtesy at the forthcoming Fair in the Maclaurin country, he went vacantly gaping through the crowd and forgot all about the indignity.   The proud Buchanan, however, was not so easily appeased, for the Balquidder Fair had been scarcely begun when a band of kilted Buchanans were seen hurrying over the shoulder of the neighbouring hill.   Not till they thus appeared did the "innocent" remember his pithy objurgations flung against the rival clan, and here they were marching hot-foot to avenge the indignity.   There was no time to lose; the "fiery cross" was despatched north and south to gather the bold Maclaurins to the war standard.   The Buchanans were amongst them before their warriors could be collected, and many a burly Maclaurin fell on Auchenleskine field on that bloody morning.   At length one of their chiefs saw his son cut down.   Claymore in hand, he uttered the Maclaurin war-cry, and flung himself among his foes.   As if by magic, the whole clan were filled with the "Miri-Cath" (the madness of battle), and turning round fought so furiously that the whole of the Leny Buchanan warriors were massacred,—cut off root and branch.   Two of them tried to escape by swimming over the river Balvie, but they were caught and slain.   And is not the identical spot still pointed out to the curious traveller, as a proof of the authenticity of the story, and known to the present day as " Linn-nan-Seichachan,"—the pool of flight or of retreat?

Of this doughty clan was old ANDREW BUCHANAN, who more than two hundred years ago was Laird of Gartacharan, near Drymen. Andrew had two sons—Allister, whose representatives still hold the estate, and George, who came to Glasgow to push his fortune. George was a staunch whig in the old "killing times" of the unhappy Stewarts, and took the field with the Covenanters, fought stoutly at Bothwell Bridge, and had a reward set by the Government upon his head. Shortly after the Revolution, however, we find him a prosperous maltster in the town, and in 1691, 1692, and 1694, deacon-convener and visitor of the trade. He was the second in rotation who held this office under William and Mary's Government.

The old borough records of Glasgow give us a curious view of the importance attached to the office, as it bears upon the comfort of the community. Here is an illustration :—

"*Item.*—It is statut and ordanit that thair be na dearer aill sauld nor Xd. the "pynt (somewhat less than one penny per half gallon), aye and quill the provest, "baillies, and counsall tak furder ordour thair anent, and that the sam be kingis "aill, and very guid, vnder the pane of XIJ's the first falt—the secund dealing of "thair brewing and breking of thair weschellis—and that the browstaris mak thair aill "patent to the taistaris, sa aft as thai ar requirit to that effect."

These "taistaris" must have had a jolly office of it, under the supervision of the maltsters. We read of occasional outbreaks against the over strict rule of those who managed the assize of the bread; but the "ailwives and tapsters" seem to have been either more honest or sweeter tempered than their brethren of the batch, for the "taister" has not had left against him any record that his jovial duties were ill received or too rigorously executed.

The old maltman, George, had a remarkable family, who were all associated with the progress and prosperity of Glasgow. His sons were—(1) George Buchanan, of Moss and Auchentoshan; (2) Andrew Buchanan, of Drumpellier; (3) Archibald Buchanan, of Silverbanks or Auchintorlie; and (4) Neil Buchanan, of Hillington. The four brothers in 1725 founded the Buchanan Society, now the oldest charitable institution existing in Glasgow, with the exception of Hutchesons' Hospital. Most of their names are to be found in the list of old John M'Ure's Sea Adventurers.

1. George of Auchentoshan, like his father, was a maltman, and seems to have been prosperous, and highly honoured by his fellow-citizens; for not only was he appointed to the office of convener and visitor of the trade, but we find him city treasurer in 1726, and a magistrate in 1732, 1735, and 1738. He built what was esteemed at the time a splendid town house, which occupied the site recently known as the warehouse of Fraser & Sons, a short way east from Buchanan Street, on the north side of Argyle Street. He was also proprietor of the whole north front of the latter street from his house eastward to the present Arcade. This formed the western section of the Lang Craft, now a very valuable property. He died a wealthy merchant in 1773.

2. Andrew of Drumpellier was still more highly honoured. He was born in 1690, two years after King William had ascended the throne; and consequently, at the date of the Union, 1707, (the very turning point of Glasgow's commercial prosperity), he was at that period of life which generally determines the future business career of every young man. Mr. Buchanan, leaving the malt that had made his father and his elder brother rich men, was among the first who took advantage of the opening Virginia trade, which he prosecuted with ardour and success; and while he was yet a

comparatively young man, we find enumerated among the shipping of the Clyde five vessels owned by the firm of Buchanans & Co.

The mode in which the Virginia trade was prosecuted at first was both prudent and characteristic. A vessel was chartered at some English port, and laden with manufactured goods suitable for the Colonial trade. A supercargo was appointed, whose duty it was to barter his merchandise with the tobacco planter; and by the time his return cargo had been completed, his instructions were to return immediately, carrying with him so much of the goods as remained unsold.[1] Of course, as the trade extended, which it did very rapidly, this prudent system was modified or abandoned; the merchants became themselves large shipowners, and engaged in extensive speculative ventures as planters on their own account. The double profits realized by this system of dealing, enabled most of them to amass, in a short time, splendid fortunes, and to extend the trade so rapidly as almost to bid defiance to competition. We have elsewhere noticed the spirit of jealousy and ill-will which this great prosperity engendered amongst the English merchant-rivals in the same business, and the efforts that were made to damage the Glasgow trade, with only partial success ; for so extensive did the import of tobacco become, that in one year out of 90,000 hogsheads entering the ports of Great Britain, Glasgow imported considerably more than one-half.

[1] "I have been told that the first adventure which went from Glasgow to Virginia after the "trade had been opened to the Scotch by the Union, was sent out under the care of the Captain of "the vessel acting also as supercargo. This person, although a shrewd man, knew nothing of "accounts; and when he was asked by his employers, on his return, for a statement of how the "adventure had turned out, told them he could give them none, but there were the proceeds, and "threw down upon the table a 'hoggar' stuffed with coin. The adventure had been a profitable "one ; and the Company conceiving that if an uneducated, untrained person had been so successful, "their gains would have been still greater, had a person versed in acounts been sent out with it. "They immediately despatched a second adventure with a supercargo, highly recommended for a "knowledge of accounts, who produced to them, on his return, a beautiful made out statement of his "transactions, but no 'hoggar.' "—*Notes by Mr. Dugald Bannatyne.*

As we have said, among those who were carried forward on this great tide of prosperity was Mr. Andrew Buchanan. In 1728 he was elected Dean of Guild, and in 1740 and 1741 Lord Provost of Glasgow. In the first year of his Provostship the whole population of the city numbered 17,034. A most remarkable circumstance in connection with the old census of Glasgow is noticed by Dr. Clelland and others, namely, that eighty years previous to this time, at the period of the restoration of Charles Second (1660), Glasgow numbered 14,678 citizens; yet such was the woeful waste of human life in the process of educating the hard-headed and stiff-necked burgesses of the town into "the religion befitting gentlemen," that at the revolution of 1688 the population had dwindled down to 11,948, and it took more than half-a-century of milder rule to restore the balance.

With respect to the position which Glasgow held among the poor towns of poor Scotland, and the changes that time effected upon her commercial status, the following table, compiled from old John Gibson's History, is worth volumes of description, showing from the Tax Roll of a few of the principal towns, the proportion of their respective wealth and standing :—

	QUEEN MARY, A.D. 1556.	KING WILLIAM, A.D. 1695.	A.D. 1771.
Edinburgh,	£2,650 Scots.	£3,880 Scots.	£14 10s. Sterling.
Dundee,	1,265 "	560 "	4 18s. "
Aberdeen,	945 "	726 "	5 18s. "
Perth,	742 "	360 "	3 8s. "
Saint Andrews,	300 "	72 "	0 7s. "
Cupar,	270 "	108 "	0 10s. "
Stirling,	252 "	174 "	1 8s. "
Montrose,	270 "	240 "	2 12s. "
Ayr,	236 "	128 "	0 15s. "
Glasgow,	202 "	1,800 "	18 10s. "
Renfrew,	101 "	36 "	0 5s. "
Rutherglen,	63 "	12 "	0 4s. "

The changes that have passed over Glasgow since Provost Andrew Buchanan bore civic rule therein are difficult to realize. At that time "The good King William, glorious and brave," had only held his baton over the heads of the passing street crowds at the Cross of Glasgow six short years, mounted upon that wonderful horse, about which old John M'Ure so enthusiastically sings—

> Methinks the steed doth spread with corps the plain,
> Tears up the turff and pulls the curbing rein !
> Exalts his thunder neck and lofty crest,
> To force through ranks and files his stately breast !
> His nostrils glow—sonorous war he hears,
> He leapeth, jumpeth, pricketh up his ears,
> Hoofs up the turff, spreads havock all around,
> Till blood in torrents overflowes the ground !!

The tremendous war horse and his rider are still with us, but where are the "eleven new lodgings," the "mutton market," and the "gate of curious workmanship" over which old John glories, that once graced the aristocratic Bell Street? or "the great and stately lodgings of pure fine ashler work, with their new buildings on both sides of the closs, and garden at the head thereof, with the well of sweet water, so useful to the tenants," of all which Gallowgate neighbours were once so proud? If the ancient Clerk of "Seisins and other evidents" were once more permitted to visit his native town, could he really puzzle out the probable whereabouts of those architectural wonders amongst the greater wonders of the modern city?

The aspect of the town during the first quarter of last century has been described as a cross, formed of two lines of street, one running east and west, the other north and south, with projecting lanes and wynds, which the old historian quaintly likens to "the teeth of a comb." Some idea of the condition of these thoroughfares may be gathered from the fact that up till 1777, with the exception of a few yards of "plainstanes" at King William's Statue, there was not a foot of pavement, nor till 1790 a single sewer, in the whole town, and the scarcity of water was such as to make it imperative that most rigid regulations should be enforced against washing at public wells, or otherwise wasting the precious commodity.

The shops of the city were mostly clustered about the Cross, little dingy booths, ill lighted and worse ventilated, situated behind heavy stone pillars, which supported the upper stories, and each little shoppie having the convenience of a "half-door," over which at idle hours the head and shoulders of the shopkeeper might be seen, as he bestowed a friendly greeting on a passing neighbour, or a kindly welcome to a coming customer. The highest shop rent was five pounds, and the lowest twelve shillings. In our busy Trongate there were thirty shops, only four of which were on the north side. Saltmarket was the business centre of the town, and could boast of no less than fifty-four shops.[1]

Such was the condition of the quaint little town, when Andrew Buchanan was elected Provost. One of his first associates in office, and immediate successor, was Provost Cochrane, who bore rule in 1745, a period perhaps the most eventful of any through which the city ever passed, and to which we would like to refer shortly before proceeding with our story.

---

[1] The first Shoe shop in Glasgow was opened in 1749 by Mr. William Colquhoun; the first Haberdashery shop in 1750 by Mr. Andrew Lockhart, in the Saltmarket; the first Hat shop in 1756 by Messrs. John Blair and James Inglis; the first Woollen Draper's shop in 1761 by Mr. Patrick Ewing; the first regular Distillery was opened in Gorbals, in 1786, by Mr. William Menzies; Messrs. Stein, Haig, and another, preceded him in a small way. The duty on Spirits was about one penny per gallon.

The manufacture of Glass was begun in 1777; the manufacture of Cudbear in the same year; the Turkey Red Dyeing in 1785; Messrs. Tennant & Co., Chemicals, in 1799.

The duties which the worthy Provost and his advisers in that year had to discharge required the utmost discretion and foresight. Prince Charles had landed at Moidart in the latter end of June, and had collected a large force of followers before his designs became public. Immediately upon his crossing the Forth he sent a letter to the magistrates of Glasgow, demanding a sum "not exceeding" £15,000 sterling, besides all the public money and arms in the town, under pain of military execution. At the time of receiving this demand, the whole revenue of the little town amounted only to £3,000. The levy, therefore, meant utter and irretrievable ruin. A meeting of the principal merchants and inhabitants was convened. It was represented that a body of rebels, four thousand strong, were within twelve miles of the town, and that little favour could be expected, because of the well-known loyalty of the community, and the part that they took in the effete rebellion of 1715. Ex-Provost Buchanan and certain other of the influential citizens were appointed a commission to meet with the leaders of the rebel army, and try to effect a compromise as favourable to the town as could possibly be obtained. In the meantime, as it was known that Sir John Cope's army had been despatched to meet the rebels, hopes were entertained that matters might take a turn for the better. The popular feeling is thus described by the Provost—"Our case is extremely deplorable, "that we must truckle to a pretended prince and rebel, and, at an "expense we are not able to bear, purchase a protection from "plunder and rapine."

Glasgow at this time was totally defenceless. A poor force of some thirty of the Royal Scotch Fusileers was quartered on the inhabitants, but these, with their one officer, were ordered to Dumbarton Castle; and although the Provost and Council entreated that Government would supply the citizens in their sore straits with some means of defence, their urgent request for more than five full weeks remained totally unheeded; and when a warrant for raising the citizens was at length received, and a regiment of enthusiastic volunteers was organized, the Government, under the impression that a supply of arms would only be the means of furnishing the rebels with greater facilities for arming themselves, refused to give either arms or ammunition, thus depriving the town of all means of self-defence. This insane apathy was felt by the community, at a time of such peril, as cruel in the highest degree. Well might the worthy Provost complain, " Sir John Cope's great distance and the " few troops appointed for Scotland give us great alarm and disgust. " No doubt the king's troops will retard and harass the enemy on " their march as they are able, but we are of ourselves altogether " defenceless. Heaven help us!"

Within a week after the meeting formerly alluded to, viz., on 21st September, the battle of Prestonpans was fought, resulting in the complete discomfiture of Johnnie Cope and his inefficient army, and leaving Scotland entirely at the tender mercy of Charles and his Highland hosts.

Four days after the battle, Quarter-master Hay, an obscure writer, who had undertaken to be the " scourge and persecutor " of the town, came into Glasgow with a party of horse to renew the previous demand. At this time, however, the rebels could afford to be more lenient, so the levy was now presented in the form of a loan, for which they offered what was represented as very excellent security, namely, the whole excise and tax duties of Clydesdale! It was no easy matter to effect an adjustment of the claim. The disaffection of the town, and particularly the part it took in the rising of 1715, were urged as a complete justification of extreme measures; yet after a hard battle the commissioner succeeded in restricting the original demand to £5000 in money and £500 in goods. A meeting of the inhabitants was called, and between borrowing from private citizens on bond, and a loan from the Earl of Glencairn (see sketch of the Glencairn family), the sum was collected and paid, and as the rebels went south shortly afterwards, the town for the present was left unmolested. Scarcely, however, had the party of horse passed the Molindinar watering ford—that then crossed the street at the foot of the Gallowgate brae—when the agitation for a band of efficient volunteers was again renewed ; and on a representation to Government, one thousand stand of arms were procured, and the Earl of Home was appointed to command the recruits. The inhabitants willingly subscribed a sufficient sum per day to each private soldier, and the officers undertook to defray their own expenses.

While the rebel army was in England a new body of rebels collected at Perth, and it was agreed that the Glasgow Volunteers should assist in preventing the Highlandmen from crossing the Forth. Bailie Allan, a substantial Glasgow burgess, and an officer in the Glasgow Regiment, gives a narrative of the situation, which is sufficiently characteristic :—" They are about three hundred " Hilenders said to be at Down and Dumblen," he writes ; " they " keep a strong gaird at the Bridg of Allan, and some of them in " small cumpanies wer shouing themselfes yestarday but a miel of " Stirling, upon a rock, and was said to be come to intercep a bark " that was coming up the watter with meall and barlie. They are " very opresife wheir they cum, they sufred non coming by the " bridg of Allan pas for Stirling yestarday, which was the market " day, but they caused pay six-pence, or ells behove to turn back. " Their is of Stirling Malichie, on companie stationed at Buckie " burn, on at Leckie parks, and on at Kippen Kirk."

About the middle of December news was received of the rebel army being in full march on their way from England, and the Glasgow Volunteers were ordered to Edinburgh to defend the Capital; and on Wednesday the 25th December, the vanguard of the army arrived in Glasgow, accompanied by the town's old scourge, John Hay. While the magistrates, in terror, were met in the town clerk's chambers, Mr. Hay came amongst them, and in great wrath reproached them for their late rebellion, and told them that the Prince, their lawful King, was resolved to make them "an example of his "just severity, that would strike a terror into other places."

On Friday the clans arrived, headed by Charles himself, but he met with a cold reception. He took up his lodgings in the Shawfield mansion, then the grandest residence in the town. He appeared several times on the streets in all his "mock majesty," only to encounter gloomy looks and disdainful silence; the ladies declined an invitation to attend a ball given by his Highland chiefs. It was even hinted by him that were the magistrates prevailed upon to present him with an address, the effect of their courtesy would be beneficial to themselves, but in the whole town he found "none so poor to do him reverence." Andrew Buchanan was selected for special notice by Mr. Hay, and a demand for £500 presented to him, with the threat held out that if he refused payment his house would be plundered. "Plunder away then," said the sturdy old bailie, "I won't pay a single farthing." Irritated beyond measure at the continued obstinacy of his self-constituted subjects, the Prince complained, that although Glasgow might be a fine town, yet he had no friends in it, and, what was worse, the people were at no pains to hide this from him.

Quarter-master Hay, therefore, resolved to make them reap the fruits of their own contumacy. Besides quartering his ragged regiments on the most respectable inhabitants, he conceived the idea of getting them all comfortably clad at the expense of the town.   He therefore issued a Royal Edict, to provide 12,000 linen shirts, 6,000 cloth coats, as many pairs of shoes, tartan hose, and blue bonnets.   It was in vain that the magistrates remonstrated. Hay told them that it was a just retribution for their rebellion, and the fear of indiscriminate plunder or worse obliged them to comply. The condition of the rebels at the time is graphically described by Dugald Graham, the town bellman, in his metrical history :—

> To Glasgow they came the next day,
> In a very poor forlorn way ;
> The shot was rusted in the gun,
> Their sword from scabbard would not twin ;
> Their countenance fierce as a wild bear,
> Out o'er their eyes hung down their hair ;
> Their beards were turned black and brown,
> The like was ne'er seen in the town.
> Some of them did barefooted run,
> Minded no mire nor stony groun',
> But when shaven, dressed, and clothed again,
> They turned to be like other men.
> Eight days they did in Glasgow rest,
> Until they were all cloth'd and dress't,
> And though they on the best o't fed,
> The town they under tribute laid.

As we intend simply to notice the progress of the rebellion as it affected the subjects of this sketch—Andrew Buchanan and his brother magistrates—we may only say further that when the affair finally collapsed at Culloden, those who took such a prominent part in the stirring scene settled down quietly to their every-day duties. A great amount of trouble was experienced, however, in the endeavour to substantiate a claim to compensation for the losses which the town had sustained in upholding the cause of royalty. The magistrates granted commissions to Provost Cochran and Bailie George Murdoch, his brother-in-law, to go to London on the town's behalf. For a full half-year they were obliged to dance attendance on Government. A strong party was formed in opposition to the claim, which they called "The Glasgow Job," or "The Duke of Argyle's Job." The Provost, in a letter to his wife, says—"I am sure I am much to be pitied. I would rather "have paid great part of what we expect, than to have had "this plague and vexation. I shall be away from my dearest "wife and best affairs for an age, losing my time and spending "the town's money, and vexing and fatiguing myself, and all "to no purpose. God pity me and give an happy end to this "vexing affair!"

The worthy Provost's description of a levee which he witnessed in London is worth notice for its quaint humour :—"Levees," he says, " are the greatest farce in nature. The King stays about five "minutes. Some are introduced to kiss his hands, others present "petitions; he speaks a little to some great lord, all bow, fawn, and "cringe, then off goes Majesty. The Prince stays about fifteen min- "utes ; he allows some one to kiss his hands—talks to half-a-dozen "people about the roads and weather, then exit Royal Highness. "The Minister's levee is the greatest and throngest of all, stars of "all kinds—Generals, Admirals, Bishops, and the Lord knows who, "bowing low; he smiling and going round the whole company "distributing his nothings. Were he to be dismissed, not one of "these flatterers would be seen in his house ; he might go where he "pleased for them. I am sick of the subject, and have not temper "to say any more. God send me to my spouse and home, I shall "be better pleased with them than ever."

Notwithstanding the fears entertained by the Provost and his friend that their mission on behalf of the town would prove a failure, a sum of £10,000 was subsequently granted by Parliament, and the following memorandum of the transaction exists in the records of the town :—" The Magistrates and Council, for themselves, and in " name of the community, being sensible of the Provost and George " Murdoch, their good services and diligence in procuring such " relief to the town, do tender them their most hearty thanks." Nor did the community content themselves with a simple vote of thanks, for during the long period of thirty years we find the Buchanans and Cochrans and Murdochs, and the sturdy citizen Bailie Allan, enjoying, with their friends, a great share of civic honours, as they well deserved.

In the year 1740—to which time, after our rambling gossip, we now return—there seems to have been a grievous failure of the crops in Scotland, for the wheat rose to what was then considered a famine price, nineteen shillings sterling per boll.   These periodic famines, as we shall have frequent occasion to notice, were very common, and we are inclined to believe that the baxters had been surreptitiously scrimping the poor man's loaf for their own benefit, despite the knowledge that Mr. Buchanan had descended from a race whose experience of the trade would prevent him from being easily hoodwinked.   So a meeting of the Magistrates and Council was called, and after making it imperative that the bread should be stamped with the makers' initials : " They furder statute and ordain, " that the baxter affix distinct figures on the bread, such as I. for " a penny loaf, II. for a twopenny loaf, and so furth for larger loafs, " and that any of the inhabitants who have any suspicion of the " weight of the bread furnisht to them, may bring the same to the " Clerk's Chambers to be weighed, and if found light the Magistrates

" are empowered to pay for the loaf, and give half-a-crown of reward
" to the person who brings the loaf so formed light."

During the scarcity Mr. Buchanan was empowered by the
Magistrates, the Merchants' House, the Trades' House, and the
General Session, to borrow from the bank £3000 sterling, " for
" providing grain for the service of the place in this straitened time,
" and the Council oblige themselves to indemnify the Provost and
" Andrew Cochran, bailie, for the bond, and any loss that may be
" sustained by purchasing grain and selling it out again to the
" inhabitants by retail."[1]

It was also agreed that during the scarcity each of these bodies
should contribute a fixed sum for three months, besides what the
inhabitants themselves should agree to contribute, and the town's
proportion it was arranged should be £15 sterling per month.
There can be little doubt that the dour loyalty of the leal town, as
manifested in the eventful 1745, took more of its force and tenacity
from an experience of this loving helpfulness to the inhabitants in
their straits, than from any spontaneous love to the Government in
power, or the " wee, wee German lairdie ;" and this opinion is
further confirmed by the fact that a resolution was adopted by the
Magistrates in 1742, and embodied in a letter to Mr. Neil Buchanan,
M.P., (Neil of Auchintorlie,) making grateful acknowledgment of
his Parliamentary services to the city, and earnestly requesting him,
in the name of the Corporation, " To promote every maxim for
" preventing and restraining all manner of pecuniary influence over
" the members of your House—*the unhappy source of all our
" calamities*—for restoring frequency of new Parliaments, and for

---

[1] There was at this time a number of the citizens who made the distilling of Aqua Vitae their
business, and as there were no excise restrictions on the trade, the liquor could be manufactured at
two shillings a gallon. On a scarcity of grain occurring, Government immediately put a stop for a
time to the distilleries.

"giving vigour to our once happy but now exhausted Constitution.
"That you be as sparing of the national treasure as the present
"exigencies will admit, and join in all the Parliamentary enquiries
"into the past conduct and management of public affairs, whereby
"His Majesty's Government will be founded on its proper basis,
"the affections of his people."

It is perhaps worthy of remark that the celebrated political
economist, Dr. Adam Smith, was elected professor of moral
philosophy in the Glasgow University a few years after the
rebellion, and that about the time this letter was written he was a
frequent and welcome visitor at the houses of the principal magistrates, and a student known even then as a profound thinker.
There is a flavour, we think, of that keen sagacity which characterised his great work on the "Wealth of Nations" to be found
in this extract. At any rate, it strengthens the belief that the
intercourse which existed between him and the shrewd Glasgow
merchants gave shape and potency to many of these maxims
in political economy which give value to his wonderful book.

The Virginia trade was resumed vigorously and successfully
when the rebellion ended. The little town grew apace, and in
twelve years the population had increased to 23,546. Under the
fostering influence of the newly established banks, merchants rapidly
acquired fortunes. Andrew Buchanan became a wealthy man ; he
purchased Drumpellier, and added field to field in his town property
on the north side of the Westergate, then owned mostly by small
lairds, and laid out as vegetable gardens. His relations and brother
magistrates, Provosts Dunlop and Murdoch, had erected at this
time, 1750, two splendid houses beyond the Westport.[1] What

---

[1] These were the old "Buck's Head," built by Provost Murdoch, and its eastern neighbour,
built by Provost Colin Dunlop.

should hinder him also from perpetuating his name by erecting a mansion that would excel them both? Alas! before his plans were fully matured he was overtaken by the great equalizer death, and laid lovingly in the old Ramshorn kirkyard.

It is indeed a weirdly suggestive fact, and one that the worthy Provost himself would probably have called "gruesome," could he have foreseen it, that in subsequent widenings and straightenings of the old Back Cow Loan to form the present Ingram Street, the Ramshorn burying - ground suffered encroachment, and the resting-place of the lordly Buchanans was swallowed up in the modern improvements. At the present time, therefore, a portion of the noisy traffic of Glasgow rumbles daily unheeded over the once bustling magistrate who a century and a half ago filled his poor brains with puzzling forecasts respecting the welfare of the little town, and the part that he himself was destined to occupy in its prospective history :—

> The mighty man of rank and power,
>   Who thought without him nought could be,
> Having lived out life's little hour
>   Is no more missed than me.

Provost Andrew Buchanan died in 1759, aged 69 years. He left two sons, both Virginia merchants of high standing like their father. James the eldest,[1] perhaps for his father's sake, likely for his own merits, was twice elected Lord Provost of Glasgow. He inherited Drumpellier, while his younger brother George acquired

---

[1] James, from the extraordinary breadth of his face and the size of his mouth, was known during his civic reign as "Provost Cheeks." One day he complained to a brother magistrate that a well-known citizen had saluted him on both sides of the face, abusing him with his nasty saliva. His friend, looking emphatically at Mr. Buchanan's capacious mouth, quietly rejoined—"If I had been you, Provost, I wad hae bitten aff the fallow's head!"

the greater part of the town property which his father had so assiduously scraped together on the north side of the Westergate, including the site of Virginia Street as far north as the Back Cow Lone.

George's first care, on coming into possession, was to carry out the plans sketched by his father, particularly that object which he knew occupied so much of the old Provost's thoughts, namely, the spacious town house. So the barns and byres and malt kilns were cleared away from the stripes of cabbage garden and corn ridge that skirted the old St. Enoch's gate, and on the north-eastern extremity of his property, then fairly out of town, a grand mansion was erected, which, without doubt, was the most elegant private residence the town possessed—for the Shawfield mansion, then occupied by Colonel M'Dowall of Castle Semple, with hard usage and the effects of the passing years, had begun to lose its splendour, and Cunningham of Lainshaw's mansion was not yet in existence. The house was styled the "Virginia Mansion," and many of the older citizens still remember its stately bearing even in its decadence forty-five years ago, when it was superseded by the still more stately Union Bank.

That exclusive style, which about this time took such a firm hold upon the upper classes of society in the city, forms a curious subject of study, delighting as it did, in anomalous contrast and trumpery display,—the great town mansion which contrasted so strangely with the thatched malt kiln, or barn, or lowly hostelry, its next neighbour,—the vanity of scarlet cloak, and silver buckles, and cocked hat, and haughty strut and stare, and its contrast of hodden grey, and Kilmarnock bonnet, and cringing obeisance,—happily these incongruous distinctions are in a great measure unknown in modern times, and held very lightly in estimation. And yet· these weaknesses were in most cases combined with a robust perseverance, and a healthy benevolence and patriotism worthy of admiration and imitation.

About 1758, George Buchanan, while he was yet under thirty years of age, was able to purchase the estate of Windyedge, in the parish of Old Monkland, upon which he erected a country house, planting and ornamenting the ground in the most tasteful manner, and in compliment to George Washington, whose Virginia estate of the same name stood neighbour to his own, he called the place Mount Vernon, a name which it still retains.

Mr. Buchanan married, early in life, Lilias Dunlop of Garnkirk, sister to Provost Colin Dunlop, who built one of the grand semi-urban mansions which graced the Westergate, and which still exists, perhaps the only entire specimen of the dwelling-places of the ancient Virginia lords. Though sadly dilapidated indeed, and reduced to the menial office of a common eating house, its ornamented drawing-room roof and panelled walls, as illustrative of a phase of Glasgow life, now past and nearly forgotten, are well worth seeing.

George did not long enjoy his city residence and country seat; four short years had only elapsed after the erection of the Virginia mansion till he was laid beside his father in the family burying-ground, in the thirty-fourth year of his age.

His eldest son, Andrew, at his father's death in 1762, was a minor, and the estate was put into the hands of trustees for the family, the principal of whom were his mother, Lilias Dunlop, her brother, Provost Colin, and her brother-in-law, Provost James Buchanan of Drumpellier, and Alexander Speirs, a Virginia merchant, who had married Mary Buchanan, daughter of Archibald of Auchintorlie.

The family of George consisted of the above-mentioned Andrew, and another son, David, both young, and one daughter, Marion, who subsequently, by marriage with her cousin, James Dunlop of Garnkirk, became the grandmother of our esteemed fellow-citizen, James Dunlop of Tollcross.

The trustees shortly afterwards sold the Virginia mansion to Mr. Speirs, who had been attracted from Edinburgh—his father being a merchant in that city—by the success of the Virginia trade. Mr. Speirs was one of four young men whose energy and enterprise has won for them the reputation of consolidating, if not creating, the great commercial prosperity of Glasgow in the middle of last century, namely, Mr. John Glassford of Dugaldson; Mr. William Cunningham of Lainshaw—who built the mansion, the wonder of its time, that is now incorporated in the Royal Exchange; Mr. James Ritchie of Craigton, who, with Sir Walter Maxwell of Pollock, established the aristocratic Thistle Bank, and whose town mansion stood on the site of the present National Bank; and Mr. Speirs, who, with his partner, Provost Murdoch, founded the Glasgow Arms Bank.

While the Virginia trade continued a mine of wealth to the Glasgow merchants, Mr. Speirs invested a portion of his fortune in the purchase of several detached stripes and patches of land, the property of certain small "bonnet lairds" in Govan, who held them chiefly by ancient inheritance. Far back in the year 1590, King James appointed a commission "To feu the haill lands of the "Lordship and Regalitie of Glasgow, without diminution of the "auld rentall, to the effect that the tenants, being thereby become "heritable possessors of their several possessions, might be in- "curadged by virtue and politie to improve that countrie!"

The Govan lairds—there were about seventy of them—held

tenaciously to the little properties thus acquired, through many changes, political and ecclesiastical ; but riches can do wonders, and Mr. Speirs, as we have said, managed to obtain possession of a goodly number of these country patches, which, with part of the ancient lands of Elderslie and the Inch, he, by a Crown Charter, got consolidated into a Barony, under the general name of Elderslie—and here he purposed to plant and build, and make his name famous in all coming time. Accordingly, great preparations were made in 1777 for building a spacious country house, and five full years were spent in its erection ; and in 1782 the family removed from the Virginia mansion to Elderslie House. But a mysterious fatality seems to have hung over these lordly seats, for before the year had closed, the proprietor of Elderslie was dead, and his death was accompanied by circumstances over which the glitter and grandeur of his new possession cast a shadow that was profoundly sorrowful.

By the marriage of Mr. Speirs into the haughty Buchanan family, he had entered that exclusive circle which formed the ruling power in the society of Glasgow. The father of Mrs. Speirs, Archibald Buchanan of Auchintorlie, was son-in-law to Provost Murdoch ; her uncles were Provost Andrew of Drumpellier, and Neil of Hillington, Member of Parliament for Glasgow ; her cousins had all been Provosts and Bailies, and connected by inter-marriage with the Dunlops, the Stirlings, the Cochranes, and the Murdochs—the very cream of the city aristocracy at the time. Moreover, nearly all that select circle were Virginia merchants, and reputed to be rolling in wealth ; and in token of their approval of the popular belief, the merchants themselves assumed a style of haughty superiority as foolish as it was ludicrous. Dr. Strang says—" For one of the *shopocracy* or *corkocracy* to speak to a

"tobacco aristocrat on the street, without some sign of recognition
"from the great man, would have been regarded as an insult.
"They were princes on the pavement, and strutted about every
"day as the rulers of the destinies of Glasgow."

During the time that the Elderslie House was building, this unnatural and anomalous condition of society came suddenly and unexpectedly to an end.

In the year 1776 the American colonies threw off their allegiance to Britain, and with their allegiance they unfortunately threw off also all their responsibilities to British subjects by whom their country had been enriched.

The Buchanans, on the outbreak of the American war, were not only extensive tobacco importers; they were also proprietors of large plantations in Virginia. Their estates therefore became, as it was considered, the legitimate spoil of the strongest party in the struggle, and in 1777 the great houses of Buchanan, Hastie & Co., and Andrew Buchanan & Co., which were considered impregnable, failed. Provost James was stripped of his Drumpellier property, and died a Commissioner of Customs in Edinburgh, in 1793. He lies beside the Earl of Morton, in Old Greyfriars churchyard, and a handsome monument has recently been erected by his friends to perpetuate his memory. Andrew, of the Virginia mansion, took up his residence in Adams' Court, and died in 1796. In 1777, the year of the crash, there died Neil Buchanan, M.P., uncle to Mrs. Speirs; William Stirling, whose wife was Mrs. Speirs' cousin; and Provost Colin Dunlop, whose sister was wife of George Buchanan, another cousin, died also in the same year. Another of the family who was ruined in the general crash was Andrew, (eldest son of maltman George, who died in 1773.) Andrew's name is still kept in remembrance by "Buchanan Street," which in his prosperous days he laid out in thumping lots of so many roods and yards *or thereby*, for the ground was of comparatively small value.   Being so far removed from the business centre of the town, it could only be used for suburban houses and gardens,   As it was, the patches collected with so much care, and that represented the eident thrift of the old maltman George, were swept from his son relentlessly in the common wreck and ruin, and nothing left him but the empty street name with which so few in the present day can associate one sympathetic idea.

Mr. Speirs was not affected by the universal disaster.   He held a large stock of tobacco when the war broke out, and was at the time a leading partner and director in the " Glasgow Arms Bank "—Speirs, Murdoch & Co.—but both himself and Provost Murdoch were involved in the Virginia trade, and we feel assured that the melancholy reverses we have tried to record must have cast a gloom over the evening of the haughty old merchant's life, which the style and glitter of his new mansion would only serve to deepen and intensify.

Thus it was that the house of Buchanan fell from its proud position for a time.   George of the Virginia mansion, as we have stated, left two sons, Andrew and David.   Andrew was all but ruined by the failure of the Virginia business, and died in 1795.   David, however, was a person of more than ordinary energy and enterprise. When the crash came he was only seventeen years of age, and with praiseworthy resolution he determined that he should at least try what could be recovered from the wreck of his family fortunes.   In pursuance of this resolution he proceeded, at the termination of the war, to Virginia, where, quietly and energetically, he set himself to the fulfilment of his allotted task, and with so much success, that in 1802 he was able to redeem the family seat, Mount Vernon ;

and on the retirement of his relative, Andrew Stirling, to London, he had the satisfaction of purchasing his grandfather's family mansion, Drumpellier, also, and thus recovering the position of the ancient and honourable race among the city aristocracy of the period. In this laudable ambition he was assisted from a quarter whence help could scarcely be expected.

When Provost Andrew and his brothers were boys, George, their father, employed, according to the custom of the time, a divinity student as a family tutor, and the family had sufficient influence to get him inducted as the parish minister of Houston, where his memory is kindly cherished to the present day. When the Ship Bank was established in 1750, Andrew, who was one of the original partners, got his old tutor's son, then a smart lad about fourteen years of age, a situation as message boy and general assistant in the quaint old Briggate establishment. This boy was the renowned Robin Carrick, one of the most heartily, and, we believe, most unjustly, maligned Bank officials ever Glasgow produced. It cannot be denied that Robin, as a member of the community, was cold, unsympathetic, grasping, and inflexible, but in his official capacity, as the guardian and distributor of the public wealth, he displayed, we think, an accurate perception of those sound monetary principles that were subsequently more fully developed by Dr. Adam Smith, and in the application of which Robin evinced an amount of assiduous attention and shrewd sagacity, that contrasted favourably with the recklessness or stupidity of so many official brethren in his own and in more recent times. At any rate he for many years piloted the good old "Ship" past many a dangerous reef and through many a troublous passage, till after eighty-six years' buffeting it found a harbour sound in timbers and cordage in the "Union Bank."

In accordance with the advice of his contemporary and namesake, Burns, Robin

> "Gathered gear by every wile
> That's justified by honour."

He yearly added house to house and field to field. No speculation was either too high or too low for him, provided it held out a prospect that it could "pay," and before his death he was reputed to be the richest man in Glasgow. Of course speculation was rife as to how or where all this wealth would find an owner when he died. His old housekeeper, who was reputed to be a more inveterate "skinflint" than himself, was almost his only relative. As for churches, and schools, and infirmaries, and similar institutions, they might be supported, he said, by those who could afford to do so, or who needed their help. At length Robin died friendlessly in the upper room of the old "Ship," which he had served so faithfully, and it was found that the greater part of his large fortune was left to David, the grandson of Andrew Buchanan, his old patron.

Although the motives of Mr. Carrick in thus disposing of his wealth were unquestioned and unquestionable, nevertheless the matter formed a nine days' wonder, and a great source of gossip at the time, especially when it became known that not one of those benevolent and useful institutions which were the pride and glory of the town benefitted to the value of a copper coin by the old man's bounty, and that even his faithful servant John—his bank porter, body servant, groom, coachman, gardener, and general *fac totum*—who carefully collected the bank candle-ends to grease the axle of the ricketty vehicle in which Robin was conveyed from his country house each summer morning, in company with a supplementary load of syboes, cabbages, and turnips, which John duly carried to the green market, and fought the kail wives over in many a wordy encounter; even poor faithful John, who had grown grey in the service of a thankless master, was entirely neglected, and died an inmate, and a highly respected one, of the old Clydeside Poorhouse.

Had the eccentric banker lived but a short time longer, there is no saying where his great fortune might have been bestowed. One of David Buchanan's Virginia partners, a cute American, raised a serious lawsuit against the firm, which assumed such proportions, that whatever way it might have terminated, would have damaged, if it did not ruin, the estate. As it was, however, the windfall enabled Mr. Buchanan to come off unscathed; yet everybody said that sharing his painfully gathered gear among the lawyers was the last thing Robin would have submitted to, could he have foreseen such a catastrophe.

Mr. Buchanan became a partner in the " Ship " when he came into this fortune, and the partnership was changed from Carrick, Moore & Co., to Carrick, Buchanan & Co. He also assumed the name of his benefactor, David Carrick Buchanan. He died in 1827.

David Carrick Robert Carrick Buchanan, his grandson, is now the representative of the ancient family in Drumpellier. He has added to the family inheritance, Finlayston, in Renfrewshire, the ancient seat of the Glencairn family, and Carradale, and Torrisdale in Cantyre.

Auchintorlie is now the property of Andrew Buchanan, the great-grandson of Archibald (third son of old maltman George), and thus one of the most ancient Glasgow families is yet represented by two quiet respected country gentlemen, who have completely passed out of that circle of active Glasgow life, which the old Buchanans filled so faithfully and so long.

Alexander Speirs and his wife, Mary Buchanan, were munificent benefactors to the Merchants' House. Their portraits are suspended in the new hall of the institution. Mrs. Buchanan has a very lovable face, which every one admires. The family is now represented by the son of the late Alexander Speirs, M.P., whose death in 1873 was so much lamented. This boy never saw his father, being born after that gentleman's death.

CHARLES TENNANT of St. Rollox,

THE MACRAES of Ayrshire,

AND

THE GLENCAIRN FAMILY.

IF a stranger were to inquire what are the two most noteworthy things to be seen about our good town, he would probably be directed to Tennant's " big stalk " at St. Rollox, and the statue of King William at the Cross ; the first a monument to commemorate the commercial energy and enterprise of the son of a substantial Ayrshire farmer, the other a memorial of a great national deliverance, and gifted to the town by the son of an Ayrshire washerwoman.

However different may be the sentiments and actions which the two monuments serve to perpetuate, they are nevertheless curiously connected, as the following true story will show.

A long time ago, when Charles the Second was King, there lived in a little cottage, near the old town of Ayr, a decent washerwoman, whose name was widow Macrae, or, as she was more commonly called, Bell Gardner. Bell had one son, Jamie, to whom she was tenderly attached, a healthy, obliging little fellow,

free to run errands for herself and neighbours, in short, a general
assistant to all around.   In course of time Jamie grew up a strapping
lad, and found little difficulty in procuring a berth in one of those
coasting vessels that traded at the Ayrshire ports; and as he was found
faithful and capable, he rose rapidly in his profession, till his mother,
with pleasure and pride, was able to call him Captain Macrae.
For a time his visits to his mother were dutiful and regular, but he
left her to enter a ship bound for India, and the poor woman
saw her wandering son no more.

As the infirmities of age gathered around the widow, sorely did
she pine for her missing son, and for the much needed shelter in
her declining years, which she had hoped to find in his filial
affection.   But year after year passed and brought no tidings from
Jamie, and as she felt her strength gradually decay, her heart failed
at the dreary prospect before her.

Fortunately for her, however, her namesake and niece, Bell
Gardner, had married a country joiner, Hugh M'Guire, and the pair
were comparatively comfortable ; for Hugh, besides being a good
and steady tradesman, was also an excellent musician, and no merry-
making in the district was thought complete without the presence
of Hugh and his fiddle, and thus many an extra shilling found its
way into the family exchequer.   Now that poor old aunty Bell was
so ill qualified for her usual task over the washing tub, and had
apparently been forgotten by her undutiful son, if still alive, the
worthy pair resolved that she should never be thrown upon the cold
sympathy of the stranger, but should henceforth, at their own canny
fireside, take her bite and sup among the bairns; and so the evening
of life fell quietly and gently on widow Macrae, till the end came,
embittered by few regrets, except the loss or the apparent neglect
of her beloved son.

Forty long years had come and gone since Jamie left Ayrshire, when his friends were startled by the intelligence that on the 18th day of January, 1725, the Honourable James Macrae of Ayrshire had taken his seat as Governor of the Madras Presidency in India.

Madras at this time was one of the most important of the East India Company's possessions, but the duties which the Governor was then called to discharge were very different from those which devolve upon him who now aspires to administer law and order to so many millions of the Queen's subjects. The whole of the Company's dominions could be included within a radius of a few miles, for which a rent was paid to some native potentate; and the Governor's duties had simply reference to the regulation of trade, and consisted chiefly in a vigilant guardianship over the monopoly which the Company claimed, in terms of their exclusive Charter, dating back to the time of Queen Elizabeth. The clerks and inferior officers in the Company's employ were miserably paid, and hardly dealt with, and enjoyed but sorry prospects generally of bettering their circumstances. Such of them, however, as were afforded these rare opportunities in the race for advancement, had splendid facilities for acquiring wealth, and the chiefs of the various departments in the employ generally managed in a short time to amass an ample fortune. Governor Macrae was one of those. At the termination of six years he gave up his office and came back to his early Ayrshire home, laden with wealth and honours, never to leave Scotland more.

We have no means now of accounting for the protracted silence of the prosperous Indian Nabob, especially to his poor mother. It is true that the Indian voyage in those days occupied the greater part of twelve months, and often longer, and we know not the struggles which the penniless lad might have to pass through before he reached that point of comfort and independence to which he had arisen, and his wilfulness or his pride might hinder him from communicating these struggles to his friends till he had attained the object of his ambition. Greatly to his honour, however, it is recorded that his first duty, on reaching home, was to find out his poor relatives, especially his cousin Bell, by whom his mother had been cherished in her old age, and to heap upon her and her family every comfort and luxury that wealth could procure. The four daughters who constituted her family were educated, and polished, and petted, and brought out ; and as it was known that the old Governor had store of wealth, they soon became objects of great attraction to the local gentry around.

It is stated, however, that old Hugh the fiddler remained intractable. What cared he either for conventional privileges or conventional restraints ? He had long enjoyed the greater privilege of being esteemed the leader and chief in all life-giving Ayrshire splores, and he would not, and could not, lay down all at once the proud pre-eminence his own talent had won for him, nor the jollity and mirth with which it was associated ; and so he stipulated with his grand relative for liberty to contribute, as formerly, his share in the popular merry-makings, to all of which he felt sure of the cordial invitation and the kindly welcome.

About this time William the thirteenth Earl of Glencairn was the chief of the local aristocracy. The Glencairn estates were said to be somewhat encumbered; the fiddler's eldest daughter Leezie— who no doubt he had seen skelping barefooted to school many a time—was now a young lady, fair, accomplished, and, better than all, had "great expectations." What could the Earl, therefore, do better than to mend his somewhat cracked fortunes by a portion of the old Indian's rupees? So Leezie became the Countess of Glencairn, with Governor Macrae's "consent and bounty;" for, on the day of her marriage, she received, by way of "tocher guid," the whole Barony of Ochiltree, which cost £25,000, as well as diamonds to the value of £45,000—altogether a very sumptuous "down-sitting."

Moreover, in the poor fiddler's daughter the Earl obtained a real "help-meet," for her life-long labour of loving duty shed a lustre over her station, which mere wealth or rank could never confer. A correspondence is still preserved which passed between the Countess and the parish minister of Ochiltree, that gives a very lovable view of her character. It details her little schemes for helping and improving the district, and especially those young women who occupied a similar station to that which she herself had filled before the change in her fortunes. One of these schemes was the establishment of a "spinning school," the whole expenses of which—such as rent, furniture, teacher's wages, &c.—she proposed to defray, out of her own private means. Her description is most characteristic. "The profits," she explains, "should be devoted to "the benefit of the scholars, and layed up as a fund for marriage,— "such as buying clothes or furniture,—or any misfortune or inabi- "lity, as every stage of the human existence is liable to miserable "accidents. We must have also some person of generous humanity, "who will volunteer himself as our treasurer and actor in disposing "of our yarn and buying our lint; for if he is not very moderate in "his demands, he may encroach on funds, charity, and good-will to "our fellow-creatures, which we must look on as sacred." Another extract further reveals her character and work :—"I beg the "continuance of your prayers for me and mine. I was sorry to see "my name in the newspaper for any little donations to a people who

"have so just a claim on my attention as your parish.   They are my
"support.   I have had for several weeks six dozen Shetland
"stockings for their use, but no opportunity has occurred to convey
"them to you.   If you hear of any, I beg you would let me know,
"as I am really anxious they, in so severe a season, should have
"the use of them."

Notwithstanding the benevolence of her work, and the amiability
of her character, the life of the Countess was on the whole a sad
and unhappy one.   Her eldest son, Lord Kilmaurs, died in 1768, in
his twentieth year.   His amiable and accomplished brother James,
who succeeded to the Earldom in 1775, died unmarried in 1791.
He was the patron and friend of Burns, and his death drew from
the poet that touching lament so replete with genuine pathos :—

> "The bridegroom may forget the bride
> Was made his wedded wife yestreen,
> The monarch may forget the crown
> That on his head an hour hath been :
> The mother may forget the child
> That smiles sae sweetly on her knee,
> But I'll remember thee, Glencairn,
> And a' that thou hast done for me !"

John became fifteenth Earl of Glencairn on his brother's death.
He married a daughter of the Earl of Buchan, and died childless in
1796.   It was while the Countess was residing with John's widow
at Coates, near Edinburgh, that the correspondence from which we
have quoted took place.   Her daughter Harriet married Sir
Alexander Don of Newton Don.   The match was an unfortunate
one, for their son turned out a profligate, who squandered the estate
by selling it, piecemeal, here and there for whatever it might bring ;
and the last of the race was a strolling player, Sir William Don,

who carried about only the poor shadow of his aristocratic connection, and who, with his wife, had some pretention to theatrical talent. Sir William died recently on his way from Australia—a sad termination to a worthy and honourable line, which, so far as can be ascertained, is now extinct.

Governor Macrae, in the year 1734, presented to the city of Glasgow the equestrian statue of King William, which has for so many long years occupied a prominent position among the sights of the town. It is not difficult, we think, to define the motives which prompted the old Governor to offer this gift. He had lived in the days when Ayrshire was the chief hunting-ground for Claverhouse and his men. No doubt he had, with his own eyes, seen the cruel excesses practised against quiet, God-fearing neighbours among the scattered farm steadings and the sandy downs of Ochiltree, and the contrast between those dreary " killing times " and the peace and liberty inaugurated by a beneficent Government, he reckoned worthy of this form of permanent remembrance.

It is curious to observe how this sentiment of loyalty to king and country filled the mind of Governor Macrae. He purchased an estate in the ancient parish of Monkton, in Ayrshire, which he named Orangefield, a name which it bears to the present day ; and the last recorded act of his life was to grant a loan of £5000 to Glasgow to meet part of the losses to which it was subjected during the memorable raid of the Highland host in 1745. At Orangefield the Governor lived quietly for fifteen years, and there he died in 1746, and was buried in the old Prestwick kirk-yard.

We should like now to notice a curious link of connection between old Governor Macrae and another remarkable individual who has given to Glasgow a monument more conspicuous still, and marking an event even more beneficial to the city than any inaugurated by the bare-legged king who has so long bestridden his steed at the Cross of Glasgow.

At the time when Bell Gardner was engaged in her humble vocation, there lived in " The Mains," Brigend of Doon, a farmer named William Tennant, between whom and the widow a friendly feeling had long existed—indeed they were near neighbours ; and as his son John and her niece Leezie M'Guire, whose story we have already told, were about the same age, they became great friends. We frankly make confession of a hankering desire to record a more sentimental bond of union existing between the pair than simply schoolfellow and playfellow ; but on this subject history is silent. This we know, however, that when, through the good offices of her grand friend, she became Countess of Glencairn, she entrusted the management of her affairs to her old playfellow, John Tennant of Glenconner ; and wisely and worthily did that " ace and wale of honest men," as he was called by Burns, discharge the duties with which he was entrusted. Mr. Tennant was twice married, and had a remarkable family. His eldest son, James, was the miller of Ochiltree—the friend, companion, and " fellow-sinner" of Burns, who, in his well-known letter to Mr. Tennant, mentions the members of the family in detail. " My auld schoolfellow, preacher Willie," (Rev. W. Tennant, LL.D.,) went to India, where he instituted a movement for the educational and moral improvement of the natives, that bears good fruit to the present day. " The manly tar my mason Billie" was a naval captain. During the French war he lost his hand. Knighthood was offered him for his services, which he declined ; on his brother asking him the reason for refusing the honour, his reply was most characteristic—" To tell the truth, I juist considered the title little better than a nickname." " Singing Sannock," for whom Burns wished " hale breeks, saxpence, and a bannock," went to Cape Colony. One of his descendants, Sir Hercules Tennant, is now (1880), and has long been, speaker in the local Parliament there. The most remarkable of the whole brotherhood, however, was CHARLES, whom the poet thus notices :—

> " And no forgettin' wabster Charlie,
>   I'm tauld he offers very fairly."

Had Burns lived till Mr. Charles Tennant had fully developed that tremendous latent energy of which the St. Rollox works were the outcome, and which even in his apprenticeship—for at the time this was written he was only in his seventeenth year—was open to the keen insight of the poet, he doubtless would have strengthened his somewhat half-hearted forecast regarding the strong-armed, strong-minded wabster laddie ; for there are very few of that noble band of comparatively self-made men whom the old town has been proud to adopt, who have left upon her commerce more distinct traces of his individual force of character than Mr. Charles Tennant. . Mr. Tennant, who was born at Glenconner in 1768, after serving his apprenticeship in Kilwinning, wrought for a short time at the loom, and in the latter part of the century we find him established as a bleacher at Darnley, in the parish of Eastwood, while yet a young man.

When the art of spinning by machinery was fairly established in Scotland, and almost every country village had become a weaving shop, it was found that the produce of the loom overtasked the capabilities of the country bleachers, in the preparation of the cloth for the market. Bleaching at the time was a tedious process, requiring long months' exposure to sun and wind. Indeed, the success of the dilatory process, like the progress of the crops, depended in a great measure on the favourable nature of the weather, and at the close of the season the cloth was generally stored in the bleacher's warehouse till the spring sun shone, and the spring showers fell, when the tedious work was again renewed.

Previous to the close of the century, indeed, bleaching on anything like an extensive scale had not been attempted in Scotland. "Customer wark," as it was called—the home spun and home woven cloth for common wear—was subjected by the thrifty goodwife to the usual exposure to wind and weather on the small corner which invariably formed a portion of the kail yard, which even the town housewife at the time possessed.

The finer sorts of linen were generally sent to the "Broomielaw crafts," then unsoiled by steamboat or foundry smoke, where the goods enjoyed the privilege of being watered from the streams of the pellucid Clyde! Anything requiring a more elaborate treatment, however, was sent to Holland, where it underwent a complicated process, which usually required full twelve months to complete. It was steeped for weeks on weeks in soured milk, and subjected to repeated boilings in caustic ley, alternated with repeated exposure to the weather, so that, by the time it reached the hands of its owner, it had often suffered considerable deterioration by the ordeal through which it had passed.

Toward the end of the century, Mons. Berthollet, a distinguished French chemist, tried to expedite this tedious process, by the application of oxymuriatic gas (chlorine), which, it had been previously discovered, possessed a remarkable power of extracting colour from all vegetable fibre. The attempt, however, was a failure. He was unable to control, in any way, the volatile gas, which, from its diffusive as well as its noxious qualities, made the process intolerable to those who were charged with its application.

The great problem to be solved, therefore, was how to restrain this diffusive tendency, so that the powerful agent could be safely applied to bleaching purposes. This hidden secret Mr. Tennant set himself resolutely to discover. We are not informed that he ever received a systematic training in the mysteries of chemistry, but we doubt not that his habits of careful observation, and his practical knowledge of the substances necessary for the process of bleaching as it then existed, led him at last to the discovery that the common substance lime possessed a wonderful affinity for the noxious gas, and hence could imprison it, so to speak, till its useful qualities could be applied in the most efficient, economical, and harmless manner.

Now-a-days, when every substance has been rummaged, and poked into, and analysed, till nature has but few secrets to communicate, there is a likelihood that such a plain discovery as the use of the bleaching liquor or the bleaching powder may be undervalued ; all great discoveries, when they become public property, appear very easy of solution. But, irrespective of the effect which this discovery has had on a great national industry, surely we cannot withhold our admiration from the shrewd practical young man as we picture him carrying about daily his precious project, and, in the condition of chemical knowledge at the time, blundering after its realisation almost in the darkness ; nor can we fail to sympathise with him as difficulty after difficulty disappear before his keen scrutiny, and he finds the grand secret at length within his grasp.

It may be explained that lime had been employed for bleaching purposes from a very early time, but owing, we suppose, to its destructive action upon vegetable fibre, it had been prohibited by an ancient and well-known Act of Parliament—unrepealed in Mr. Tennant's time—which empowered the Government inspector, the manufacturer's " bogie," to enter bleaching warehouses, and, on discovery of the forbidden material, to seize the cloth found on the premises, suspend all bleaching operations for two years, besides coming down upon the offenders with the inevitable pecuniary penalties; in short, it gave him power for the offence to ruin the offender. We do not think that the triumph of the discovery would be lessened, in the estimation of the keen-sighted young man, by the fact that he had found what he sought in a substance so common and so unsuspected, and one, moreover, that he well knew would subject him, by its use, to the penalty of having his business and prospects ruined for all time; and we feel persuaded that had the incautious inspector paid a visit to the Darnley warehouse in the hour of triumph, the reception given him would have been " on the north side of friendly."

The advantages of the discovery were at once appreciated. Here was a process that enabled the manufacturer to do the work of months in a few hours. The economy of the discovery, too, was immediately felt. It has been calculated with great plausibility that in the first year that the invention came into use (1789), no less a sum than £166,800 was saved by the process in Ireland alone.

A few years thereafter the Glasgow Chamber of Commerce sent a memorial to Government, praying that, in view of the great importance of the discovery to the whole nation, it should be purchased from Mr. Tennant and thrown open to the public. There is no record of any response to this request. Mr. George Macintosh the younger, mentions that the trustees for the promotion of the Irish linen and hemp manufacture voted a sum of money to the inventor; but he adds—" This proved truly a *Hibernian vote;* " not one penny of the money ever reached the inventor's hands, who " was paid with a cock and bull story, in the usual style of official " honesty."

In the latter end of 1802, Mr. Tennant brought an action

against a firm of bleachers for infringement of his patent. The firm, in fact, represented the bleachers of Lancashire, who had entered into a combination to resist the claims for compensation for the use of the bleaching liquid which the patent conferred.

The case was tried before Lord Ellenborough, who found that, owing to some confusion in the phraseology employed in the specification, as well as to the fact that *one* material mentioned had been in use previously, therefore the patent should be held invalid— a decision which even at the time was generally held to be partial and unjust.

By this time, however, the chemical works had been removed to Glasgow, and had assumed considerable dimensions. Messrs. Charles Macintosh, James Knox, Alexander Dunlop, and Dr. William Couper—all gentlemen of substance and talent—had become partners in the concern. A new patent, more carefully framed, was obtained for the manufacture of bleaching powder, as it was called, the former patent having reference to the impregnated substance in a liquid form. Fortunately the new patent remained unchallenged till the firm had so extended its various manufactures, and so established its reputation, that it could bid defiance to legitimate competition.

Mr. Tennant was a gentleman of remarkable business energy. The manufacturing establishment at St. Rollox, under his vigorous management, was rapidly extended in all its branches, till it became the largest of its kind in Europe ; and, notwithstanding a constitutional hesitancy or nervousness, somewhat remarkable in one possessing such a robust and healthy physical frame, Mr. Tennant entered ardently into most of the schemes which his brother merchants projected for the progress and welfare of Glasgow at the time. The Garnkirk, and the Edinburgh and Glasgow Railways—the former the first railway opened for public traffic in Scotland—owe much to his advocacy and help; indeed, the Garnkirk may be said to have had its origin in his own mind, and to owe its completion entirely to his individual exertions. He was an intimate friend of the great railway engineer, George Stephenson, and was present with him at the opening of the Liverpool and Manchester Line; and he witnessed the melancholy accident that cost the amiable and talented Mr. Huskisson his life.

After a busy life, full of good to the city of his adoption, in which he enjoyed the privilege of being respected by all classes of the community, Mr. Tennant died suddenly at his own residence, Abercrombie Place, Glasgow, in 1838, in the seventy-first year of his age. His friend, Mr. Henry Ashworth of Manchester, thus gracefully and lovingly estimates his character and worth :—" Mr. " Tennant was an earnest and indefatigable promoter of economical " and educational improvement—an uncompromising friend of civil " and religious liberty; while his own inborn energy of character and " clear intellect placed him among the foremost of those men who, " by uniting science to manufactures, have at once extended their " field of action, and entitled their occupations to be classed among " the ranks of the liberal professions."

A little episode in the life of Mr. Tennant, which was repeated to the writer by one of his relatives, is worth recording. At the time he first established his bleachfield at Darnley, in company with his friend, Mr. Cochrane of Paisley, one of his neighbours was the late Mr. Wilson of Hurlet, whose house overlooked the bleaching field. Mr. Wilson was then understood to occupy a prominent place in that distinguished circle or " caste," which we have elsewhere described, and out of which the mere tradesman or dealer was rigidly excluded; but being himself a gentleman of great business energy, he took no pains to conceal his admiration for any who might be imbued with a kindred spirit. For some time the new industry was regarded with little favour by the grand neighbour. As the old man, in his younger days, however, had acquired a habit of early-rising, he observed, one summer morning, a smart, good-looking young man, long before the usual business hours, wandering in the green field with his large watering-can, dispensing its refreshing showers over the snowy croft carpet ; next morning there he was again, before the lark had left its nest ; and the next, and next. On inquiry, he learned that this industrious young man was no less a person than the proprietor and vigorous manager of the new work. His sympathies were at once attracted towards this enterprising neighbour, who was forthwith invited to visit the big house, and on further acquaintance he fairly won the confidence of the old man. Not only so, but Mr. Wilson's fair daughter also was captivated by her new acquaintance, and, in a reasonable time, after going through the usual preliminaries, Miss Wilson became Mrs. Tennant, and thus formed an important link in the chain that still binds the honourable name of Tennant to the fortune and progress of our good town.

On the death of Mr. Charles Tennant, in 1838, his son John carried on the works. He also was a gentleman of uncommon energy and ability, and was esteemed one of the most honourable and upright of the merchants and citizens of Glasgow ; and every movement for the social, commercial, or educational advancement of his native city, found a ready claim to his support. Especially was the goodness of his heart manifested in sympathy with the various agencies in the city for the relief of the destitute and the afflicted, irrespective of station or denomination,—the last act of his useful life being a liberal donation for the relief of poor humanity during the Indian famine.   He died in 1878, aged 82 years.

His son, Charles Tennant, M.P. for Peebles-shire, inherits no small share of the family energy and probity.   His genial courtesy makes him a universal favourite, while his quiet unostentatious wisdom and prudence favour the anticipation widely entertained, that as in his private and business life, so also in his Parliamentary career, he shall justify the confidence reposed in him, and be found a worthy representative of the honourable name he bears.

A word or two regarding the multifarious and onerous duties which devolve upon Mr. Tennant, may fitly close this record of a remarkable house, honoured equally with the noblest in the land. Some idea may be formed of the extent of the works belonging to the firm of Charles Tennant & Co., of which he is principal partner, when it is mentioned that they are estimated to cover one hundred and eighty acres of ground, and to absorb about £120,000 of yearly wages.   He is owner of an estate in Peebles-shire, and takes a great interest in agriculture.   He is also one of the most extensive West Indian planters, his estates producing from eight to nine thousand tons of sugar per annum.   He is chairman of the Steel Company of Scotland, situated near Glasgow—an extensive industry, the first of its kind in Scotland—and also of the very successful Tharsis Copper and Sulphur Company.

After this enumeration, surely we cannot withhold from Mr. Tennant our kindliest wishes, that he may be long spared to perform his many duties worthily, and enjoy the reward of his labours in the esteem of his constituents and his fellow-citizens.

DAVID DALE of Rosebank.

OF all the individuals that pass before us in our hasty survey of the old Glasgow Commercial Aristocracy, there are perhaps none more worthy of our respect and admiration than DAVID DALE, who, from lowly circumstances, raised himself to independence and fortune; whose whole business life was most earnestly devoted to the moral and material welfare of this city, and who has left a reputation which constitutes the best memorial of his worth.

Mr. Dale was born at Stewarton, in the year 1739. His father was a small shopkeeper in that town. His first occupation outside of the little shop was that of a "herd laddie," a very common employment for the sturdy boys of the country towns at that time. The condition of the small farmers of Ayrshire at the period when David pocketed his first "penny fee,"—if, indeed, he received any-thing at all in the shape of money compensation for an irksome and onerous task,—has been described graphically by Colonel Fullarton of Fullarton, Chancellor of the Burgh of Prestwick, and the descrip-tion is worthy of reproduction. "In 1760 there was scarcely a "practicable road in the country. The farm houses were mere hovels "moated with clay, and having an open fire-place in the midst of "the floor—the manure heap at the door—the cattle starving and the

"people wretched. The land was overrun with weeds and rushes,
"and gathered into serpentine ridges. The scanty soil gathered on
"the top of the ridge, and the furrows drowned with water. No
"straw yards—hardly a potato or any other esculent root; no garden
"vegetables, except a few Scotch kail which, with milk and oatmeal,
"formed the principal diet of the people; no hay, except a scanty
"portion of the coarsest quality gathered from the bogs. The
"quantity of manure produced was of small avail, and that portion,
"little as it was, the farmers dragged on cars or sledges wanting
"wheels, or furnished with what were called tumbler wheels, which
"turned on their wooden axletrees, the wretched vehicle hardly fit to
"carry and draw five hundredweight. The ground was scourged
"with a succession of oats after oats, as long as it could pay for seed
"and labour, and afford a small surplus of meal for family use, and
"then it was allowed to remain in a state of absolute sterility, or
"overrun with thistles, till rest had enabled it to produce another
"series of scanty crops.

"Many of the farm leases were granted for three times nineteen
"years. The rent was mostly paid in 'kind.' One-half of the
"crops went to the landlord, and the other remained with the
"tenant to support his family. The tenant was expected, moreover,
"to assist his landlord in ploughing, leading peats or crops, working
"hay, and other operations, which, from their nature, interfered
"with the attention requisite on his own farm.

"As there were few or no enclosures, the horses and other
"cattle were either tethered during the summer months or entrusted
"to the care of a herd and collie dog, by whom the poor starved
"beasts were kept in constant agitation, being impelled by starva-
"tion to fly from bare leys, and commit continual depradations
"on the growing crops. The cattle—starved during winter, hardly

"able to rise without aid in spring, and perpetually harassed during
"summer—were never in a fit condition for the market; indeed,
"very little butcher meat was used, excepting the 'Mart,' which
"was generally the most unsaleable of the flock, and which farmers
"generally salted at Martinmas, to serve for food through the
"winter. A small portion of this, with groats or home-made
"barley[1] and kail, was the usual dinner, and with porridge,
"oatmeal cakes, and milk, and, on rare occasions, the luxury of
"butter or a bit of cheese, formed the only food of the people. So
"small was the consumption of butcher meat at this time, that not
"more than fifty head of cattle were killed annually in the county
"town of Ayr, although it contained a population of from four to
"five thousand.

"There were no manufactures in the country, excepting bonnets
"at Stewarton, and shoes, and a growing trade in carpets at
"Kilmarnock.

"Exports and imports at the harbours of Ayr, Irvine, and
"Saltcoats, were very trifling. The finest lands were let for two or
"three shillings an acre; and as there was hardly any substitute for
"oatmeal, the people were entirely at the mercy of the seasons. If
"the seed-time was unfavourable, the summer bad, or the harvest
"late and stormy, a dearth or famine unavoidably ensued. In these
"seasons of misery, the poor people have not unfrequently been
"obliged to resort to such shifts as bleeding their cattle, that with
"the blood so obtained, boiled with oatmeal or herbs and roots,
"they might be enabled to eke out a scanty existence."

In circumstances such as are here described, young David Dale
received his initiatory experience of life, and while he gathered

---

[1] The "knocking mell and stone," for the manufacture of groats and pot barley, were, in old times, invariable adjuncts to the farmers' establishment.

health and strength at his solitary task, we doubt not that he was also slowly acquiring that shrewd and thoughtful character which constituted a marked feature in his career. The peasants of Ayrshire at this time were strongly imbued with a sound religious principle and feeling, transmitted down from the old persecuting times, when their fathers testified to the sincerity of their convictions at the risk of sacrificing worldly comfort, and even life itself; and although some "professors" did provoke, and might have deserved the bitter castigations of the poet Burns, yet we like to conjecture how much guiding and strengthening influence those good old God-fearing men and women exercised over the mind of the docile herd boy.

When the time came round that David must take an independent part in the battle of life, many earnest consultations, no doubt, were held in the back parlour of the little Stewarton shop. All sorts of work requiring strength of arm and limb were then miserably remunerated, and there were few openings in the poor little town of Stewarton for the well-conditioned and thoughtful lad. At length it was decided that David should be sent to the weaving trade, by which, in course of time, he might be enabled to earn his twelve or fourteen shillings weekly, or, if steady and dexterous, as he gave fair promise to be, a still greater rate of wages; nay, he might even aspire to the ultimate dignity, responsibility, and emoluments of a "bowl cork," or dealer in yarns.

Kilmarnock, as we have mentioned, was now growing in repute for its carpet manufactures, and it was probably matter of discussion also, whether David should become an item in the "creeshie nations" that "fidged and clawed" through the old town. It was finally determined, however, that he should go to Paisley, and in that ancient town accordingly he served his weaving apprenticeship.

It is worthy of remark that this was long before the use in Scotland of the "fly shuttle," and all kind of weaving work was then accomplished by dexterously pitching from hand to hand a heavily-laden iron-shod shuttle, an occupation requiring strength, aptitude, and perseverance—qualifications, we may presume, with which the young man was largely gifted. After his apprenticeship was finished, he wrought for some time as a journeyman in Hamilton, and about the year 1763 we find him employed as a clerk in a drapery establishment in Glasgow.

This was the turn of his fortune, the outlet of that keen sagacity which was his prevailing characteristic. Shortly afterwards, guided by the experience he had acquired when a humble journeyman weaver, now fortified by further insight as to suitable markets and fair prices, the result of his habits of observation while employed as a drapery clerk, he ventured upon what might be esteemed a bold step on the part of a comparatively penniless lad, namely, to try his fortune, sink or swim, in the great whirlpool of Glasgow commerce. The boldness of the enterprise will be more apparent when we consider that the winning prizes of trade, as well as of social and civic standing, were in the hands of a distinguished caste, who had guardedly surrounded themselves by a distinctive circle, to which we have scarcely anything corresponding in modern society, and of which we can only form a vague idea. From this circle the small tradesman and the petty shopkeeper were rigorously excluded. The adventure on the part of David Dale, however, was very unobtrusive. He took a small shop in an old-fashioned building, known as "Hopkirk's land," a few doors north of the Cross, in High Street. The shop rent was sufficiently moderate, being only five pounds yearly ; and here he set up in a small way, as a dealer in yarns, a growing trade, the benefits of which he no doubt foresaw. And lest the shop rent should lessen too much his anticipated margin of annual profit, he contrived to portion off a fair division of the accommodation to a watchmaker, who in return paid an equal share of the rent. What a queer combination! We like to picture the round-faced, thick-set, brisk lad, bustling among his dusty yarn bundles, or haggling over their price, in one corner of the little low-roofed ware-room, and on the other side a solemn gentleman peering into one of those strange-looking turnip-shaped watches, while ranks of old-fashioned eight-day clocks, with their sober faces, are swinging their pendulums hither and thither along the walls. However incongruous the partnership might seem, there it continued for many a long year, during which Mr. Dale's speculations throve wondrously. He became one of the most extensive importers of French and Flemish yarns in the city, and year by year increased in riches and honours ; and we cannot help surmising that it would be with feelings of deep regret he parted with his old companion the watchmaker, when he was appointed, in 1783, first agent in the city for the Royal Bank, and the watchmaker's shop was converted into a banking office.

We henceforth lose sight of the poor weaver lad trying his little shifts for the bettering of his fortunes in the busy city, and are now introduced to the prosperous Glasgow merchant, who, by virtue of pure force of character and intelligence, had fairly broken down that wall of distinction which once separated him from the great tobacco and sugar lords, and could now wear his cocked hat jauntily, display his silver knee buckles showily, and take the place of honour on the crown of the causeway with the proudest of them all. How we wish for some occult science that might enable us to lift the veil of intervening years, and peep into the back parlour of the "little store of a' things" in Stewarton, and there listen to the expressions of opinion and gratulation interchanged between the good old shopkeeper and his "vaunty" wife respecting the career of their weaver boy!

When the Chamber of Commerce was instituted in 1783, Mr. Dale threw the whole force of his energies into the scheme. He was one of the first board of directors; he officiated as chairman in 1786 and 1787; and for twenty-one years acted as one of its most honoured and trusted directors.

In 1783 the celebrated Sir Richard Arkwright, inventor of the spinning jennie, visited Glasgow, and was invited to a banquet, got up by the merchants of the city, in honour of his visit. David Dale was present—it need scarcely be said with that sagacious head of his, filled with the prospective benefits likely to accrue from the wonderful invention. He afterwards persuaded Sir Richard to accompany him to the upper reaches of the Clyde, to find where the river could be most advantageously and easily applied, for the purposes of the new branch of industry. We are inclined to believe that the whole details had been arranged and forecast in Mr. Dale's practical judgment previous to the visit. Be that as it may, the result of the survey was, that a boggy hollow—the property of the notorious Judge Braxfield, situated within a short distance of the county town of Lanark, and described as a mere morass, utterly worthless for any other purpose—was fixed upon as a suitable site for the new industry; and so satisfied was Sir Richard with the advantages of the situation, that he voluntary offered to become a principal partner in the speculation, and held that position for some years.

No time was lost before operations were commenced. Land was cleared and building immediately begun, but owing to the difficulty of excavating a rocky hill that interfered with the necessary supply of water, spinning did not commence till March, 1786. The first mill in operation was accidently destroyed by fire, shortly after its erection, but was speedily rebuilt; and in the course of five years no fewer than four mills were in operation, employing 1334 hands. The manager of the works was Mr. William Kelly, father of the late Mr. Kelly, cotton broker, well-known in this city. Mr. William Kelly, in 1792, invented and patented a self-acting spinning machine, which was expected to supersede skilled labour entirely, and to require only such attention as could be given by children. The invention, however, turned out, in practice, a failure, and the patent machinery was found less profitable than the old system of hand guidance by trained spinners. Mr. Kelly, although he applied for, and took out a patent for his invention, never insisted upon his patent rights, and we believe that the principle of his machine has been applied successfully in the self-acting spinning machine of recent times.[1]

A great proportion of the population about the new working establishment were Highlanders. About the time that the Lanark mills commenced operations, sheep farming on an extensive scale was introduced by some of the Highland lairds in the northern districts of Scotland. This broke up many a little group of labourers' dwellings, whose inmates were obliged to seek

---

[1] Mr. Kelly was an ingenious country watch and clock maker in Lanark, and was employed by Mr. Dale for his mechanical ingenuity. The appointment fully justified Mr. Dale's sagacity. Mr. Kelly not only managed the work faithfully and efficiently, but he also entered with enthusiasm into all the schemes which Mr. Dale organized for the well-being of the little Lanark community, and was a loving and persevering co-worker in all Mr. Dale's benevolent undertakings. A handsome clock of his own construction still points out the time, through so many years, in the warehouse, graced by his name at 23 Exchange Square. If the old thing were gifted with intelligence, what a tale of progress and of change it could unfold! The present respected head of the firm, Mr. Anthony Hannay, and the late lamented Mr. John Matheson, Jun., were both clerks in the counting-house of Kelly & Co.

for themselves employment in the large towns, or to cross the Atlantic and find homes in the wildernesses of Canada. Government took alarm at the prospective dearth of soldiers and sailors that this emigration threatened, and used all its influence to stay the exodus. David Dale and his friend George Macintosh, a gentleman of similar sympathies, as well as kindred force of character, exerted all their energies in the same direction, more, perhaps, from benevolent motives than from patriotic principle. A ship-load of poor Highland emigrants, numbering about two hundred, were put back by stress of weather, and landed at Greenock in very destitute circumstances. Mr. Dale prevailed upon them all to become helpers in his works. He made known his desire to receive poor Highland families, and grant them such sustenance as they required, until they had gained sufficient skill in the work to enable them to earn their own livelihood comfortably.

The greater part of the preparatory operations in the cotton manufacture were then done by hand, and as this kind of work (teasing, picking, &c.,) depended more on dexterity of fingers than strength of body, large numbers of children were employed in the work. Hundreds of poor children were apprenticed from orphan asylums and poorhouses in Edinburgh and elsewhere. A large boarding-house was erected for their accommodation. They were well fed and clothed, and their education and moral training were conscientiously attended to; yet we learn with pain that, of 795 boys and girls employed in the work, no fewer than 523 were under fourteen years of age, and of these, 297 ranged from six to ten years. Moreover, all these children, even the youngest, we are told, began work at six in the morning, and continued till seven in the evening, with an interval of half an hour for breakfast, and an hour for dinner. This was the daily routine, after

which they were expected to attend school till nine o'clock each
night.   Poor little wretches!   Yet it is testified that in seven years'
time, notwithstanding the severity of the ordeal, only five of the
small drudges had died.[1]

The concern proved highly remunerative.   Spinning factories
were established at the Firth of Dornoch, at Blantyre, at Catrine,
at Lochwinnoch, and other places.   With many of these Mr. Dale
was connected.   With his friend, Mr. Macintosh, he set up an
establishment for dyeing turkey red, a new and untried industry.
This work was further developed subsequently by the family of
James Monteith of Anderston, till it became not only the first but
the most important establishment of the kind in Scotland.   Mr.
Dale started an inkle factory also, which turned out highly
remunerative.   He became immensely rich; civic honours were
showered upon him; he was appointed a city bailie in 1791, and
again in 1794: and yet, with all the burden and temptation of
honour and riches upon him, he remained plain unspoiled David Dale
still.   The little shop in Hopkirk's land, with its modest banking
business and its dusty yarn bundles, was retained up to 1798, when
Mr. Dale removed to St. Andrew's Square, then newly built, and
esteemed the great commercial centre of the city.

Of Mr. Dale's works of kindness and charity many instances
are preserved.   In 1799–1800, there was a grievous failure of the
crops in Scotland.   The pressure of distress and want was sorely
felt by all, but of course fell most heavily upon the working classes.
The defective system of agriculture, to which we have already
alluded, and the restrictions placed upon the importation of food by
the iniquitous corn laws, intensified the distress.   Old people still

[1] See Mr. Lockhart's article on New Lanark, in Sir John Sinclair's "Statistical Account of
Scotland, 1796."

remember the stories which once formed part of the winter fireside entertainment, about the battling over the single "peck of meal" to which every family was restricted ; of the weary waiting for hours on the precious dole ; of the terrors of the military array which guarded the treasures, and kept the eager and hungry crowds at a distance. These were just the circumstances to call for all the energies of Mr. Dale. It is recorded that he chartered a vessel to proceed to America, with orders to bring home a full lading of grain —any kind that could most speedily be procured. When the vessel returned, the pressure of want was very severe. The bulk of the ship's cargo was Indian corn, then little known. This was received with demonstrations of joy and gratitude, and many a hungry family blessed the "benevolent Magistrate," as he was commonly named, for his much needed and highly prized "sma' peas." The Magistrates and Councillors most nobly responded to the appeal of want. Conjointly with the benevolent merchants of the city, they imported food to the value of £117,500. This they sold and distributed among the inhabitants, with a final loss to the contributors of £15,000,—a large sum in these days. This charity was long remembered with feelings of gratitude and love to the memory of those by whom the loss had been sustained.

In Jones' Directory of 1789, the following address is inserted :— "Mrs. Brown, dealer in cotton and cotton yarn, first flat, Lang's land, Prince's Street." Mrs. Brown was a widow, whose history is curious. Her husband was a shoemaker, who, when he died, left a large stock of leather and ready-made boots and shoes. As the widow had but little experience in the business, she applied to Mr. Dale for his advice as to how the stock should be disposed of. He suggested that the leather should be speedily wrought up into shoes, and consigned to a well-known American merchant, with instructions to return the value in raw cotton, for which he assured her she should find a ready sale and a good profit; and as the cautious widow expressed her fears respecting the risk she ran of losing her precious stock, Mr. Dale promised to take a share in the adventure. When the cotton arrived Mrs. Brown again waited on Mr. Dale for further guidance. He advised that it should be placed in the hands of a careful agent and sold. " Na, na," said she; " I'll juist sell it "a' mysel', and that'll save commission, ye ken." So, providing herself with a stout leather pouch, which she filled with cotton samples, she sold her stock so advantageously that she was induced to enter into the cotton trade on an extensive scale, and soon became the first in that business. Dr. John Buchanan says—" She " passed more value through her hands than any woman in " Scotland." In the disastrous year 1794, Mrs. Brown was seques-trated, but she seems to have recovered, in a short time, the credit of her house, and, abjuring the conversation and sympathies of her own sex, she to the last carried round her samples, and made her sales in her own way—a queer specimen of the cautious and thrifty merchant of the period. The late Mr. Robert Henderson —of Robert and John Henderson, well-known Glasgow merchants —when a lad, was employed by Mrs. Brown as a clerk in her cotton warehouse.

However strange it may appear, Mr. Dale was a sectary in religious matters. He left the good old Establishment, and one of its most popular ministers, Dr. Gillies of the College church, and became a dissenter, and a dissenting preacher. Three gentlemen were the prime movers in this matter—Mr. Dale, Mr. Archibald Paterson, and Mr. Matthew Alexander,—the latter gentleman was great-grandfather to three well-known Glasgow merchants of the present day, viz., Edward, John, and George Alexander.

To account in some measure for this secession, it may be stated that, in the little New Lanark community, there lingered a strong flavour of the old Jacobite feeling, and of the old religious persuasion that gave it vitality. Mr. Dale and his friend, George Macintosh, both employed large numbers of Highlanders, who, no doubt, were trained from their earliest years to cherish these sentiments reverentially, and both these gentlemen stipulated that all their workers should enjoy full freedom of religious opinion. In the middle of last century, a crusade against Popery and everything tinged by this form of faith was got up in Glasgow. One of the town ministers received the thanks of the General Session for a violent speech which he fulminated against the doctrine and its professors, wherein he depicted " The awful signs of the Divine displeasure " displayed in the encouragement given to the growth of that system " whose distinguishing doctrines and usages are according to the " flesh, after the working of Satan in all deceivableness of unrighte- " ousness." We have a strong persuasion that Mr. Dale, although perhaps scarcely free from the prevailing prejudices of the times, felt that this want of charity, which had become incorporated with the very essence of Church polity, was more than he could patiently bear, especially when it evinced itself, as it did soon after- wards, in acts of violence and outrage.

This bigotry, conjoined with the cold morality of the pulpit, must have provoked in the mind of the good man involuntary comparison with the humble and simple thanksgiving for that love which bestowed the "unspeakable gift" so earnestly acknowledged in the nightly "exercise" at the Ayrshire farmer's fireside, or in the back room of the Stewarton shop; and the kindly sympathies of Mr. Dale impelled him to share with others the experience and blessing of an influence that he himself found could be the surest guide in life, and the greatest comfort at death.[1]

The ostensible cause of the rupture with the Established Church, however, was the question of Patronage, the Magistrates and Council having appointed an unpopular minister to the Wynd Church, notwithstanding the repeated protests of the congregation.   Mr. Dale at first connected himself with the Albion Street Church,[2] an offshoot of this disruption ; but growing dissatisfied with several points in the practice of all Presbyterian churches at the time, and especially with that which he esteemed a neglect of the duty and privilege of Sacramental communion, which he thought should be partaken of more frequently, he, with a number of personal friends, hired a small room for their own social worship.   The accommodation soon became too limited for the little congregation, and one of their number, about 1770, erected a meeting-house, in Greyfriars Wynd, capable of accommodating about 500 worshippers.   The modest building, from the circumstance that it was got up by a wealthy candlemaker (Mr. Archibald Paterson), was then and subsequently known as the " Caunnel Kirk."

An inveterate prejudice existed at this time against the sad and sorrowful defection of Independency, arising from the belief, not yet wholly extinct, that soundness in the faith was somehow linked with Presbyterianism alone ; so the new sect found but little public sympathy.   The first teaching elders in the communion, Mr. Dale and Mr. Ferrier—who had been a minister in the old church

---

[1] " The truth is, a more decided idea of Evangelism than had been generally preached by the "pastors of the Kirk of Scotland began to take possession of the public mind ; and, consequently, "where that peculiarity of faith was most insisted on—as was always the case in the pulpits of the "Independent churches—it is not difficult to account for the number of proselytes which that body "obtained."—*Strang's* " *Glasgow and its Clubs*," *page 348.*

[2] The old dingy building still exists, and is now used as a leather store.

of Largo—were hustled on the public streets, and found themselves often obliged to take shelter under some friendly roof. Even the modest "Caunnel Kirk" came in for a share of the common rough usage, till the authorities were called upon to interfere. The prevailing dislike then assumed another form. Crowds of mischievous lads filled the little church to turn the service into ridicule. On one occasion, it having been announced that a certain Mr. Smith was to take part in the services, some of these wicked wags got up a signboard in imitation of a country blacksmith's, which was fixed above the door of the church, with the inscription,—"Preaching done here by David Dale, Smith and Ferrier!" All these annoyances Mr. Dale soon lived down. The little congregation grew in numbers and influence, and some of its old adherents—for the Communion still exists, under the name of the Old Scotch Independents—tell with justifiable pride of the ranks of carriages that stood in the Grammar School Wynd, waiting on the "skailing" of the Candle Kirk.

But soon a more grievous influence for evil fell upon the little congregation, and one which might easily have been predicated as inevitable in a society of terribly conscientious individuals, each tenacious of his own convictions, and with no higher board of arbitration than brethren of similar earnestness and similar obstinacy. Questions arose regarding the frequent and regular use of the Lord's Prayer; about standing during the service of praise; about the audible repetition of the "Amen" after prayer, &c. On these and similar questions, Mr. Dale, as might have been expected, counselled forbearance, but a large party were obstinate, and, under the leadership of his co-pastor, Mr. Ferrier, broke off, and joined the Glassites, whose religious system enjoined the duty of holding love feasts; the washing of each others' feet ; of abstinence from the use of things strangled and of *blood*, a duty that, in view of the time-honoured institution of the " Mart," was anything but acceptable. A community of goods was also enjoined ; and what must have been esteemed as little short of sheer insanity in these Presbyterial days, the support and countenance of the sect were given to theatrical representations, and similar entertainments. Their place of meeting was known as the " Kail Kirk," that much esteemed dish forming an invariable item in the "love feast." There can be little doubt that this first secession grieved the kind heart of Mr. Dale, but greater perplexities were in store for him and his little church. The practical question arose whether a leading elder could lawfully marry a second wife. Paul had expressly said, "An elder must be the husband of *one* wife." Would not a second marriage, therefore, be a direct violation of an explicit Scriptural injunction? Besides, grave doubts arose, especially in the minds of the poorer brethren, regarding the inequality of worldly possessions amongst them, in view of the good Apostolical practice of having all things in common, a practice which, in the cautious mind of the founder of the church, seems to have been contemplated with little favour. The result was another break in the little congregation. But the saddest breach of all was yet before him. Controversy again rent the congregation, regarding their duty and obligation with respect to adult baptism, and in the dissensions which this question raised his own wife bore a part, and with blamable contumacy, as we think, took up the side of the argument in opposition to him whom she should have been the first to honour. With all these dissensions to vex his spirit, the good man, Mr. Dale, struggled on, comforted and strengthened by the grand old Apostolic philosophy, upon which he preached his first sermon,—" I am debtor both to the wise and to the unwise, so, as

" much as in me is, I am ready to preach the Gospel to you ; for I
" am not ashamed of the Gospel of Christ, for it is the power of
" God unto salvation to every one that believeth."

When Mr. Dale was first elected a magistrate for the city, it
was the practice to attend in official state, on certain Sundays,
at one of the City churches, accompanied and preceded by the
town's officers in scarlet coat and cocked hat, bearing the glittering
Lochaber axe,—"A terror to evil doers." Great perplexity took
hold of the minds of the civic brethren as to how Mr. Dale was
to be disposed of in the grand parade. Common courtesy forbade
that he should be asked to the "laft seat" in the Tron, and their
respect for him was far too sincere to permit even a shadow of
neglect. A few of the guard of honour were therefore "detailed
off," with instructions to convey Mr. Dale with due pomp and
circumstance to the " Caunnel Kirk ;" and doubtless the procession
—the appearance of which it is by no means difficult to realize—
would create a profound impression ! It was the custom in the
little church at that time (a custom which, with some modification,
is still continued), to set before every member, at mid-day, a slice
of bread and cheese, the dry morsel being washed down by con-
tinuous applications to a large tin flagon or "loving cup," well
replenished with good cauldron ale or porter—tell it not in
teetotaldom!—and circulated amongst them from lip to lip ; and we
have often tried to picture the sombre faces of the red-coated
gentry, when, in those days of deep dramming, the sapless bite and
sour browst was the only reward for their important and august
services !

Mr. Dale, some years before his death, bought from Mr. John
Dunlop, of Carmyle, the house and small estate of Rosebank ; and
here, on the banks of the yet unpolluted and beautiful Clyde, he

spent the latter years of his active and useful life. Among his last appearances as a director of the Chamber of Commerce was to do honour to his old and tried friend, Mr. Gilbert Hamilton, the Secretary, when his brother directors presented him with a well merited testimony of respect for his long and faithful services. After the death of Mr. Henry Riddle, who died while chairman of the Chamber, his kindly countenance was seen no more at the meetings of the Board. He was able to walk about in comparatively good health till within a short time of his death. The late venerable Dr. Jamieson thus lovingly describes the last scene of all. "Feeling "his end approaching, he sent for some leading members of his "church, whom he exhorted to remain steadfast in their Christian "profession, and gave them the dying testimony of his faith in the "Gospel—asked them for forgivenness if on any occasion he had "given them offence, and prayed for a blessing on them; after "which, as the elders of Ephesus did to Paul, 'they all fell upon "his neck and kissed him, sorrowing most of all for the words that "he spake, that they should see his face no more.' Exhausted by "this parting scene, he rapidly sank, and on the following day, the "17th April, 1806, he departed in the sixty-eighth year of his age, "deeply regretted by all parties: by the church, who loved and "revered him as their faithful pastor; by the poor, who largely "participated in his liberal charities; and by the general community, "who esteemed him both as a man and a Christian."

The following tribute to the memory of Mr. Dale was written by Dr. Wardlaw, whose father was a Glasgow merchant, and an associate in many good works with Mr. Dale. It appeared in an obituary notice inserted in *The Glasgow Herald* of 1806:—

"Mr. Dale had not, in the outset of life, enjoyed the advantage "of a polished or liberal education, but the want of it was greatly

"compensated by a large share of natural sagacity and good sense,
"and extensive and discriminating knowledge of human character,
"and by a modest, gentle, dignified simplicity of manner peculiar
"to himself, and which secured to him the respect and attention of
"every company and of every rank of life. A zealous promoter of
"the general industry and manufactures of his country, his schemes
"of business were extensive and liberal, conducted with singular
"prudence and perseverance, and, by the blessing of God, were
"crowned with such abundant success as served to advance his
"rank in society, and to furnish him with the means of that diffu-
"sive benevolence which rendered his life a public blessing, and
"shed a lustre on his character rarely exemplified in any age
"of the world. His ear was never shut to the cry of distress;
"his private charities were boundless; and every public institu-
"tion which had for its object the alleviation or prevention
"of human misery received from him the most liberal support
"and encouragement. Like the patriarch of old, he was 'eyes to
"the blind, feet to the lame, and he caused the widow's heart to
"sing for joy.' In private life his conduct, actuated by the same
"principles, was equally exemplary; for he was a kind parent, a
"generous friend, a wise and faithful counsellor, a lover of hospi-
"tality, a lover of good men, 'sober, holy, just, temperate;' and
"having thus 'occupied his talents,' he has entered into the joy
"of his Lord."

The denomination which Mr. Dale founded still exists. Their
place of meeting is in Oswald Street. There are twelve churches
in the connection in Scotland and England, and one in the
United States. They profess no peculiarity of faith or doctrine,
but preach the Gospel in all simplicity. They claim the privilege
of managing their own affairs without control; they have a plurality

of pastors and deacons, whose labours must be gratuitous, "except when circumstances require it to be otherwise;" baptism they administer to the infants of members in the usual way; the Sacrament of the Supper is dispensed every week; and the seats in the church are free to all.

Mr. Dale had one son, who died young, and five daughters, who all survived him. Two of these were married to clergymen of the Church of England, and one to the notorious socialist, Robert Owen, who for some time was manager of her father's Lanark mills, and was, at the date of their marriage, a principal owner.

It is pitiable to think how the handsome fortune left to Mr. Owen—the hard won fruits of the old man's industry—was literally thrown away in vain efforts to renovate society after a model which neither past experience, sound philosophy, nor even good common sense could sanction; and of which efforts not a single trace now remains, but such as demonstrate their utter folly, and exhibit to the world the whole life's aspirations of poor Mr. Owen as a miserable failure.

GEORGE MACINTOSH,

OF DUNCHATTAN.

ANY of our philosophical readers who may feel a desire to trace the commercial development of our wonderful city to its first beginning, would do well to take a meditative stroll up Ark Lane, past Tennant's old Brewery, in what is now known as the Dennistoun suburb. Here are to be seen mysterious, purposeless fragments of high brick walls, mixed up with and aimlessly intersecting rows of pretentious modern cottages and villas, with here and there little nests of old ruined houses now entirely fallen into decay,—the whole presenting a scene of striking desolation, and of fantastic contrast, such as can seldom be seen except in troubled dreams.

These ruins are all that is now left of the Cudbear Manufactory of George Macintosh & Co., which enjoyed a vigorous existence before a thread of machine-spun yarn or a yard of machine-woven cloth was known in Scotland.

The life of GEORGE MACINTOSH, like that of his friend David Dale, is closely associated with the mercantile and manufacturing prosperity of Glasgow. Indeed, the business career of both these gentlemen presents many points of striking resemblance. Both began life comparatively poor and friendless; both were animated by the same upright and honourable motives, and guided by the same prudence and sagacity; both were highly successful in business, and devoted the fruits of that success to the promotion of the noblest purposes ; and the names of both have come down to the present day, hallowed by loving remembrances ; whilst many of their associates, with larger pretensions, and occupying more distinguished social positions, are now fairly forgotten.

Mr. Macintosh was born in 1739. His father, Lachlan Macintosh, was tacksman of a farm in Roskeen, Ross-shire, the cultivation of which enabled him to live with his family in comfort and independence. Young George, after going through the usual initiatory routine of country farm work, and finding that the position of a fourth son on a small Highland holding offered but sorry prospects of future worldly advantages, resolved to seek his fortune in Glasgow. Accordingly, with a good stock of health and hope, a fair amount of education, and plenty of Highland enthusiasm, he entered as a junior clerk in the large city tanwork, situated on the classical Molindinar.

The art of tanning and manufacturing leather has been one of the leading branches of industry in Glasgow for ages. Far back in the reign of Charles II. the following curious entry was inserted, and still exists in the records of the burgh :—" The saide day the saids " Provest, Bailies, and Counsall, maid report that they had con- " siddered John Woddrops petition, with the loss of his hydes that " was takin out of his holls and laide on vpon the sydes of the " houssis for saving them from the lait fyre in Gallowgaite, which " they fund to be very considderable, and therfoir for helping to " repair the samyne they thought fitt to gif him vp his band of " nyne hundreth and fyftie merks monie, &c."

The Glasgow historian, John M'Ure, in the beginning of last century, thus discourses upon the Molindinar tanwork :—" Bell's " tannarie is a prodigious large building, consisting of bark and

"lime pits, store houses, and other high and low appartments, with
"all conveniences whatsomever for carrying on that great work;
"the buildings are so considerable that it is admired by all strangers
"who see it."

Gibson, who wrote his history of Glasgow in 1777, mentions the
somewhat striking fact, that, while the whole iron trade of Glasgow
at the time was valued at £23,000, the value of the boot and shoe
trade could be fairly estimated at £32,000, or, including saddlery
and tanned leather, £85,000 per annum.

Most of the leading merchants of the city were partners in the
"Spoutmouth Tannerie" about the time when Mr. Macintosh
entered as a clerk in the business, and we find in the list of partners
the names of Mr. Glassford of Dougaldston, Mr. Campbell of
Clathic, Mr. Speirs of Elderslie, Mr. Bogle of Daldowie, Provost
Bowman, and others—all men of rank at the time.   Perhaps the
most remunerative branch of the old tannery business was the
manufacture of boots and shoes for home sale and exportation.
The double profits upon exported manufactures and imported
produce had already made many a handsome fortune, and this, no
doubt, Mr. Macintosh had sufficient sagacity to perceive.   The
various steps which led to the first change in his commercial
position are not recorded, but we find him, in 1773, in the thirty-
fourth year of his age, with 500 boot and shoemakers in his
service, and fairly established as a formidable rival to the original
tannery company in this branch of business; and although he
must have had little practical knowledge of the business, yet, by his
careful superintendence, the speculation prospered, and was prose-.
cuted with energy for many years.

About this time he was also connected with a glass manufactory, and, to a limited extent, with the West India trade, but

these speculations were soon abandoned in favour of that one great industry to which the greater part of his vigorous energies were henceforth to be devoted. This was the manufacture of "Cudbear" —a dye stuff which, in the age of the purple duffle and the distinguishing state cloak, which marked the rank of the Virginian merchant, was destined to come into extensive use.

The discovery and introduction of this material is curious and romantic, and worthy of record. In the early part of last century, a decent copper and tinsmith of the clan Gordon left his Highland home to prosecute his business in London. In the ordinary course of duty he was employed to repair an old copper boiler in a metropolitan dye-house, famed for producing the Orseille or Archella dye, an ancient art said to have been practised by the Italians, and brought to this country from Florence. While Mr. Gordon was engaged at his task, he was struck with the great similarity of the different processes that he saw going on around him, to those which he remembered to have seen at his own mother's fireside. There, most assuredly, was the well-known lichen or rock-moss, which, under the familiar name of "crottal," he had gathered for dyeing purposes when a boy, and the lustre of which might have graced his own first "philabeg." Its connection with his home in the Highland glen, therefore, was quite as ancient —yes, and as interesting and respectable too!—as with the old Florentines; for, had not the same process been followed by his grandmother and great-grandmother, and the whole Gordon clan, away back into the far remote generations? It so happened that Mr. Cuthbert Gordon, his nephew,—a shrewd, long-headed young Highlander—was at this time following his studies as a chemist, and to him Mr. Gordon communicated his theories respecting the ancient and valuable dye. A course of experimental investigations resulted in confirming the correctness of Mr. Gordon's conclusions, and also in the discovery of a method for procuring the dyeing extract in a concentrated form, which, in honour of the young man who had made the valuable discovery, was henceforth to be distinguished by the somewhat unmusical modification of his own name, "Cudbear."

The manufacture of cudbear on a large scale was first attempted at Leith, by the Messrs. Gordon, uncle and nephew, in company with the brothers Alexander of Edinburgh; but the speculation, although prosecuted with considerable energy for some time, was ultimately unsuccessful, probably for want of the necessary capital to carry on operations on a sufficiently remunerative scale. While in this languishing condition, the business attracted the notice of Mr. Macintosh, who was struck with the ingenuity of the process thus improved, and its importance as a new and profitable manufacture. Besides, one of the most striking features in his character was his intense "clanishness," as it was called, and his love for all that could remind him of the Highland hills and his early home; and there can be little doubt that the new industry would receive additional value in his estimation, from the circumstance that he also must have often seen the common dyeing process, as practised in his boyhood, at the fireside of the old shieling of Auchinluich, among the braes of Roskeen, his own Highland home.

At any rate, he set about the resuscitation of the decaying industry with his accustomed vigour. He had sufficient influence to organize a wealthy co-partnery to take up the business, comprising the names of many of the most substantial merchants in the city; a piece of land was purchased in the eastern outskirts of the town, "by the Craig's park," subsequently extended to about seventeen acres; and to this place the works were removed from Leith in 1777. According to the original arrangement, the Messrs. Gordon conducted the practical details of the manufacture, but the business department in all its details was under the sole charge of Mr. Macintosh from the first.

In order to preserve the valuable secret of the cudbear manufacture, the most stringent precautions were taken. A strong wall, ten feet high, was built all round the works; within this wall an elegant and substantial house was erected, in which Mr. Macintosh resided, and which he named Dunchattan (the hill of the Macintosh). Here he surrounded himself with trusty Highlanders, all solemnly sworn to secrecy on entering the service, and mostly all residing within the walls, for the convenience of hearing the Gaelic roll called nightly, and each answering to his own name—a ceremony that was never neglected. So exclusively Highland was the little community, and so markedly isolated from the outside world, that it is said many of the members lived and died within the walls, without the ability of making themselves understood in decent English.

The manufacture of cudbear is now well understood, and may be shortly described as the art of extracting a vegetable dye from a species of *lichen*, that grows chiefly upon sea-side rocks, by macerating the vegetable in ammonia. Some idea of the extent of the operations conducted by the cudbear company may be gathered from the fact, that the consumption of the lichen from which the dye is obtained amounted to about 250 tons annually. Indeed, the supply in this country was in a short time exhausted, and Norway and Sweden were resorted to for fresh supplies, with this result, that the material rose in price from £3 per ton to £25, and in war time even £45; and it was found that, on a moderate calculation, no less a sum than £306,000 was remitted to these countries during the time their connection with the cudbear company lasted. There is another striking fact in connection with the business. One of the waste products of the town was found to contain a sufficient amount of ammonia for extracting the dye; and as the material could be obtained for the cost of collecting, it might be supposed that this item of expense would be trifling, yet we are assured that it cost the company £800 annually.

The confidence of Mr. Macintosh was sorely tested by the defalcation of one of his trusty Highlanders, who left his service shortly after the establishment of the cudbear works, to instruct a rival London company in the art and mystery of cudbear manufacture. A conciliatory arrangement, however, seems to have been effected with this company, who were never very prosperous, and soon abandoned the manufacture altogether. The Glasgow works were highly prosperous, notwithstanding this rivalry, under the management, first of Mr. Macintosh, and afterwards of his son Charles, and subsequently of his grandson George, and the late well-known and greatly respected Mr. John King of Levernholm, up till the year 1852, when the old firm of George Macintosh & Co. ceased to exist, having enjoyed a prosperous existence for the long period of seventy-five years.

Old Dunchattan House still sturdily resists the ravages of time and change. A few of the ancient orchard trees yet toss their leafless branches in the summer sky, and here and there, as we have said, scraps and fragments of the original boundary walls wander upwards and downwards, and indications are not wanting of where a dwelling once stood ; but the little Highland village, like the small community who gave it life and interest, has passed away for ever.

Before leaving this subject, we should like to notice a circumstance which pleasingly illustrates the feeling of reciprocal obligation that existed between master and servant in the old cudbear factory.

When the business was finally wound up, not one of the old workers was forgotten or neglected. Every individual able to work was in some way provided with employment, or supported till so provided for, while the aged or infirm received a pension. Indeed, very few years have passed since the last of these old pensioners died, and till the present day kindly remembrances are cherished with respect to the faithfulness, the probity, the intelligence, and the piety, manifested by many of the old servants in the nearly forgotten firm of George Macintosh & Co.

Cudbear as a dyeing material can only be applied to textures of wool and silk. In the latter part of last century the mode of dyeing cotton goods was little known ; indeed, the knowledge of this art was comparatively useless, as the only form in which cotton was then used to any extent was in the manufacture of a coarse kind of handkerchiefs with linen warps and hand-spun cotton wefts, which received the name of "blunks." About the year 1780, Mr. James Monteith of Anderston warped the first web of pure cotton that is supposed to have been woven in Scotland, and the introduction, shortly afterwards, of the art of cotton spinning by machinery gave such an impetus to the manufacture of cotton cloths, that it was found necessary, if Glasgow was still to hold the place which it had assumed in this branch of industry, that a more intimate knowledge of dyeing cotton fabrics should be acquired. The art of producing the beautiful colour known as adrianople, or turkey red—which had its origin in the far east, although it was commonly practised by continental dyers—was, at that time, a secret to the dyers of this country. There can be little doubt that the mystery which enshrouded this branch of industry did sorely exercise the keen intellect of George Macintosh, for in 1785 we find him in communication with a French dyer, Monsieur Papillon, who had practiced the art at Rouen, and in that year, in conjunction with his friend, David Dale, Mr. Macintosh had the honour of establishing at Barrowfield the first dye-work that ever produced that much prized dye in Britain. Great interest was manifested in the productions of the firm. A committee of the House of Commons was appointed to examine the goods, and to report. A grautity of several thousand pounds was awarded to Mr. Macintosh "for his exertions in introducing the art of turkey red dyeing into Great Britain,"—a reward, by the way, which never reached that gentleman.

Of course, precautions were taken, somewhat similar to those which had existed at the cudbear manufactory, for the preservation of this valuable secret; but Monsieur Papillon did not remain long in the service. He seems to have been troublesome and contumaceous, and two years had scarcely elapsed when his connection with the Dalmarnock dye-works terminated. In the summer of 1787, Mr. Macintosh, writing to his son Charles, says— "Papillon has now left us entirely. We could not manage his "unhappy temper. I have made a great improvement in his "process. I dye in twenty days what he took twenty-five to do, "and the colour better. We paid him his salary up to October, so "as to be quite clear of him." Monsieur Papillon, in fact, appears to have been, both by nature and education, unfitted to stand the keen scrutiny of the shrewd Highlandman. Mr. Macintosh's grandson, George, states that, in 1790, M. Papillon received a premium from the commissioners of Scottish manufactures, in consideration of his communicating to Dr. Black, then professor of chemistry at Edinburgh, a description of his process; but that this description was so incongruous as to lead any scientific reader to suppose either that M. Papillon wished wilfully to mislead, or that he possessed no chemical science whatever.

In 1787 an intimation was made in the Glasgow Chamber of Commerce that Government had purchased the secret of dyeing turkey red, according to the method practiced by a certain Mr. Basil, and that the secretary had procured a description of the process for the use of the Chamber. This document, which is still preserved, was accompanied by a letter from Mr. Rose, Secretary to the Treasury, intimating the desire of the Treasury Lords that, in the meantime, the process should not be made public; and the secretary was therefore instructed to show the same to any of the members who might desire to see it, but not to give it out, nor allow a copy of it to be made, until further directions should be given. It is worthy of notice that both Mr. Macintosh and Mr. Dale, as directors, were present at the meeting when this announcement was made; and we may conjecture with what feelings it might have been received by these gentlemen, threatening, as it did, the prosperity of their newly found source of prosperity.

With regard to the secret involved in the process of turkey red dyeing we may say that it chiefly refers to the mode of preparing the cotton fibre for absorbing the dye, and this was at first effected by successive treatment with barilla, alum, galls, oil, and animal substances; and although many improvements have subsequently been introduced both in the materials employed and in the mode of their application, these, we believe, have been mainly simplifications of the original complicated routine, which in a modified form is still carried out in a manner similar to the old Barrowfield dyeing process.

The utensils necessary for prosecuting the business on anything like a large scale, as these are elaborately stated in the old document alluded to, present such a curious contrast to the extensive apparatus in use at the present day that the description is worth a passing notice. Two large copper pans are described, the dimensions of which are particularly noted. One must be 26½ inches deep, 36 inches in diameter at top and bottom, and 43 inches in the middle. The other pan must be one-third of this size, but "the form of no consequence." These are to be fitted with suitable fire places, and each provided with two lids— one of wood and one of copper—in each of which there must be a hole three inches in diameter covered with a hinged lid. This hole, it is explained, is left for the convenience of raising the cotton fabric out of the pan during the process of dyeing, and this is effected by means of an iron hook fixed on the end of a rope which runs through a pulley inserted in a strong beam overhead. In addition, seven tubs must be provided, and an extra large one "capable of holding sixty gallons." Upon this, one of the largest tubs must be supported, the bottom of which must be overlaid with "a handful of straw, covered by two gallons of clean pebble stones." This vessel is pierced "near the bottom with gimlet "holes partially stopped with the upper end of straws." With this primitive apparatus, we are gravely informed, that "sixty gallons "of liquid can be run off in forty hours." And, lastly, a pail, a set of dye sticks and poles, and a box-wood wringing peg and pin, constituted the full complement of dyeing apparatus.

In similar form, and on a like scale, we may presume that the art of turkey red dyeing first took shape at the Barrowfield works, and, in view of the vast proportions which this art has at present attained, we can scarcely repress a smile while we go back in thought to the little array of pans and tubs from which the great industry took its origin.

The extension of the art of dyeing " Dale's Red," as it was locally known, kept pace with the growth of the cotton manufacture ; and after enjoying a prosperous existence for twenty years, the Barrowfield works were sold in 1805 to the late Henry Monteith of Carstairs, under whose vigorous management the beautiful modifications of the process, as applied to Bandana handkerchiefs and to calico printing, have won for the works and their owners a world-wide reputation.

In 1791 Mr. Macintosh and some of his friends established a cotton mill and weaving factory on the Firth of Dornoch, in Sutherland. This was the greatest failure in all his prosperous business career, and yet it is impossible to study this transaction in its various bearings without greatly increasing our respect for the memory of the good man, and our approval of his benevolent aims and purposes.

It may be necessary to take a glance at the domestic and social condition of Sutherland at the time, in order to understand the reasons which induced Mr. Macintosh and his friends to undertake this manufacturing project. The situation was simply deplorable. The isolated position of the county, situated in the far north, surrounded and intersected by rugged mountains, and crossed and recrossed by rapid flood-bearing rivers, the total want of roads and bridges, and the absence of wheeled vehicles of every kind, greatly limited the intercourse of the inhabitants with each other, and almost forbade all intercourse with strangers. The nearly obsolete " Feudal system"—which, after the Revolution, was in a great measure superseded by influences tending to civilisation and improvement—still lingered in the wilds of Sutherlandshire long after these influences had reached and ameliorated the condition of many of the neighbouring Highland counties. The chieftain still maintained his nominal supremacy; but as he no longer required to summon his adherents for the prosecution of domestic feuds, the clans had settled down into peaceful pursuits, and the small holdings, to which, as the followers of their respective chiefs, they claimed a right at a trifling rent, were ruinously over-populated. These holdings, consequently, were divided and sub-divided, until they became quite inadequate to support the swarming multitudes who filled dale and glen, where they scraped and exhausted every available spot with successive crops of oats upon barley, and barley upon oats, so long as they could be made to yield a bare subsistence. The rent was paid by the sale of cattle. A full grown cow was valued at 30*s.* or £2, and a sheep sold at from 2*s.* to 4*s.* The services of an able-bodied man could be procured for 6*d.* per day. Mr. Bethune, the parish minister of Dornoch, who describes the country, remarks somewhat querulously, that sometimes 8*d.* was "demanded." A hired male servant got from 30*s.* to £2, with board, per annum, and a female servant was worth 20*s.* to 30*s.*, and in harvest could earn 6*d.* per day. The authority already quoted states that it was found profitable to sow the grain, especially pease and barley, on the bare ley, and then "plough it down!" Every man was his own carpenter; few implements were required, and one blacksmith served a whole district. The little wooden plough had no iron about it save the coulter and sock, and took four horses to draw it, yoked abreast, the driver taking his place in front, and walking backwards! When a new house was to be built the neighbours far and near were invited to assist, and a day or two was sufficient for the work. Four walls were constructed of divot or turf; on these wattles, from the neighbouring glen were laid, which in turn received a covering of lighter divots. A large stone was sunk in the middle of the floor—that was the fire-place. A rudely constructed frame work, with two folding boards, was built in the wall—that was the window. An old butter kit was fixed in the roof, or, perhaps, a hole left there—that was the chimney—and so the house was finished. One end served to accommodate the whole family, great and small; the other was devoted to the comfort of the domestic animals—cows, horses, pigs, and dogs. This arrangement was mutually beneficial, inasmuch as it served to economise heat, a most important consideration in that chilly climate. The greater part of the summer work consisted in cutting, drying, and carrying home the necessary winter fuel from the distant peat bogs. We can now scarcely form a faint estimate of the difficulties to be surmounted in the carriage of peat from these distant and nearly inaccessible morasses. On the summer afternoons, long ranks of half-starved *garrans* (ponies) might be seen winding slowly up the mountain side, each carrying his double *crubags* (creels), strapped to a wooden saddle, which rested on a straw mat for the prevention of friction. When the moss was reached, the ponies were left to pick a scanty meal in the neighbouring bog, while the men, under the shelter of the next broom bush, slept till the morning. And this dreary routine was repeated while the season or the necessity lasted. Mr. Bethune, in his description, observes :—" The great distance, " badness of the roads, weakness of the horses, and scantiness of " pasture, impose this cruel necessity, which is peculiarly injurious " to health."

Scraping together, thus, a scanty subsistence from day to day, isolated from the rest of the world, and left entirely at the mercy of the seasons, it is little wonder that, in such a variable climate, the poor Highlanders were often made to feel the pinch of famine. In the years 1782, 1783, and 1784, the crops were very scanty in Sutherlandshire. So severe did the pressure of want become, that the hungry multitudes came down from the interior to the shores of the Dornoch Firth, that they might scramble for shell-fish and sea-ware to stay the pangs of hunger. When intelligence of these privations reached the ears of Mr. Macintosh, all his sympathies were aroused, and, with the assistance of Mr. Dale and several Glasgow friends, whose hearts were ever open to the appeal of want, a vessel was despatched with a cargo of food for the starving Highlanders, part of which was sold at prime cost, and part distributed gratis. It is recorded that eighty poor persons received their periodical dole while the scarcity lasted.

In 1786 Mr. George Dempster of Dunnichen purchased the estate of Skibo, on the Dornoch Firth. Mr. Dempster, who for twenty-eight years represented the Dundee and St. Andrews district of burghs in Parliament, when he came to the estate, was most assiduous in devising measures for improving the condition of his neighbours and tenants. He was a man of great benevolence, and till his death, in 1818, enjoyed the respect and esteem of all classes of the community. This gentleman was the prime agent in the manufacturing speculation which we have mentioned. The estates owned by himself and his brother were about 18,000 acres in extent, but excluding three farms, upon one of which the mansion house was situated, yielded little more than £500 of yearly rental.

Here, then, was an abundant and healthy population in such straitened circumstances, that the offer of fair wages for light work must have appeared to the poor Highlander a welcome prospect, to be gratefully received.

The situation, too, was admirable. An arm of the Firth running up some miles formed a beautiful harbour, where vessels of large burden could find shelter in the stormiest weather, and the water privileges for driving machinery were of the very best. In short, everything promised that the speculation would turn out a great success. A copartnery was soon formed. Nine Glasgow gentlemen took shares in the concern—viz., Mr. Macintosh and Mr. Dale, William, James, and Andrew Robertson, Robert Dunsmore, Robert Bogle of Daldowie, Robert Mackie, West India merchant, and William Gillespie of Woodside. The other partners were mostly local gentlemen. The work was begun with great energy and high hope. A large spinning factory and weaving village were built. Instructors in the various departments were sent from Glasgow, and a second village was got up in haste near the principal harbour ; and that the villagers might have nothing to distract their attention from their duties, the various services which they were in the habit of rendering to their superiors were commuted by a money payment. Secure tenures of dwelling-houses, gardens, and other requisites were granted, and Spinningdale, as it was called, promised to be a great mutual benefit. Mr. Bethune, however, whose remarks we have already quoted, thus sketches the Highlander of the period, upon whom the success of the factory depended :—" Petty frauds and offences against society " are prevalent here as well as elsewhere ; little disingenuities, " pilferings, and wilful encroachments, are also committed. The " people cannot be called industrious ; but they are tenacious and ' frugal of what they get. If they can but live without much " exertion, they are content to live sparingly ; and if they relax of " their usual parsimony at fairs and other occasional meetings, they " know how to make amends, by habitual economy and abstemious-

" ness." And Mr. Dempster says that " Nothing can exceed the
" wretched condition of their habitations, where an iron pot for
" preparing food constitutes their principal furniture ; and although
" the women can only earn by spinning about threepence a day,
" yet the men pass the winter round peat fires, and do very little
" work."

These habits and conditions were found to be positively fatal to
the success of the new enterprise. Why should an active man be
doomed to finger among paltry cotton threads, in the midst of
noisy and evil-smelling machinery, from week's end to week's end,
especially when the partridge and muir hen are on the wing, the
trout and salmon are leaping in loch and river, and the broom
bushes are gleaming like the beaten gold? And besides all that—
here are these inflexible and intolerant Sassenachs, too, with their
unreasonable restrictions regarding the use of the tobacco and the
dram, and their forgetfulness of the fact, that Donald Ruach and
Shamus Gordon, our renowned progenitors, fought side by side
with King Robert Bruce, at the battle of Bannockburn!

There was no help for it ; with deep disappointment Mr.
Macintosh and his friends saw all their magnificent schemes for
the improvement of the Highlands doomed to failure, without
a particle of sympathy from those for whose benefit all that
toil and expense had been wasted. Moreover, all the partners
in the speculation, except Mr. Macintosh and Mr. Dale, and
another gentleman who held a small share in the business,
cautiously withdrew from the concern. It was in vain that the
partners appealed to Government for help. They were informed
that the funds set aside for improvements in Scotland were to be
applied only " for specific purposes of a general nature," whatever
that might mean. A letter sent to Mr. Macintosh by Mr. Dempster,

in 1804, is very emphatic; he writes—"I was prepared for the "unpleasant tidings of the result of your patriotic efforts to serve "your native country. I am sorry that the work is to be aban- "doned, and still more that it has been attended with loss to you. "Alas! bonny Spinningdale. Alas! poor Sutherland." Regrets were vain. This year the works were sold for a mere trifle to an individual who took the precaution to insure them, and imme- diately afterwards they were wholly consumed by fire; and thus ended Mr. Macintosh's grand plan of help for "poor Suther- land!"

We have now to consider the character of Mr. Macintosh from a point of view in which it appears strangely incongruous. As we have already seen, the habitual tendencies of his mind were essen- tially benevolent—in fact, wherever want, or misery, or ignorance, presented themselves, there George Macintosh was found labouring with the whole force of his energetic disposition, to alleviate the distress. How, then, are we to account for the seeming inconsistency of this good man, devoting the same energy for years to the work of amateur recruiting for the army? literally entreating or entrapping thoughtless young men to offer themselves for a miser- able remuneration as "food for powder!" The motives that could impel a heart the kindest and a hand the most beneficent to this work are worthy of consideration.

We believe that, among the thousands that swarm through the busy streets and lanes of our city at the present day, there will not be found one who can cherish a distinct personal recollection of the trepedation and mistrust and dismay that fell upon all classes of the community in the disastrous year 1793. Then the population of Paris madly rose against their rulers, and with sanguinary ferocity, which shall continue a reproach and shame while the world lasts, murdered their king and queen, with many of the best and wisest of the citizens, overthrew all restraints, sacred and secular, and, under the plausible name of liberty and equality, set up a system of government and social order, which was nothing short of anarchy. In blind rage even the tombs of their own kings were ravaged, and the national churches pillaged; even heathen rites were publicly sanctioned, and a noted strumpet was set up on the altar of the Cathedral to receive the public homage of the citizens. The National Convention, too, in their pride of power, declared war against all systems of government that they thought could interfere with their newly-found liberty; especially against the King of Great Britain and the Stadtholder of the United Provinces was their rancour directed, To enable the Convention further to carry out a plan of universal subjugation, a Decree was submitted and received with great approbation, proposing that " Till the moment when all the enemies of France shall be driven " from the Republic, every Frenchman shall be in permanent readi- " ness for service in the army. The young men shall march to the " combat; the married men shall forge arms, and transport provi- " sions ; the children shall make lint of old linen ; and the old men " shall cause themselves to be carried into the public squares to " excite the courage of the warriors, and preach hatred against the " enemies of the Republic!" Further, provision was made for wash- ing all the cellars in Paris to obtain saltpetre,' and for the national edifices being converted into military storehouses, and used as the quarters of district battalions, in preparation for a general rising at the word of command. The whole force to be marshalled under

---

' A French chemist had just made the discovery that the burial .vaults of Paris were a perfect mine of nitre. Could this be the reason for rifling the vaults in which lay the bodies of the French kings? If so, what a weird idea it gives us of the "base uses" to which even royalty may be put !

military banners, inscribed—"THE FRENCH NATION RISEN AGAINST TYRANNY!"

Early in the year 1794, the English Government set itself in good earnest to devise measures whereby this formidable military power, now in active preparation for being poured upon our shores, should be met. "Letters of Service" were immediately despatched to the friendly chiefs in the northern counties of Scotland, imploring help in the nation's great need—to Gordon of Huntly, Mackintosh of Aberarder, M'Donell of Glengarry, Colonel Fraser of Inverness, and the great chief of the clan Chattan, Æneas Mackintosh—all loyal men and true. The brave chieftain of the Mackintosh, who had fought stoutly in the American war, in a letter to his namesake and friend in Glasgow, says:—"I believe "that I (who have already had a pretty long trial of the fighting "trade) must again gird on my sword, and collect our scattered "tribes. I must begin to feel their pulses, to know if they beat "high in their country's cause, and for the honour of clan Chattan, "under whose saffron banners they have formerly done such "feats of arms." What his experience had taught him, after the operation of "feeling the pulses" of the clan, is revealed in another letter to Mr. Macintosh. He says—"Times are altered in this "country. Men do not now go out at the call of their lairds, unless "for valuable considerations, such as leases for nineteen years, or "a lessened rent." And he adds—"Manufacturing towns are "the proper situations for recruiting, but even there, had not such "a friend as yourself stepped forward, our chances would have been "small."

In these circumstances, we think there is a ready solution of Mr. Macintosh's zeal. Independently of his habitual "clannishness," that could so ill brook the idea of his kith and kin, even in a

" Highland degree," having their aims frustrated, here was the spectacle of his beloved country as sorely in need of timely help as ever were those starving masses, from whom his ready aid and bounty had never been withheld. We must also keep in remembrance that the sentiments of loyalty to king, constitution, and church, which were cherished in the social circles to which Mr. Macintosh was attached, although they may now be fairly characterised as rank Toryism, had been gradually gathering strength since the memorable 1745, and were held with a tenacity of affection and reverence scarcely conceded, now-a-days, to our most valued moral convictions; indeed, the contrast between the horrors of democracy, and the rule of right and safety embodied in the British Constitution, as both were exhibited at this time, strengthened the national determination to support the Government at whatever sacrifice.

In the midst of the general alarm occasioned by the anticipated invasion, and the universal gloom which it cast over trade and commerce, it is curious and diverting to note the common opinions entertained with regard to the much vaunted military prowess of Britain's foes. Burns sang, and his sentiments found ready response in the popular mind :—

> " Their gun's a burden on their shouther,—
> They downa bear the scent o' pouther ;
> Their bauldest thought's a hankerin' swither
> To stan' or rin,
> Till skelp,—a shot,—they're aff a' throuther
> To save their skin ! "

And, subsequently, our own street Homer, Blind Alick, quite as emphatically, although perhaps less euphoniously, expressed public sentiment thus—

> "As for the Emperor Napoleon Bonyparty,
> And some of the French Imperial Guards,
> They thought they had no more to do
> Than to take our gallant Scotch lads:
> But very soon, on the contrary,
> The Royal Greys they let them ken
> They might go and tell the tyrant Bonyparty,
> They cared not a —— for either him or his men !"

These opinions formed a capital ground of encouragement, then, to the new recruits, but unfortunately they were held quite as tenaciously by our foes in depreciation of British valour, and it required many weary years of hard fighting, and the expenditure of much bloodshed and treasure to decide the question ; and through all these years, so long as his life extended, did Mr. Macintosh, with a perseverance and success which can only be accounted for by the great respect and confidence which his public life and character had acquired for him, continue his patriotic labours unwearyingly. However averse we may feel to the idea of establishing truth and justice by means of "hard knocks," it would be sheer ingratitude to forget that, under Providence, we owe a deep debt of gratitude to the memory of such men as old George Macintosh, to whose patriotism and energy we are indebted for the privilege of sitting so many years under our own vine and fig trees in peace and comfort.[1]

[1] "Assuredly there were few towns throughout the length and breadth of the land where a more "intense feeling of joy or of grief, resulting from the war, might be expected to be expressed than in "Glasgow, as in none did the British army find more recruits than in the Scottish western metropolis. "Several, indeed, of the most conspicuous regiments were filled almost to a man from Glasgow."— *(Strang's Clubs, page 377.)*

Whilst yet a young man, and still a clerk in the old tanwork, Mr. Macintosh married Mary, daughter of the Rev. Charles Moore, minister of Stirling. Mr. Moore was a native of Ireland, and the son of an officer in King William's service. Both directly and collaterally Mr. Moore's progeny were greatly distinguished. His son, Dr. John Moore, the author of Zeluco and other works, was much respected and admired, no less for his amiable disposition and goodness of heart than for his great literary accomplishments ; and his grandson was Sir John Moore, who fell at Corunna, and whose heroism and military skill have gained for him a deathless name. Sir John Moore, it is worthy of remark, when a young man, entered as a clerk in the Dunchattan House, and the training he there received, under the careful superintendence of his uncle, Mr. Macintosh, we may assume, were of the greatest service to him in the formation of those prompt methodical habits which were the main sources of his military success in after life.

The married life of Mr. Macintosh seems to have been, so far as its social and domestic aspects are concerned, a very happy one. In the last year of his life he writes of his wife as his "loving companion of forty years;" and Dr. Ritchie, at his death, bears testimony "that the deep affliction of his widow gives heart-"piercing witness to the purity and constancy and tenderness of "their conjugal affection."

When the Chamber of Commerce was instituted in 1783, Mr. Macintosh was one of its most zealous and active promoters, and through the long period of twenty-four years, with the exception of a few short intervals, he served as one of its most respected and useful directors. In fact, he held office as chairman of the Chamber at the time of his death ; and unless we are greatly mistaken, his life was unduly shortened by his active services on behalf

of the Chamber and the town.   In the years 1806 and 1807, when
Mr. Macintosh was chairman, several matters were brought before
the Chamber, deeply affecting the commercial welfare of the community.   One of these was the small number of Custom-House
officers and tide waiters appointed to do duty at Greenock and
Port-Glasgow, then the shipping ports for the city, and the multi-
tude of uselessly complicated forms which they were called
upon to enforce; and although the Chamber had hitherto only
asked such modified restrictions and privileges as were in use at
the ports of Liverpool and London, their moderate requests
remained unheeded.   Another grievance was that the drawback
of duty granted on English rock salt—a material which was found
indispensable in the manufacture of "chlorine" for bleaching
purposes—was shamefully unequal in England and Scotland respectively, to the prejudice and loss of the Scotch manufacturers
employed in making the much-prized bleaching powder.   Government had also proposed a duty of forty shillings per ton on iron, a
large per centage upon its total value.   The merchants and shippers
on the west coast were anxious for an increase in number and
efficiency of their Lighthouses.   And lastly, an Edict had been
promulgated by Government, declaring that apprentices under
indenture who might be enlisted in the army could not be claimed
by their respective masters.

In the spring of the year 1807, these matters were discussed in
the Chamber, and at the last meeting over which Mr. Macintosh
presided, he was appointed to take part with the magistrates of
the city in any plan of action that they might think likely to remove
the evils complained of.

There are many things, as it appears to us, strikingly pathetic
in this last meeting of the good old man with his brethren in the

Directorate. The attendance was fairly representative, and yet, when he looked around him, excepting the secretary, Mr. Hamilton, then within a single year of his removal also, there was not an individual of the strong and sympathetic band present who, twenty-four years before, held wise counsel with him around that table. The membership of the whole Chamber had in that interval nearly changed, and few indeed of the old mercantile aristocracy, his early companions, remained. Besides, a great shadow had fallen upon his own household. His youngest daughter, a lady of varied and uncommon accomplishments, to whom he was tenderly attached, was stricken with rapid consumption, and taken away ; and his "loving companion for forty years," Mary Moore, was fairly prostrated by the calamity, and rendered unable to rise from her bed. In view of these circumstances, what an amount of pathos do the few words assume which had been recently spoken by him on the death of his oldest friend, Mr. Malcolm M'Gilvra, the patriarch of the little social circle, the Gaelic Club, of which Mr. Macintosh was president. "The father of the Club is gone—the oldest in years— "the gayest in all juvenile and innocent amusements—the first in "the dance—the last to part with a social friend. His venerable "countenance and grey locks created respect, while his cheerful "good humour diffused mirth. In all his dealings and conversa- "tion he was strictly just and honourable, in religion and piety "sincere. We have lost one of our best members, and many poor "their best friend." And then, in the usual form at the meeting, he proposed a sentiment or toast in memory of their aged friend, expressed in his beloved Gaelic, we presume, the language ever so musical in his ears—

> " May we all live in health and comfort to the age of Callum,
> And when we cease to be members may we be regretted like Callum ! "

Shortly after the meeting of the Chamber, to which we have just alluded, Mr. Macintosh set out for England. What the particular objects were that could induce him to undertake a long and tiresome journey at his advanced period of life, and especially at the time when his wife was enfeebled by a great family affliction, we are not informed. We may feel assured, however, that they must have been both urgent and important, and there is no incongruity in the supposition that they had reference in some way to the duties imposed upon him, in respect of the claims of right and justice advanced by the Chamber and the city, both of which he loved so well.

On his journey homewards he was seized at Moffat with an alarming illness of an inflammatory character. Intelligence was immediately despatched to his son-in-law, Mr. Balfour, W.S., Edinburgh, and his son Charles, at Glasgow. The letter to Charles contained a postscript, which, considered as probably the last words Mr. Macintosh ever wrote, is striking and characteristic. He says—" The people of the inn are the most attentive and most " civil I ever saw—*wonderfully so indeed.*" On receiving the alarming intelligence, Mr. Balfour and his wife, with his son Charles, hastened to Moffat, taking with them the best medical aid that could be procured, only to find the good old man rapidly sinking and beyond help; and when Mrs. Macintosh reached Moffat—having risen from her sick bed, and in company with one trusted servant hurried to her husband's relief—she found that her loving companion was dead. She is said to have borne the shock with Christian fortitude, and her family and friends wondered at her exemplary patience and cheerful resignation. Alas! the loneliness of Dunchattan and its accompanying associations were too much for her enfeebled constitution to bear, and in a few months she was laid by the side of him she had mourned so truly, in the old Cathedral churchyard. "They were lovely in their lives, and in death they were not divided."

George Macintosh died on the 26th day of July, 1807. On the Sunday following his funeral, as a mark of esteem for one so universally lamented, a sad procession walked to St. Andrew's Church, consisting of the children of the Highland Society—one of the numerous charities which received a great share of Mr. Macintosh's sympathy and assistance—accompanied by the directors of the Society and their friends, the members of the Gaelic Club, headed by his old neighbour and friend, Provost James M'Kenzie, and the body of Magistrates, most of whom were brother merchants, and all of whom knew the worth of the deceased, and mourned his loss.

In sketching the character of Mr. Macintosh, Dr. Ritchie, the minister of the church, said:—" Mr. Macintosh possessed an eleva-
"tion of soul superior to that ignoble spirit of a corrupted age
"which casts off even the forms of religion. He feared God; he
"worshipped Him who made heaven and earth; he was not
"ashamed of the Gospel of Christ—he believed in its doctrines, he
"acted upon its laws. While his profession of religion was con-
"scientious and fair, it was free from affectation. He was pious
"without enthusiasm—the friend of substantial godliness without
"fanaticism. The bigotry of prejudice, the gloom of superstition,
"the contempt of those who adopted modes of worship different
"from his, never disgraced his creed, never soured his temper,
"never polluted his conversation; in him, piety was combined with
"charity, and the love of his God with the love of his neighbour.
"Piety is the parent of charity; how profound, therefore, was the
"piety which reigned in the heart of Mr. George Macintosh; its

"spirit smiled through his eye when he looked kindness, opened his
"hand when he bestowed benefits, and rendered him the willing
"agent to distribute, as the almoner of Providence, a portion to
"the children of poverty. Wherever the 'still small voice' of
"charity was heard craving in confidence immediate relief in urgent
"pressure, there stood by her side George Macintosh, animating
"by his countenance, prompting by his words, and constraining by
"his example, the benevolent exertions of others. His good works
"were a gently flowing stream, winding softly through the haunts
"of poverty and disease."

We think these remarks, the truth and beauty of which were
willingly acknowledged at the time, throw a radiance around
the few simple and characteristic observations offered by Mr.
Macintosh on the death of his old friend, the father of the Gaelic
Club, and show his own character, as sketched unwittingly by
himself, in a most pleasant and amiable light both "Godwards and
manwards."

Thus lived and died George Macintosh. Among the Glasgow
commercial aristocracy of the present day we have yet left many
whose beneficence keeps pace with their prosperity; but amongst
them all we feel assured none will be found unwilling to acknowledge how much the good old town is indebted for its present
prosperity to the energy, the benevolence, and the true stamp
of piety exhibited by such men as David Dale and George
Macintosh.

JAMES MONTEITH,

OF ANDERSTON.

AT the time when so many of our Glasgow merchants were making splendid fortunes by trading with the American colonies, and while their princely mansions were appearing amongst the picturesque and romantic, but somewhat squalid, dwellings that lined the Westergate, there might also be found on the outskirts of the town straggling groups of unpretentious houses—each with its room and kitchen, its loom shop, and its kail yard—whose occupants were yet to influence the future progress and prosperity of the city in a way that they themselves could never have anticipated. Among these old Glasgow worthies, James Monteith of Anderston claims special attention for that robust perseverance which marked his life and associated his name with the growth and stability of the city.

Mr. Monteith, like his friend George Macintosh, was a Highlander, and inherited all the dour tenacity of purpose characteristic of the race. His grandfather, James Monteith, had been a small Highland laird somewhere in the neighbourhood of Aberfoil, in those troublesome times in which might was right; and, unfortunately, his near neighbour was that rank reiver Rob Roy, who founded his moral creed on the simple principle—

> "That they should take who have the power,
> And they should keep who can."

More unfortunately still, this maxim was not in accordance with old Mr. Monteith's code of moral ethics, and so, with his independent honesty, or, perhaps, his Highland stubbornness, he refused to acknowledge the claims of the MacGregor Mohr on him for "black mail." The usual result followed. Once, twice, and a third time he was made the object of a Highland "raid," harried of all his possessions, and forced to begin the world anew. The last ruinous visit is said to have been too much for the old man to bear, and he died of a broken heart, leaving one son, Henry, and three daughters, slenderly provided for. Henry, unwilling to undergo the same ordeal that had ruined his father, disposed of his small Highland possessions, and became a market gardener in the village of Anderston, near Glasgow.

About the year 1734 the little straggling clachan of Anderston was purchased by Mr. John Orr of Barrowfield. Although in subsequent years Anderston was honoured by being the principal cradle of Glasgow manufactures, at the time it became the property of Mr. Orr—which, we believe, may have been about the date also of Mr. Monteith's coming to reside there[1]—the little place could scarcely claim the title of a village, as it consisted only of a few thatched houses, and one house built of "divots" (or turf). This house was occupied by an ingenious weaver, who produced the first check handkerchiefs woven in this country, which were subsequently known by the name of "Half-ell-half-quarter-ell Divoties."

In the memorable 1745, Glasgow, to show its loyalty to the Government, raised two battalions of six hundred men each. As might have been expected, Henry Monteith willingly shouldered his musket against his old Highland antagonists, and fought them

---

[1] Rob Roy died about 1736.

stoutly at Falkirk, where, however, the King's forces and the Glasgow regiment were obliged to turn their backs and flee. This was a sore and delicate subject to the sturdy Highland gardener ever afterwards. After the battle of Culloden, when the rebellion finally collapsed, Mr. Monteith quietly returned to his kail yard and his syboes, and died a staunch Presbyterian of the old school, universally respected.

Henry Monteith left one son, James, the subject of our sketch, who was born in 1734. Fortunately for himself, and for Glasgow also, James did not follow his father's occupation, but in early life was instructed in the art of hand-loom weaving.

The condition of the weaver in the middle and latter part of last century was one of comparative comfort. Every bien house-wife then, with all her female servants and family, plied the spinning-wheel late and early, for a store of napery was ever a thrifty Scotch matron's pride. Moreover, all those little luxuries that were supposed to hover upon the borders of the forbidden, such as the tea or the snuff, could only be stealthily provided by the sale of the dozen of eggs or the hasp of yarn, both of which were readily disposed of at the little store of "a' things," or at the loom shop of the " wee cork."

Many of our elderly readers must have frequently seen the perambulating merchant-weaver carrying round his great bundle of household napery, and may remember his cheery greeting, and the hearty welcome he received to the best seat at the fireside, and also the friendly wrangle that ensued when the precious bundle was unloosed. Thus, when stock accumulated or trade was dull, the thrifty weaver managed to make a comfortable addition to his family income.

But over all these advantages this was the principal : suburban homesteadings were so cheaply and easily acquired, that every healthy man, by the exercise of ordinary diligence and thrift, might secure the room and kitchen, the six-loom shop, and the kail yard, the very pinnacle of a weaver's ambition; and thus sitting nominally rent free, he could demand his weekly shilling of rent for every loom occupied by his journeymen, and receive, besides, a profitable proportion of the earnings won by his active apprentices; and by furnishing them all with home-bought yarns, his profits enabled him gradually to add loom shop to loom shop, till his little factory had become a thriving business, and he himself was on the fair way to independence.

We know not what were the circumstances that combined to elevate Mr. Monteith in the social scale. The old gardener had been thrifty and successful, and James was his only son. In the latter part of last century we find him the acknowledged chief and leader among the prudent and industrious Anderston "wee corks," then a numerous, respectable, and thriving fraternity.

Before the introduction of machine-spun yarns, Glasgow manufacturers, besides the usual customer work, as it was called, were limited to the production of plain and figured lawns and cambrics. The home spun yarns were found to be unsuitable for these delicate fabrics, being, except in very rare cases, coarse and irregular, and it was found necessary to import from France, Belgium, and Holland, the yarns suitable for the finer manufactures. Into this business Mr. Monteith entered with great energy and success. He was the largest importer of yarns at the time, as well as an extensive cambric manufacturer, and he added to his many branches of business the old-fashioned system of croft bleaching for his cloth. His bleachfield was on the north-west corner of Bishop Street, where his warehouse and dwelling-house were also situated, his garden being separated from the churchyard by a low stone wall.

The principal goods manufactured at this time for export were cambrics. These all required to pass through the hands of the stamp-master, therefore the quantity stamped for export could be correctly ascertained. From an old document preserved in the Chamber of Commerce, we learn that the total export of this material from Scotland in ten years, 1775-1784 inclusive, was as follows:—

		Yards.
From Nov., 1774, to Nov., 1775,	- - - -	29,114
" " 1775, " 1776,	- - - -	34,433
" " 1776, " 1777,	- - - -	44,192
" " 1777, " 1778,	- - - -	52,972
" " 1778, " 1779,	- - - -	51,175
" " 1779, " 1780,	- - - -	45,998
" " 1780, " 1781,	- - - -	45,921
" " 1781, " 1782,	- - - -	44,385
" " 1782, " 1783,	- - - -	56,304
" " 1783, " 1784,	- - - -	83,438

Making a total of 487,932 yards. Average value, 6*s.* 6*d.* = £158,577 : 18*s.*

We give the figures in detail to show the gradual yearly increase, and, in view of the fact that Scotland was a principal seat of this manufacture, the figures are very suggestive.

Comparing this branch of industry with the great staple trade of Glasgow in the middle of last century—namely, the import of tobacco—the contrast is very striking. In the year 1771, the import of this latter commodity is given by Mr. Gibson, the Glasgow historian, as 46,055,139 pounds, or about £2,250,000 value.

Gibson states that, although the commerce of Glasgow

took its rise at the date of the Union with England, when the restrictions imposed upon the traders of Scotland were removed, and trade with the colonies was thrown open to the merchants of Glasgow—a privilege they were not slow to take advantage of— yet it was not till about 1750 that the real progress of the city began. The establishment of banks had then put it in the power of industrious tradesmen to obtain money. "Schemes of trade "and improvement," he says, "were put in practice, the under- "takers of which in former times would have been called madmen. "Luxury advanced with hasty strides every day, and from this era "we may date all the improvements which have taken place, not "only in Glasgow, but over the whole of the west of Scotland."

We get a curious glimpse into the domestic condition of the working classes at this period from the same venerable historian. He informs us that the mechanics of Glasgow upon an average will earn seven shillings per week each man, and that although Glasgow is by no means a cheap place to live in, "such wages are more than "sufficient to supply liberally all his wants, and he must save "money." This he accounts for by the moderate diet which contents a Scotch mechanic, in comparison with his more extrava- gant English brother. "His ordinary breakfasts and suppers from "choice," he says, "are oatmeal pottage with a little milk or small "beer, and his dinner barley broth, or potatoes and salt herrings. "A peck of potatoes, weighing 48 English pounds, can be obtained "for 7*d*. Three pounds of these, with a couple of salt herrings," he gravely informs us, "do not exceed in value one penny half- "penny, and are a sufficient dinner for any labouring man "whatever."[1] He also waxes quite didactic, almost eloquent, upon

---

[1] Oatmeal at that time was sold for 11*d*. per peck, 8 lbs. of 22½ oz.; butter cost 6½*d*. per lb., 22½ oz.; cheese, 2½*d*. ditto; beef, 5*d*. ditto; eggs, 6*d*. per dozen; spirits, 1*s*. 6*d*. per pint; and house rents ranged from 30*s*. per annum, upwards.

the advantages of the Scotch mode of living, and with reference to a favourite dish at this time in Glasgow he discourses thus :—
" Seldom does a year pass in England without complaints being
" made of the high price of provisions. Could an English
" mechanic condescend to eat *herrings*, here is a cheap, healthy,
" and tasteful food : eating of butcher meat daily, in whatever
" manner you may dress it, must certainly pall the appetite; by
" sometimes making use of these herrings it would at least be a
" change of food, and would make them return to the roasted beef
" with double keenness. This would prove the means of increasing
" the number of our brave seamen—the supporters of our greatness
" as a nation—and it would be attended with this happy effect, that
" it would introduce wealth into the most northern part of this
" island, whose inhabitants are ready upon every occasion to turn
" out in defence of the country; besides, it would be an effectual
" method to reduce the price of butcher meat !"

Indeed, Mr. Gibson was a perfect master of this species of special pleading, and, even at the risk of being esteemed prolix, we should like to lay before our patient reader another specimen of old John's reasoning, especially as we get through it a curious illustration of popular opinion, which when read at the present day is abundantly diverting.

He is discoursing about the operations of fashion upon every species of manufacturing industry, and lamenting that while Scotch manufacturers were exerting themselves to extend the manufacture of cambric and lawns, their own extravagant wives and daughters were wearing muslins, "a fabric of the Indies!" Yet, seeing that our Scotch fashions were not likely to be introduced at "Court," what, therefore, should prevent the people of Scotland from daring to have a fashion of their own? And he adds :—

"People prone to start difficulties will say, who is to lead this
"fashion, and which way is it to be brought about? My answer
"is, that there is nothing more easy. Let the people who fix the
"fashion be such whose quality and fortune elevate them above the
"rest of mankind, and let this fashion be changed three times in
"every year in the following manner:—Let there be a public
"breakfast in Edinburgh upon the 14th of February annually; let
"the different manufacturers produce before this assembly the
"respective kinds and patterns. of their goods; and let it be
"determined by the company present what species of goods are to
"be in fashion for the whole dress of both men and women, to
"commence on the 4th of June, and to continue to the 11th of
"November." (The same process to determine the winter and
spring fashions, changing the dates.) "Let the ladies treat every
"gentleman who does not give obedience to the mandates of these
"assemblies as an unfashionable creature, and as one inimical to
"the welfare of his country; and let the gentlemen look upon
"every lady who does not appear dressed in the manufacture of
"her country as an extravagant woman unfit to attend to the
"concerns of a family!"

The leading Anderston manufacturers at this period were Mr.
Monteith, Messrs. John and James M‘Ilwham, who subsequently
became famous for their enterprise and wealth; Mr. John Semple,
who was also a bleacher at the little village of Finnieston; Mr.
Allan Arthur, who married a daughter of James Monteith's, and
was grandfather to Mr. Arthur, recently of Henry Monteith &
Co., and also to our worthy townsman, Mr. James Hannan, of the
same firm; Messrs. Grant & Fraser,[1] who established a large manu-

---

[1] Dickens' delightful portraits of the brothers Cheeryble owed their origin to the brothers Grant, of
Grant & Fraser, the Anderston manufacturers.

factory at Manchester, which still exists; Mr. William Gillespie of Woodside, cotton spinner and manufacturer, who was subsequently an office-bearer in the first Anderston congregation with Mr. Monteith; Mr. Robert Hannan, father of Mr. James Hannan; Mr. Robert Thomson of Camphill; and Mr. James Wright, who bore the suggestive soubriquet of "cash doun."

The names of these gentlemen, with the exception of Mr. Semple, do not appear in the old Glasgow Directories. We, therefore, conclude that none of them, with the exception mentioned, had places of business in the town.

Previous to 1781, when the Tontine Rooms were opened, it was the custom of suburban manufacturers to transact all their business in some little public-house over a gill and a "farl" of oaten cake. It is said that the Anderston corks met in " Pinkerton's," opposite the Tron Steeple, and that, business or no business, the daily meeting was held for the sake of the social " crack," and the moderate " twal oors " before specified. Indeed, this custom assumed something like the form of a moral duty, for when, in the course of events, misfortune had overtaken any well-known family, either by the death of its principal bread-winner or by the ordinary reverses of trade, then, as a testimony of sympathy and respect, some member of the family, generally the eldest daughter, was set up in a little half-door'd shoppie in a quiet court. A few casks were provided, filled with Stein, or Haig of the Brigend's, bead 24,[1] which, as it only paid about one penny per gallon of duty, could be sold by them at about three shillings, with a fair profit. A row of shining pewter measures was also provided, something like two egg cups wanting the stalk stuck together,

---

[1] The degree of alcoholic strength in spirits was determined by numbered beads, and particular qualities were often asked for by their appropriate number. The practice is not yet extinct.

bottom to bottom, and each cup fashioned to hold its appropriate mouthful, the whole called a tass or tassie.

> "Gae bring to me a pint o' wine,
> And fill it in a silver tassie."—*Burns.*

These, with a few rough chairs or forms and a fir table, furnished a house of business and entertainment, in which its promoters and the public could enjoy a temperate meridian while performing their daily duty, all made pleasant with the conviction that it was strictly in harmony, not only with the charity that thinketh no evil, but also with that better charity that is productive of much good.

There can be no question that at a time when deep drinking was esteemed a gentlemanly accomplishment, and when the means for indulging to excess were so easily procured, the practice was too common; yet we notice it in connection with the life of Mr. Monteith from a conviction that his character, as a true gentleman and a consistent Christian, received no tinge from what we now regard as a most reprehensible practice.

As a peculiar characteristic of the period, we would like to notice a grievous annoyance to which the manufacturers of the old times were subjected, and which, fortunately for the comfort of those in business at the present time, is unknown—namely, the vigilant and incessant interference of the inspector or stampmaster. This official, armed with powers conferred by an ancient Act of Parliament, was esteemed a sort of "old man of the sea" on manufacturing industry. Before the lint seed was sown by the farmer, he was presumed to be there with the inevitable "penalty," in case of fraudulent dealing with the commodity. Through all the preliminary processes—steeping, dressing, spinning, assorting—the vigilant eye was never withdrawn. In the event of fraudulent reeling, he was empowered to seize the yarn, and "break, burn, and utterly destroy" the defaulting reel, and fine or imprison its owner. The five pounds penalty hung daily above the head of every man who ventured to sell a yard of cloth without the inspector's license, or wanting the inevitable "stamp," which implied a modicum of the profits to Government, and a small lick as well to the stampmaster for his pains and trouble.

It so happened that, in the end of last century, before the introduction of the cotton trade, a certain Cadwaller. Colden was appointed to this unpopular office in the Hamilton district. It is to be feared that Mr. Colden performed the duties of his onerous office in a somewhat perfunctory manner, for various pieces of cloth were finding their way into the market without Mr. Colden's mark, which was scarcely fair to those who had previously come through his hands, and some of those had the temerity to tell the fiery Welshman so to his face. They were, doubtless, imprudent, for down he came on the whole quarter with all the pains and penalties of the old Act. Unfortunately for his own sagacity, however, the first person he pounced upon was no less a person than a Hamilton Bailie, even Bailie Gray, the great manufacturer, a gentleman whose sense of the social proprieties was quite as tender as that of Mr. Colden himself.

The atrocity is described in a memorial to the Chamber of Commerce, in which the feelings of the worthy Bailie find expression with unmistakeable emphasis. Mr. Monteith, most of his brother Anderston manufacturers, many of the Glasgow merchants, and Paisley weavers as well, all testify to the extent of the indignity.

They relate how, when Mr. Colden was refused admittance into the Bailie's warehouse, " He has beset our Doors with a posse of

" officers at his Tail, demanding our Keys in a menacing tone, and
" upon refusal threatening us with a Prosecution upon the statute,
" and he has lodged a complaint against some of our Number, and
" has been going about soliciting some of the Justices on this head.
" Whether, therefore, Mr. Colden's behaviour proceeds from im-
" becility or avarice, the memorialists cannot help thinking that he
" is deviating from the design of the appointment."

The Chamber remitted this matter to a committee, consisting
of douce David Dale, John Brown, jun., of Lanfin, Dugald Bannatyne, and Walter Stirling of Miller Street. These gentlemen
reported very much in accordance with the conclusions of the
aggrieved parties, and after some further correspondence, the
matter was dropped.

The story of Mr. Monteith's connection with the first church
erected in the little village of Anderston has been often told, and
is worth repetition. In 1741, Mr. James Fisher, who, eight years
previous to this date, had seceded from the Established Church,
along with Mr. Ebenezer Erskine and others, was admitted the
first minister of the Secession Church in Glasgow. Six years
thereafter, a schism arose in the little congregation with regard to
the liberty which a conscientious Christian could claim in relation
to the oath which it was imperative that every guild brother should
take before he could enjoy municipal privileges. That section of
the oath referring to the obligations laid upon the brethren to
support Protestant principles, and to renounce the Pope and all
his works and ways, was plain and unobjectionable; but, then, what
about adhesion to the Government in power, with all its leanings
toward Episcopacy, Erastianism, Antinomianism, and other objec-
tionable isms? Much acrid controversy took place over this knotty
question, which resulted in an open rupture. The party who

declared themselves unable to take the oath separated from their brethren of the Original Secession, and built a church in the Havannah, subsequently known as the Duke Street Anti-Burgher Church.

In this church Mr. Monteith held office as an elder for many years. His opinions on various subjects were much in advance of his brethren, and especially in relation to the position which the denomination held toward the brethren of the old connection and to other Evangelical congregations. Indeed, we are somewhat at a loss to account for his connection with the body at all, unless upon the supposition that the old Highland gardener Henry took such a part in the original controversy as influenced the decision of his son. At any rate, upon the question of brotherly love matters came soon to a crisis. A pamphlet was distributed in the congregation advocating a more Christian spirit among the warring brethren. Mr. Monteith and three of his brother elders were accused of having to do with circulating the book, which was the cause of much disturbance in the congregation. The case was referred to the Presbytery, who were unable to come to a decision, and from them it was sent back to the session, with special instructions to find out whether the suspected offenders "could give their hearty approbation of the present testimony for "a Covenanted work of Reformation, now in the hands of the "Associated Synod." The answer was so far satisfactory that the matter was dropped at the time, not without an expression of great dissatisfaction that the session had not proceeded against the offending elders—"by the censure of the Lord's House—according to the rule of the Word!" Perhaps no rule of the denomination was more rigidly applied than that which enjoined the church's censure against "promiscuous hearing." It mattered little whether the "cauldrife doctrines" were promulgated by ministers of the Establishment or the Relief,[1] or the Burgher connection, all were included in the same censure ; and woe betide the brother whose itching ears prompted to this particular form of carnal indulgence.

While the kirk-session were in this frame of mind, it happened that, one summer Sunday morning in 1768, Mr. Monteith and his wife were, as usual, on their way to the Havannah Church. Mrs. Monteith was weak and wearied, for it was her first day out after a severe illness. The pair had scarcely reached the middle of the Trongate when they were overtaken by a sudden summer storm, a loud peal of thunder, followed by a deluge of rain. This was long before the introduction of waterproofs or umbrellas, and, as the rain still continued, they ventured into the old Tron, then under the pastoral charge of Dr. Corse or Cross, who had been its minister since 1743. This was, in the opinion of the Session, a plain perversion of congregational rule—an unmistakeable case of "promiscuous hearing" that could not be allowed to pass with impunity. Accordingly Mr. and Mrs. Monteith were summoned to undergo the usual censure. They were, however, obstinate ; and although a good deal of angry feeling was evinced at the time between the Havannah session and the public, who expressed much sympathy with Mr. Monteith, he, after flatly refusing to submit himself to Church censure, seems to have taken no further interest in the matter.

The little village of Anderston—chiefly owing to the manufacturing energy and enterprise of Mr. Monteith and others—

[1] A small Relief Church, under the Pastoral care of Mr. Cruden, existed at this time in Shuttle Street. The congregation was composed chiefly of members of the Wynd Church, who had seceded on account of patronage. When Mr. Cruden left them for London, part of the congregation went back to the Establishment, and part formed the Dowhill Relief Church. Mr. Dale, who was a member, formed the "old Scotch Independents," still in existence.

was beginning at this time to assume respectable proportions, and the kail yards and washing greens were being slowly transformed into thriving streets, but hitherto there had been no church within its bounds. The petty tyranny exercised against Mr. Monteith had attracted on his behalf much kindly sympathy, which manifested itself in a movement for the erection of a church for the district and village. With his accustomed energy and liberality, Mr. Monteith headed the movement, and in less than two years (1770) the little Anderston Relief Kirk, with its plain exterior, was opened for public worship.

Mr. John Ewing,[1] a good man who had been an elder in the little congregation assembling in the small Relief Church in Albion Street, along with their newly-appointed minister, Mr. Neill, and Mr. Monteith, constituted the first session. It may be sufficient to state further in connection with this subject, that the Anderston Relief Church from that time until the present has held a distinguished position among the churches of the city, both as respects the numbers and respectability of its members, and the worth and ability of its ministers. Their first minister was Mr. Joseph Neill, who, before he came to Anderston, was an English Nonconformist preacher. He died in 1774. He was succeeded by Mr. James Stuart, a reputed son of the Pretender, "Royal Charlie," a gentleman of great learning, earnestness, and ability. In the course of his ministry the church was considerably enlarged. He collated the first Relief Hymn Book, and wrote an able introduction to the collection, which was first used in his own

---

[1] Mr. Ewing's son, Joseph, died quite recently, a member of the Anderston kirk-session, an office which his father filled with credit and usefulness more than a century previously. Mr. Ewing was an interesting link in the chain that binds the history of the old Anderston church—the oldest surviving church of the denomination in the city—with the present times.

congregation. He died in 1819. Regarding his successor, the good and talented Dr. Struthers, little need be said. His name is still held in kindly remembrance in the churches. He died in 1858. Dr. Logan Aikman, his successor, now fills the pulpit of the Anderston Relief Church with acceptance. The old building has been superceded by a handsome modern structure, that stands among the graves of many generations who have witnessed the chances and changes which the little suburban village has undergone.

Mr. Monteith's house was situated in Bishop Street—one of these low-roofed, old-fashioned, but commodious houses, so common at this period, full of home comfort and kindly associations. It was the invariable custom in the family, even after they had separated and had got homes of their own, to meet in the Bishop Street mansion every Saturday afternoon, to dine with the old folks, and renew the old household intercourse. At these meetings the conversation often took a political tone, when the stirring events of the time, especially those connected with the revolt of the American colonies, were warmly discussed. On that and other matters the old man strongly denounced the policy of the British Government, and his views were warmly supported by all his sons, with the exception of Henry, subsequently one of Glasgow's most honoured men, who rose to the dignity of Lord Provost and Member of Parliament for his native city. Henry defended the action of the Government with much energy and talent, greatly to the annoyance of the good elder. One day, when the discussion among the young folk had become unnecessarily warm and protracted, the old man rose, and thus addressed his ambitious, and, as he judged, mistaken son:—"O! Harry, Harry, a' things will be set right, "man, when ye're made Lord Provost o' Glasgow, and, may be,

" Member o' Parliament as weel!" The good old father did not live to see his bantering forecast realised, but it was remembered when his talented son had attained the highest honours that his fellow-citizens could confer upon him.

Another of these gossiping stories which shed a pleasant lustre over the homely life of the old Bishop Street residence has been preserved. Mrs. Monteith was one of those busy, bustling housewives, whose whole "but and ben" was a model of orderliness, comfort, and cleanliness. As, however, there were around her fireside many hungry lads to feed, and her house was distant miles from the Bell Street and Princes' Street markets, she prudently provided that, on the approach of winter, the pickle tub should be duly replenished with the yearly "Mart;" and, of course, the manufacture of those dearly prized kitchen ornaments, so "bien" in appearance, and so delicate in flavour, the rows of puddings, white and black, was her own peculiar care and her pride. It was her practice every Sunday morning, when fully arrayed for church with best Sunday peaked bonnet, to take a housewifely look into the kitchen ; for these "glaiked taupies," Peggy and Nannie, frequently left the place in such a state of "tapselteerieness" as sorely unfitted her for profiting by the admonitions of the minister.

One Sunday morning the usual inspection revealed some slight disarrangement in the ornamental ranks that hung so gracefully from the low roof. To mount upon a stool and set the whole in a sightly fashion only required a minute's time, and then the good lady followed her husband, who, douce man, had slowly plodded before her on his way to the wee kirk. By the time she could overtake him he had bestowed his usual nod on the elder, and dropped his usual offering in the plate; when, hurrying after him, she was surprised by a tap on the shoulder from Davie of the plate, who thus addressed her :—"Ye'll excuse me, mem, but there's a black puddin' stickin' on ye're bannet!" Sure enough, the unique ornament had dropped upon her head unobserved, and she had carried it through the streets, and was only prevented from displaying it in the eyes of the great congregation by the timely warning of the obliging elder. We are not informed how it was finally disposed of, but we may safely conclude that it found its way to the Bishop Street frying pan, in the capacious side pouch of Mrs. Monteith, and in the goodly company of the newly-introduced "Hymns and spiritual songs agreed upon by the Presbytery of Relief."

As the useful life of the good old man drew near its close, like many of the ancient patriarchs he increased in riches and honours. His sons grew up prosperous and respected, and the little church also, that, next to his own family, occupied the largest share of his affectionate regards, was abundantly successful, and a blessing to the inhabitants of the growing Clyde Bank village; and thus surrounded by all that makes life most pleasant, and death least dreaded, Mr. Monteith passed to his rest, loved and lamented by the whole community which he adorned, and among whose descendants his name is revered to the present day. In the session-house of the old church a likeness of Mr. Monteith was suspended. The portrait, although reputed an excellent likeness, is not very valuable as a work of high art. When his enterprising family of sons in after years had become merchants of the first rank in Glasgow, they very naturally tried to get possession of this relic, but the managers of the church could not be prevailed upon to part with what they esteemed a precious remembrance of their friend and benefactor; and in the new building it fills the place of honour which it occupied in the old.

As we have stated, a low stone wall separated the kirkyard from the little Bishop Street garden. At this wall Mr. Monteith had erected an ornamental summer house, where in the evenings he could rest, or hold kindly communion with his family or friends. Not many yards from this pleasant bower they laid the good old man when he died, and a plain, unpretentious tablet in the wall indicates the spot in that solemn city of the dead where he rests.

The old kirkyard has lost all its rural amenities. The summer bower and pleasant flower garden attached to the Bishop Street dwelling have long ago disappeared, and have been replaced by a blackened brick factory of some kind, whose small peering windows seem to frown down upon the place of graves ; yet to every thoughtful person the plain mossy gravestones read like a good book, while they tell of that earnest desire for sympathy and remembrance which is so natural to us all ; and in the case of many lying here who have left behind unmistakeable traces of their individual energy and goodness, and whose very names are now almost forgotten, the simple " Here lies " is very touching and suggestive.

Mr. Monteith left six sons, all of whom were gentlemen of great energy and ability.

John Monteith, the eldest, was a frank, manly gentleman, but in his business habits bold and speculative to rashness. In 1801 he established a company, who erected a weaving factory at Pollok-shaws. This was the first power-loom factory in operation in the West of Scotland. Eight years before this time, Mr. Robertson, an ingenious doctor in Glasgow, had brought two looms from the hulks on the Thames, where weaving by power, the invention of a benevolent clergyman, Rev. Dr. Cartwright, had been practiced for some years, and was there employed for economising convict labour.

Mr. Robertson's working room was a cellar in Argyle Street, the motive power being a large Newfoundland dog, which was trained to walk in a drum or cylinder. The whole thing seems to have been more of an experiment than a serious attempt to manufacture for the market. The proprietors of a bleach-field at Milton, on the Leven, however, erected a few looms driven by power, which attracted the notice of Mr. Monteith, and he, as we have stated, erected a factory at Pollokshaws containing 200 looms. His chief partner about this time was Mr. Scott Moncrieff, better known as the Glasgow agent for the Royal Bank, which had its office in St. Andrew Square. Mr. Moncrieff seems to have been embued with the canny philosophy of the elder Nicol Jarvie, "Never to put his hand further in than he could conveniently draw it out again;" so, getting somewhat alarmed at what he considered the reckless ventures of his fearless partner, he signified his desire, as old "Senex" informs us, to sever the connection. This was done, and Mr. Patrick Falconer took his place in the new concern, which was then changed to Monteith & Falconer. John has been described as one to whose fingers "a guinea would never stick." He died in 1834.

James, the second son, whose address is given in Jones' Directory, 1789, as a "dealer in cotton twist, Cambuslang," bought from David Dale, in 1792, the then newly-erected cotton spinning factory at Blantyre. The following year, 1793, was a most disastrous one for Glasgow. The events which followed the French Revolution paralysed commerce everywhere, and, of course, fell with the greatest weight upon such manufacturing establishments as that at Blantyre, which was only in the first stage of its existence. Mr. Monteith was in despair, and, in fear of total ruin, waited upon Mr. Dale, and urged upon him to rescind their agreement; but old David was inexorable, and so there was no help for it but to make the best of a bad, a *ruinous*, bargain, as it was considered. About this time an establishment was started in London, chiefly through the instrumentality of Provost Patrick Colquhoun, we believe, for the sale of cotton and linen cloth by *vendu*—a modification of the Auction Mart—and it occurred to Mr. Monteith that if he could but get his unsaleable yarns quickly manufactured into cloth, here was a channel through which he might have them disposed of, if not with profit, at any rate with no great loss. The work was prosecuted with great energy, and so successful did the scheme turn out that, in the course of five years, Mr. Monteith, instead of finding himself a ruined manufacturer, as he had at one time anticipated, found that he had realised a fortune of £80,000. By the time that this was accomplished, however, some of his brother manufacturers had found out the secret spring of his wealth, but it was too late of being discovered; yarns had risen in price, and the sale by *vendu* had lost further potency for creating riches.

Mr. Monteith married a daughter of Thomas Buchanan of Ardenconnal, and had no family. He was the chief partner in the firm of Henry Monteith & Co. He died in 1802.

Mr. Monteith's third son, Henry, born in 1764, was the best known and most highly honoured of the remarkable family. In early life he was sent to get a practical knowledge of the art of weaving, a course that was generally followed in the case of gentlemen's sons who expected to take part in the business of manufacturing. He used to boast that on the very first day he mounted the loom he earned " half-a-crown."

While quite a young man he established an extensive manufacturing business in Anderston. He had fallen on evil times, however. A vigorous competition at home and abroad, as well as recent improvements in the art of weaving, had made it necessary, in accordance with the ordinary laws of supply and demand, that wages should be reduced. This, of course, was received with cries of oppression and injustice. A bill was framed by the weavers for fixing the price of weaving by Act of Parliament, and loud complaints were expressed because it had been received with so little favour. The popular discontent at last found vent in open rupture, and in 1785, when Mr. Monteith was only twenty-one years of age, his warehouse windows were broken, and he himself seized and roughly handled, for his "queue" was ruthlessly cut off, the loss of which would doubtless be regarded as a great degradation, being ostentatiously worn by every young man who aspired to follow the fashion. Notwithstanding this opposition, Mr. Monteith's success in business was very marked. In 1802 he established at Barrowfield a large factory for weaving Bandana handkerchiefs, which was very prosperous; and on the death of his brother James, in that same year, he took the principal management of the whole extensive business of the firm, which was then known as Henry Monteith & Co., and which, besides the Bandana factory, carried on bleaching, and subsequently extensive turkey red dyeing and calico printing, as well as cotton weaving and spinning on a large scale. His mills at Blantyre comprised at the time—as they do still, with all the accommodation required for the comfort of the operatives—an entire town.

So greatly was the commercial energy and practical wisdom of Mr. Monteith appreciated, that in 1815 and 1816, and again in 1819 and 1820, he was appointed Lord Provost of the city. These years were perhaps the most eventful that the town had ever passed through. In the first period there occurred that terrible commercial depression following the war with France, which we have tried to picture in the sketch of the Stirlings of Cordale ; and the second period comprises the events of the Radical risings. Looking back over these stirring periods, especially the latter, from our present standpoint, we may feel disposed to take exception to certain proceedings and decisions, for which the magistrates in council are chargeable ; but, taking a dispassionate view of the social and political exigencies of the time, we must admit that, on the whole, the difficult and onerous duties of Mr. Monteith's position were discharged in a manner that reflected honour on his civic rule. This opinion is further confirmed by the fact, that in all this popular ferment and disturbance, there was no loss of human life, and very little destruction of property in Glasgow. Indeed, so cautiously and leniently did he rule, that the Lord Advocate for Scotland, Sir William Rae, complained bitterly of his want of firmness and decision, and declared that, unless more stringent measures were adopted by him, there would be no safety for life or property in the town.

But it was not so believed in Glasgow ; for in 1821 Mr. Monteith was elected Member of Parliament for the Lanark-shire district of Burghs, and having discharged the duties with acceptance for five years, he was re-elected to the same honourable position in 1831.

He purchased the estate of Carstairs, near the town of Lanark, and in 1824 he erected the magnificent mansion now owned and occupied by his son Robert. As a country gentleman and a land-lord, Mr. Monteith was highly respected; but his political creed, which was pronounced at the time violently Tory, found little favour among the Lanark weavers, who were as violently Radical, and, therefore, his visits to the county town were not highly honoured.　He died in 1848; and although a splendid cenotaph was erected to his memory in the Necropolis, he sleeps under the shadow of the Ramshorn steeple, and a granite tablet marks his resting place.

The fourth son, Robert, died in the prime of life.　One son, Alexander Earl Monteith, was sheriff of Fife ; another son was minister in the Established Church, Dalkeith.　He left the church at the Disruption, and became a minister in a small Highland charge in Argyllshire,

The fifth son, Adam, died also in the prime of life　He left one daughter and one son.　This lad was taken as a clerk into his uncle's warehouse.　The gruff old book-keeper ordered him to perform some menial office which he esteemed beneath the dignity of a Monteith, and so he walked quietly out the door and home to his mother.　James Hannan, a grandson of Mrs. Allan Arthur, old James Monteith's only daughter, was sent for in haste to fill the situation.　The little lad was found capable and obedient, and there he remains to the present day, the sole business representative of an ancient and honourable line ; and who that knows the good magistrate can refrain from wishing that he may for many years to come, worthily represent a house to the members of which the old city is so much indebted.

William, the youngest son by a second marriage, died unmarried, a comparatively young man.

THE STIRLINGS OF CORDALE

AND

DALQUHURN.

IN the year 1537 there fell, in a feudal fight with a neighbouring chieftain called Campbell of Auchenhowie, Robert Stirling of Lettyr, a chief of an old Royal stock, who could trace his descent back to William the Lion, and whose claims to be the representative of the Royal race of Stirling were therefore undisputed. We hear little of this family again till about the middle of last century, when there arose a curious controversy between three separate families, each of which asserted its claim to the exclusive privilege of direct relationship with the old chieftain—namely, the Stirlings of Keir or Cadder, the Stirlings of Kippendavie or Kenmure, and the Stirlings of Cordale. The last named family so far established their claims, that Provost Andrew Stirling of Drumpellier obtained the right to appropriate the family insignia and crest of the old Lettyr chieftain.

Irrespective of race or pedigree, however, the connection of the Stirling family with the progress of Glasgow has been so intimate, and so ancient, that it well deserves an honourable place in any record of the prosperity of the town.

We have evidence of the intimate association of the family with Glasgow in the fortunes of Walter Stirling, merchant, Dean of

Guild in 1639 and 1640, and commissioner appointed to represent
the town in the old Scottish Parliament and in the General
Assembly.   He married Helen, daughter of David Weems, first
Presbyterian minister in the Inner High Church after the Reformation.[1]   He thus allied himself with a family whose services to
Glasgow, in the days of her insignificance, are still beneficial to its
inhabitants.   We may be pardoned the digression to notice them.

Helen Weems was the widow of Mr. Peter Low, surgeon, whose
somewhat versatile character has for so many years attracted public
attention, as recorded in the quaint old doggrel verses displayed on
his tombstone in the High Church burying-ground—

> "Who of his God had got the grace
> To live in mirth and die in peace."

Dr. Low was associated with his father-in-law in the negotiations
which resulted in the production of the Letter of Guildry, the
present Constitution of the Merchants' House, which had its origin
in the following circumstances :—A violent schism had long existed
between the merchant and trades ranks in the town, chiefly relating
to the claims of precedence put forth by the respective bodies,
which claims neither of the parties would cede to its rival.   In the
year 1605, the controversy had assumed proportions so grave that,
rather than take the good old way of adjusting the dispute by
means of the "quhinger and yrne staff," as at one time was
threatened, it was wisely resolved to submit the whole question of
difference to arbitration; and a commission was appointed for the

---

[1] Mr. Weems was inducted in 1572.   In 1584 the Provost of Glasgow, John, Earl of Montrose,
by command of His Majesty, placed the excommunicated Bishop Montgomery in his pulpit.   Mr.
Weems was elected Rector of the University in 1593, 1595, 1598, and 1602.   In 1600 he was found
to be "declinand in doctrine, negligent in preparation, and oft times overtaken with drink."   He
died in 1615.

purpose, consisting of Provost Sir George Elphinstone,[1] three of the town ministers—one of whom was the minister of the Inner High Church, David Weems—and, curiously enough, Mr. Walter Stirling for the merchant rank, and Dr. Peter Low for the trades rank, likely from the barber profession, then included in "the short gowned surgeon" corporation. These gentlemen produced a wisely framed document (subsequently ratified by Parliament in 1672), defining the powers and privileges of the respective bodies, and which to this day regulates the procedure of the Merchants' House.

Although it tends to break up somewhat the continuity of our narrative, we should like to take a glance at an Act of the old Scottish Parliament, which, so far as can be ascertained, is the first attempt to consolidate the laws which govern the Guild brethren, and which dates back to the reign of Alexander III. (A.D. 1284). The glimpse which the Act affords of the organization and social condition of the ancient fraternity, must be our apology for the reproduction of the following extracts :—

"THE LAWIS OF THE GYLD.

" *Item.*—we haf ordanit that na barganour vthin the boundis of the guild sall
" ber a knyff with a poynt, the quhilk giff he dois, he sall amend with xijd.

" *Item.*—giff that ony with a staffe or with ony yrne wapyn vyolently drawys
" blud of ane other or makis ony mutilacioun, he salbe contampnyt efter the will of
" the aldirman."

*   *   *   *   *   *

[1] " Sir George Elphinstone of Blythswood rose, by the favour of James Sixth, to be a great " man. He was knighted and made a Lord of the Session and a Gentleman of the Bedchamber. " Charles First raised him to be Lord Justice Clerk, and he held the office till his death. But, " behold the instability of human greatness! for he was the only burgess in all Scotland that came to " the highest office and made the greatest figure, and yet died so poor that his corpse was arrested " by his creditors, and his friends buried him privately in his own chapel adjoining to his house.— *M'Ure's History of Glasgow, page 34.*

His town mansion was a queer castellated building on the east side of Main Street, Gorbals, recently demolished.

"*Item.*—Giff that ony of the brether of the gyld hapyn to disses, and has not
"to bring him to the erde as afferis, or to ger sing for his saule, the brether sal tak
"of the faculteis of the gyld and ger his bodye be honestly layd in erde.

"*Item.*—Giff that ony of the brether, efter his desces leyff a dochter of his
"spousit wyffe borne, the quhilk be of loffabill conversacione, and of gude fame,
"geyff scho haf nocht of hir awin quhar off it may be purwayt hir of a man, (or of a
"religiouse house gif that scho lyk,) efter the estimacioun of the aldirman and the
"faculte of the gyld, it salbe purwayt til hir of a husband, or than a house of
"relygione, &c.

We return now to the Stirlings. Mr. Walter Stirling died honoured and lamented in 1655. By his wife, the stately and good looking Nelly Weems, there was left, with other children, a son, John, who had a remarkable family. Of John it is recorded that, along with many other merchants of the town, he was summoned to appear before the King's Privy Council at Edinburgh, to answer to the grave charge of hearing "outed ministers." For this offence, the whole of the merchants were sentenced to be lodged first in the Glasgow Jail, and afterwards to be kept fast in the Edinburgh Tolbooth for three months. Several Glasgow citizens who did not obey the summons were denounced and "put to the horn, and letters of caption raised against them."

John's family were John, William, and Walter. Walter, we know, was a magistrate in Glasgow, and he gave his name to Walter Stirling of Miller Street, his nephew, who is still gratefully remembered for Stirling's library and its endowments which he left for the benefit of his fellow-citizens.

William Stirling, the father of this gentleman (Walter), and second of old John's family, was a surgeon and apothecary in High Street. It is to him that Graham's Hall Factory owes its origin. James Loudon, merchant, David Loudon, weaver—who probably took the practical management of the business—and John Gordon, surgeon, were all associated with the apothecary in the speculation. The old historian, John M'Ure, who wrote 1736, in recording the manufacturing projects of Glasgow, mentions particularly the great establishment at Graham's Hall, near Glasgow, "for weaving " all sorts of Hollan-cloth wonderful fine, performed by fine masters " expert in the curious art of weaving, as fine and well done as at " Haarlem, in Holland." "The masters of this improven manufac- tory," he further informs us, " are now united to such perfection that " noblemen, barons, gentlemen, and citizens, and their ladies, buys " of them, and wears their linen, and binds their sons to them to " be their apprentices, and the Hollan-cloth is wonderfully whiten'd " at Dalwhern's (Dalquhurn) bleaching field."

It is worthy of notice that Tobias Smollet served his apprentice- ship in the little shop of this Mr. Gordon, apothecary, in High Street ; and it is somewhat characteristic of the relation that existed between the pair, that when the apothecary was taunted with regard to the mischievous proclivities of his erratic apprentice, as compared with certain other lads of more staid demeanour, Mr. Gordon always expressed his sympathy with his own "bubbly laddie that aye carried a stane in his pouch!" Duncan Niven, too, the barber, and prototype of Smollet's Strap, hung out his basin in Bell Street, almost within sight of the small repository of pills and ointments over which Smollet usually presided. Mr. Niven went out with the trades' regiment during the rebellion of 1745, and rose to a very respectable rank in his profession. In 1763 we find his name in the list of bailies of Glasgow, and in 1778 he had the honour, as Deacon of the trade, to be presented to King George in London.

The eldest son, John Stirling—third of the name—was one of the best known and most enterprising of the Stirling family. He and his brother Walter were both Glasgow bailies, and he ultimately rose to the dignity of Lord Provost of the city. In 1725, while Mr. Stirling was bailie, the popular tumult, known as the Shawfield riot, took place. In that year the Government imposed a tax on malt, and as home-brewed ale at the time was an indispensible article of common food—"the poor man's wine"—the tax was highly unpopular. Mr. Daniel Campbell, of Shawfield, was Member of Parliament for the city, and it had become known that he had used his influence in favour of the obnoxious tax. He therefore became an object of popular hatred. When the time came that the impost took effect, there was no small commotion in the town. Crowds of turbulent idlers, chiefly boys and women, collected, who violently hustled the officers charged with carrying out the duty of exacting the tax. Of course, the dignity of the law required to be upheld, but, unfortunately, there were no military in the town, and the mob had the best of it. As there was little prospect of a peaceful settlement, two companies of Lord Delorain's regiment of foot were sent for in hot haste. When the soldiers arrived, Provost Miller ordered the guard-house to be cleared for their reception; but the doors were locked and the keys had been carried off, so the soldiers were billeted, in the usual way, on the householder, and the worthy Provost and his friends, under the impression that all was over for the time, spent the evening in their tavern or club.

Fourteen years before this time, Mr. Campbell of Shawfield had built a spacious mansion house, which, with its great garden, stood upon the site of what is now Glassford Street, then entirely out of town. As its owner wisely kept out of the way, the mob, having provided themselves with axes and hammers, proceeded without challenge to demolish the house, the furniture of which they knocked to pieces, with loud shouts of " Down with Shawfield's house!" "No malt tax!" and, doubtless, they would have carried out their threat to pull down the house, had not the Provost and magistrates interfered, and persuaded them to desist. Next day the soldiers obtained possession of the guard-house, which stood on the south-west corner of Candleriggs ; but the mob, collecting in still greater numbers, began to pelt the sentinels with stones. The soldiers were thereupon formed in hollow square, and were ordered by Captain Bushell, their commander, to fire, which they did, killing two persons. Immediately the rioters broke open the town magazine, took possession of the arms, rang the fire-bell, and alarmed the whole town. On the persuasion of the magistrates, Captain Bushell and his company left the town for Dumbarton Castle, not without a vigorous attack from the enraged citizens. In this riot, nine were killed and seventeen wounded.

On the day of the riot, Mr. Stirling was out of town ; yet, on the charge of complicity with the rioters, he, along with Provost Miller and his brother magistrates, were carried to Edinburgh, guarded thither by a party of the Royal Scotch Dragoons, and after going through a form of trial they were dismissed. On their way home they were met by jubilant bands of their fellow-citizens, and conveyed through the town with ringing of bells and other demonstrations of public rejoicing and welcome. Three years afterwards Mr. Stirling was elected Lord Provost of the city.

Mr. Stirling was one of that confederation of Glasgow merchants who, in the beginning of last century, opened up and extended the foreign trade of the city, and whom M'Ure calls " The great com-" pany undertaking the trade to Virginia, Carriby Islands, Barbadoes, " New England, St. Cristophers, Montserat, and other colonies in " America."

Mr. John Stirling had a son, James, who was minister in the outer

High Church.   His memory, however, is perpetuated to the present day in Glasgow, through his son, William, the founder of the firm of William Stirling and Sons.   Mr. William Stirling was a gentleman of remarkable energy and success.   His town residence is described as a plain unpretending two-storey house, which stood in a small garden at the end of a range of straggling houses, called, in M'Arthur's old map, Stirling's Closs.   His next neighbour was Mr. George Bogle of Daldowie, between whose house and Mr. Stirling's there was a private friendly entrance.   Mr. Bogle's house stood on the north-east termination of a narrow lane, closed up at its north end by a heckler's shop, and known afterwards as the Police Lane, the main entrance of which was off Bell Street.   The lane is described as having on one side a wood-yard and a vegetable garden, and on the other a range of dingy buildings with outside stairs, one of which was occupied as the bleaching and manufacturing warehouse of Henry Hardie & Co., better known, subsequently, as Carrick, Brown & Co.   Mr. Brown, of the firm, lived up one of these stairs, with no more pleasant view from his windows than the narrow and dirty lane thus described.

Mr. Brown, the Glasgow historian, states that Mr. Stirling at first printed cloth on commission, the work being done chiefly in London.   About 1750, however, he erected a small work at Dalsholm, on the Kelvin, which he carried on with considerable success.   Finding that he could work with more economy on the banks of the Leven, he erected the work at Cordale, still in operation there, about the year 1770.   The warehouse of the firm stood, as in the old Directory address, "by 42 High Street," nearly opposite Blackfriars Wynd ; and here for many years their sample cards of patterns attracted crowds of the bien burgess' wives, who wished to consult the latest fashion in sprigs and wavelets, as that delightful gossiper "Senex" tells us was the common practice at the time.

It will thus be seen that the old printing establishment of William Stirling & Sons has been in existence at the present time (1881) for the long period of one hundred and thirty years.[1] How many have been the changes which the town has seen during these years, and how few existing firms can claim such a worthy antiquity?

Andrew, John, and James Stirling, whose names stand in the original list of the Chamber, and who were among its principal promoters, were the sons of old William. One of his daughters, Elizabeth, married Professor Hamilton, and became the mother, with other children, of Thomas Hamilton, author of "Cyril Thornton." Another daughter married Dugald Bannatyne, so well known and affectionately remembered in connection with the progress of the city, and the father of two gentlemen recently passed away who will long be remembered in Glasgow society— Andrew and Dugald John Bannatyne, writers.

Andrew Stirling, the eldest son of the family, was born in 1751, immediately after his father had built the Cordale Printworks. At his father's death he was 26 years of age, and not quite in the prime of his manhood. It is a somewhat suggestive fact—which we have noticed elsewhere—that the old man died in the very year, 1777, when the unsettled condition of the American colonies, resulting in their "rebellion," as it was then considered, had produced such disastrous consequences upon the chief source of industry in the city—the great Virginia trade in tobacco. Andrew, on his father's death, purchased the estate of Drumpellier, in the parish of West Monkland, which his grandfather, Provost Andrew Buchanan, had

---

[1] Old Dalquhurn was first started as a bleaching field in the year 1723, and can now boast a busy life of upwards of a century and a-half.

acquired, and at his death left it to his sons. The situation at this time must have been an exceedingly pleasant one. Mr. Bower, the parish minister of Monkland, says that "the place is like an "immense garden," and he adds :—"The monks, who usually "fixed upon a fine situation, had a residence here. Their superior "skill in agriculture and gardening rendered the places they fixed "upon at once pleasant and valuable."

Seven years previous to the time when Mr. Stirling had made this purchase, an Act of Parliament had been obtained for making a canal between the Monkland collieries and the city. The object of the undertakers was to open up a cheap and easy mode of communication with the coal districts, and thus reduce the price of coals to the inhabitants and manufacturers of Glasgow. The object was a good one, but the reverses caused by the revolt of the American colonies had so crippled the resources of those who were the original projectors of the scheme, among whom the Drumpellier Buchanans took a prominent part, that the project was given up, and the stock sold by public auction in 1784. The Messrs. Stirling purchased the largest share of the stock, and ultimately became the sole proprietors.

The construction of the canal, under the vigorous management of the Stirling firm, proceeded with great alacrity, and by the end of the century it was in full operation, to the manifest advantage of the city. The works on the Leven were also prosecuted with much energy; Cordale was enlarged; and in 1791 old "Dalwhern," by arrangement with their surviving relative, Walter of Miller Street, was transferred to Messrs. William Stirling & Sons; but it was not till 1816 that the new and highly-prized turkey red dyeing was begun there. In short, the responsibilities of the firm became enormous, and, with the view of still further extension, Andrew, in the following year, 1792, went to London, and under the firm of Stirling, Hunter & Co., established the first commission house in the metropolis for the sale of Scotch manufactures.

In the meantime, the principal management of the Glasgow business devolved upon the second son of the family, John, a gentleman with a fine presence, and possessed of great business talent and energy. While living in the quaint little house at the end of the old-fashioned lane, he woo'd and won his next door neighbour, Miss Janet Bogle, daughter of George Bogle, one of the old respected tobacco lords. Two of their sons are well remembered by the merchants of Glasgow, George of Cordale, and William, the eldest brother, whose sons, until very recently, managed the works, and are still living amongst us.

Andrew, as we have already stated, had gone to London; James bought the estate of Stair, in Ayrshire; and the business of the firm fell chiefly upon John, who possessed all his father's energy, but perhaps could scarcely lay claim to the old man's caution and prudence. At any rate, the firm had fallen on evil times, and became unfortunate in 1816. Before that event occurred, however, John was beyond praise or blame, having died in 1811.

In the first three months of that disastrous year, the liabilities of bankrupt firms in Glasgow alone amounted to upwards of two millions sterling. The distress was not confined to one section of the community; every industry, commercial and agricultural, was paralysed. Nor was the depression confined to one part of the kingdom; for in the rural districts of England it is recorded that the poor rates had increased to such an extent as completely to swallow up the whole income of those who had anything to pay them; and large tracts of country bore every appearance of desolation and desertion, which might be supposed to follow the fiercest ravages of war or pestilence; while in Ireland the evil was still more extensively appalling.

Lord Brougham, contrasting the condition of the nation at this period with its state during the great commercial crisis which followed the revolt of our American colonies, said:—"On the "opening of last session of Parliament, the Prime Minister "(Mr. Pitt) congratulated the country upon the extension of its "commerce, the flourishing state of its manufactures, and the "increase and increasing amount of its revenues! Who could "employ such language now? On the contrary—and it was one of "the most portentous differences between the conclusion of this "and of all former contests—our calamities have almost entirely " begun with the peace, and each succeeding period, since the war "ended, only makes things worse. The distress, at first confined "principally to agriculture, has spread to every branch of our trade "and industry, and the national misery has reached a height wholly "without precedent in our history since the Norman conquest."

The causes of this unexampled distress were manifold, but all had special connection with the highly artificial condition in which this country had been placed by the length and persistency of our war with France. During the continuance of that war, many things had transpired to stimulate the highest exertions of our manufacturers. In spite of Buonaparte's edicts and blockades, this country had continued to supply the whole Continent with merchandise and manufactures; in fact, Britain had become, if not the only, at any rate the principal, entrepôt for the whole colonial trade.

Some time before the war terminated a Bill was passed for increasing the duty on corn, which raised the price of that commodity from sixty-three shillings to eighty shillings. Besides, a confederation of speculators had bought up all the grain in the Baltic ports, for the purpose of retarding the supplies till an extravagant price had been obtained. This threw upon manufacturers the burden of a very considerable rise in the wages of operatives, to meet the increased rate in the price of food, and added greatly to the cost of manufactures.

At the termination of the war, the manufacturers of this country, under the impression that the demand for British goods in those countries recently under the sway of Napoleon would be immensely increased, prepared and shipped goods of all kinds at a reckless rate. They were mistaken, however; for the demand bore no proportion to the actual supply, and Foreign Governments, becoming alarmed at this prodigious tide of imports which threatened to overwhelm the industry, in self-defence increased their import duties till they became positively prohibitory; and thus two principal causes of depression were created, namely, excessive supply on one hand, and inadequate demand on the other.

While these and similar causes of distress weighed so heavily upon national industry, their intensity was increased to a ruinous and unprecedented degree by a change in the currency. A growing feeling of dissatisfaction had begun to manifest itself with respect to the privileges and profits of the Bank of England. The popular discontent found expression in bitter animadversion before Parliament in the session of 1817. Whether the change that worked so disastrously might have its rise in a sagacious forecast of the coming scrutiny we cannot say; but the directors of the Bank of England, suddenly and without warning, restricted their circulation in 1816 to the extent of three millions, and, of course, the circulation of the local and country banks was restricted in a similar, and, in most cases, even a greater degree.

Thus, the liberal accommodation, which in the latter years of the war was abundantly supplied, suddenly came almost to a dead stop. It is unnecessary to explain how these restrictive measures, combined with the other causes we have mentioned, affected a crippled commerce, and, especially, what their operation was upon fixed property like that of the Monkland Canal, whose annual revenue bore such a disproportionate return.to its real value.

As we have mentioned, John Stirling died five years before this great calamity fell upon the city. His sons, William and George, set themselves in right earnest to bring back the prosperity of the old firm. In this object, as is well known, they were completely successful; and under the careful management of the next generation, James, William, and Charles, all sons of William, the works were so extended that they have became a wonder of modern industry. If any of our readers will take the trouble to peruse a very able treatise upon Banking and the Distribution of Capital, written by the eldest son of the family, James, we think he can hardly fail to perceive the honourable principles by which that success has been obtained.

These are old-world stories now, and, like the generality of mundane affairs, are fast falling into oblivion. We merely mention them, certainly with no desire " to point a moral or adorn a tale," but simply to indicate the immense difficulties that environed the merchants of our good town, at a period when the very existence of the national prosperity was endangered, and the determination by which many, like the Stirlings of Cordale, won the victory.

The old firm has now passed into other hands, of whom the late respected John Matheson, jun., was the head. How many like the writer have cause to lament the sudden death of Mr. Matheson, whose clear judgment and warm heart will long be held in loving remembrance in the circle which he adorned, and by all who knew his worth!

Mr. Matheson was an able and active Director of the Chamber of Commerce for many years, and President in 1872 and 1873. He died very suddenly in December, 1878. The following verses were written many years ago by Mr. Matheson, and will be read with interest. To those who knew him most intimately, no apology is needed for the apparent incongruity of inserting the lines in this place :—

"CONCERNING THEM WHICH ARE ASLEEP."

"But I would not have you to be ignorant, brethren, concerning them which are asleep, that ye sorrow not, even as others which have no hope."—1 THESS. iv. 13.

Shadows o'er the evening falling,
　　Softly gather, gently creep,
Where, silent till the Trumpet's calling,
　　Lie those that sleep ;
For there the earth, with bosom swelling,
　　Guardeth love's treasures in the deep,
And calm and hallowed is the dwelling
　　Of them that sleep.

Sunbeams from the morning flowing !
　　Downward from the mountains leap,
And linger with your brightest glowing
　　O'er those that sleep ;
For folding them in sheen of glory
　　A seemly vigil there ye keep !
So bright and shining is the story
　　Of them that sleep.

Hearts that know not how to falter !
    Eyes that cannot choose but weep !
Hold fast your priesthood at the altar
      Of them that sleep !
For life is but a stinted measure,
    Swift to the goal the moments sweep ;
Beyond ye have a laid-up treasure
      In them that sleep.

Sowers in the vale of sadness !
    Halcyon harvests shall ye reap—
Yet glean on earth some fruit of gladness
      In them that sleep ;
For, from beyond Heaven's star-built portals,
    Blazoned on the midnight steep,
Responsive love is shed on mortals
      From them that sleep !

HENRY RIDDELL.

M R. RIDDELL was one of the old tobacco aristocracy, a successful merchant, and West India trader. When the Chamber of Commerce was instituted, Mr. Riddell was one of the first Board of Directors, and was elected President of the Chamber in 1792 and 1793, and again in 1800 and 1801. He was also associated with the directorship of the Merchants' House, with the erection of the Tontine, and, indeed, with most of the projects that were advanced in the latter part of last century for the prosperity of the city. In 1781 he married Anne, daughter of Mr. John Glassford of Dougalston, and in a few years afterwards he took up his residence in the new and somewhat aristocratic suburb of George Square, being amongst its first tenants. Previous to 1786 the Ramshorn Meadow, or Lang Croft— on the north-western corner of which the square was built— was so far removed from the centre of city business that it was frequently resorted to as a quiet and most convenient place where the worn-out horses of the town could be slaughtered and skinned. Moreover, the whole of this corner was simply a hollow marsh, whose centre was graced with a pool of stagnant water, which was found serviceable as a means for getting quit of the stray dogs and cats that might be found troublesome. In 1786, Mr. Dougald Bannatyne organised a building society for the purpose of erecting a class of houses designed to meet more fully the growing wants of the prosperous city merchants, and among the first sites selected by this society was the Lang Croft. The rubbish of malt kilns, byres, and time-worn houses that required to be removed to make room for the buildings already in progress in the new west-end, found a ready receptacle in the mud beds of the Ramshorn Meadow,[1] and in the year 1789, Anne Glassford and her husband removed, as we have said, to their new residence on the west side of the quiet country square, with many pleasing associations, we doubt not, on the part of Mrs. Riddell, arising from the neighbourhood of their home to the locality where she must have spent so many happy days when her father inhabited the grand old Shawfield mansion, whose garden was skirted by the tenantless back Cow Lone, now our busy Ingram Street.

Many of even the most wealthy Glasgow merchants at this time were huddled together in ill-lighted and low-roofed flats, in some dingy "land" or "court," having a common stair for the accommodation of a miscellaneous neighbourhood, where all arrangements for domestic comfort, or even decency, were simply execrable; and no doubt it would be with feelings of pleasure and pride that orders were issued by the new tenants in George Square to the bare-footed servant lass to be careful that the back windows were each morning duly "lifted," so that the unusual and pleasant fragrance of the orchards and flower gardens of Meadowflat, which they overlooked, and which stretched away far into the country, should come in and fill each room.

Even in this comparatively early stage of the progress and

[1] In the spring of 1879, numerous complaints were expressed in the usual meetings of the Magistrates and Council of the city regarding the slushiness of George Square, and it was resolved that the whole should be laid with flagstones, as the only available remedy for the evil complained of.

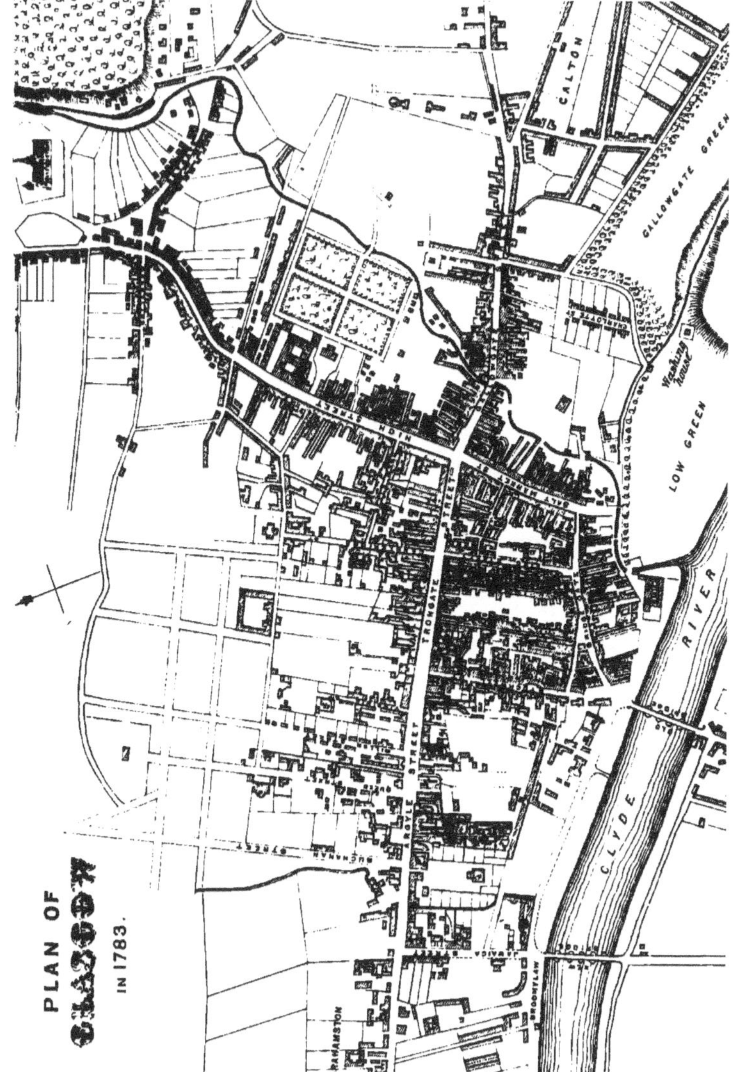
PLAN OF GLASGOW IN 1783.
CALTON
GALLOWGATE GREEN
Washing house
LOW GREEN
RIVER
CLYDE
TRONGATE STREET
ARGYLE STREET
GALLOWGATE
SALTMARKET
STOCKWELL STREET
BUCHANAN STREET
BROOMIELAW
GRAHAMSTON

extension of Glasgow great changes had taken place in the aspect of the city. It was little more than twenty years from this time when old Johnnie Anderson, the town's herd, stumped in his kilts each morning from "Picken's Land," in the Rottenrow, down the High Street, along the Trongate, and up the hedge-skirted Cow Lone—now Queen Street—awakening the echoes with the strains of his cow horn melodies, warning the Glasgow housewives to turn out the "milky mothers," so that they might be driven past this Ramshorn Meadow, up the Crackling-house Brae —now Dundas Street—and on to the common meadow of Cowcaddens. But now Johnnie and his office had passed away, and with him many a well-known rural lane and quiet meadow and pleasant flower garden, the remembrance of which could only be cherished now as a far-away vision.

The quiet square in the fields must have been, nevertheless, a desirable place of abode, even taking into consideration the drawbacks by which its amenities were accompanied. At this date water—that essential element to household comfort—could only be obtained by scrambling for it at the corners of public streets, or, it may be, battling or begging for it at private garden wells, or buying it from the perambulating water seller at so much a "gang." Sanitary appliances were considered troublesome and unnecessary, and sanitary inspection intolerable. Country and suburban roads— even the public streets—knew not Macadam,[1] and many of them were simply mud beds, which every passing shower converted into open quagmires, through which, muffled in duffle cloaks and balloon head pieces, called "calashes," Glasgow beauties might be seen paddling to kirk and market elevated upon iron pattens. In the

---

[1] In 1777 the first flagstone pavement was laid on part of the east side of Candleriggs. The pavement at King William existed before this time.

whole town, too, at this period, not a single sewer was in existence
to carry off superfluous drainage, which was, therefore, permitted
to fester in the air, or to soak into the walls,[1] and with the exception of a winking oil lamp here and there in the most frequented
streets, that could scarcely make the surrounding gloom visible, the
whole town was in absolute darkness,[2] so that when the wintry
evening fell, and the moon was down, the universal "tin bouats,"
perforated with tiny holes, or the more genteel horn-cased lanterns,
carried by the ubiquitous "servant lass," might be seen flitting like
meteors in the darkness, to warn " master and mistress" where the
dangerous mud pit, or the more treacherous cart or barrow, stabled
on the open street, betokened damage to dress or limbs. How
difficult it is for ourselves, the "feckless" successors of that sturdy
generation, to conceive that such conditions could once exist where
now stands the wilderness of monotonous streets, gas lit and police
protected, with which we are all familiar.

The final connection of Mr. Riddell with the Chamber of
Commerce is very touching. He was the last of the original
Board of directors who held office as chairman. Only seven of
these were then in office; the rest had either retired or were
dead. Of nearly two hundred of the Glasgow commercial aristocracy forming the original Chamber eighteen years before this
date (1801), about thirty only remained, most of whom had
retired from active commercial life. At the last meeting of the
directors over which Mr. Riddell presided, on 17th June, 1801,

---

[1] The first common sewer in Glasgow was laid in George Square in 1790. It ran westward to
Buchanan Street, at the foot of which it was emptied into St. Enoch's Burn, till this time a trouting
stream.

[2] In 1780 the magistrates ordered that nine oil lamps should be put up between the Laigh Kirk and
the Stockwell.

the sederunt numbered twenty-one, and only two of these—viz., Mr. John Laurie, founder of Laurieston, and Mr. John Stirling, of William Stirling & Sons—were members of the first directorate. On the next day of meeting, Mr. Robert Dunlop announced, with expressions of deep regret and sincere respect, that their chairman, Mr. Riddell, had died since their last meeting.

JOHN COATS CAMPBELL,

OF CLATHIC.

(*Signature*, JOHN CAMPBELL, *see foot of First Column*, *Lithographed List.*)

IN the latter part of last century there were few of the merchants of Glasgow who held a more honourable name, or one more distinguished for enterprise, than Mr. CAMPBELL, the subject of our sketch. His father, Archibald Coats, was, like his son, a substantial and respected merchant in town, and held a high position among his fellow-merchants. This is manifest from the fact that, when the rebel army visited Glasgow in 1745, they carried off with them two of the most substantial and influential citizens as hostages, that the terms they had forced upon the inhabitants might be duly implemented—Bailie George Carmichael and Archibald Coats; and we may feel assured that, in the subsequent business career of these gentlemen, the inconvenience they had been put to on behalf of the town was not forgotten.

Mr. Campbell was one of the most active business men amongst the old Glasgow commercial aristocracy. He was an extensive tobacco importer, as well as general merchant and trader. Besides his estates of Clathic and Ryding, he held a considerable amount of city property. He was elected Lord Dean of Guild in 1767–68, and in 1775–76 and in 1781–82 he was re-elected to the same office. In 1784–85 the honourable distinction of Lord Provost was conferred upon him; and when the Chamber of Commerce was instituted in

1783, he formed one of its first Board of Directors, and all through his life he took a deep interest in its welfare and usefulness.

At the time Mr. Campbell filled the civic chair, the trade of Glasgow was in a most unsatisfactory condition. The disastrous and ill-advised war which resulted in the loss of our American Colonies, and brought disgrace upon the arms of Great Britain, had just been concluded, and, besides the lamentable alienation of all friendly sympathy which the conflict had engendered, it had brought ruin upon many a prosperous Glasgow business. Previous to the war, almost the whole trading capital of the city was employed in the importation of tobacco from America, and the export thither of manufactured goods, the greater part of which was the production of the city and neighbourhood. Now that great source of wealth and prosperity was hopelessly lost, and the whole trading resources of the city appeared to be confined to the uncertain and somewhat unremunerative manufacture of hosiery and domestic fabrics, and to a limited intercourse with the West Indies. The great cotton industry was yet unknown ; and it is no wonder that the hearts of the city merchants were filled with fear, while they tried to forecast the future of the hitherto prosperous little town.[1]

A deeper shadow had been thrown over this cheerless picture by the action of certain English merchant rivals in the tobacco trade, who created a cruel suspicion against the honour and honesty of the Glasgow merchants engaged in the business. Although the calumny had been demonstrated to be both malicious and baseless before a Parliamentary commission, it had nevertheless been made a pretext for introducing a complicated and unnecessary system of petty Customs' restrictions, annoying and hurtful in the greatest degree.

---

[1] In 1783 the inhabitants of Glasgow numbered about 44,000.

And now that the war taxes required increased vigilance in their collection, and almost everything fit to eat or to wear required to come under the Government stamp—even the working clerk in the merchant's office was taxed—these imposts, under strict and often intolerant surveillance, were a great oppression. The annoyance was further intensified by the fact, that at this time Glasgow had no harbour of her own near the city; her merchandise, therefore, could only be shipped at Greenock or Port-Glasgow, or delivered at Glasgow, by means of the clumsy gabbert on the shallow river, or the carrier's waggon over so many miles of wretched road. Not only were the regulations applicable to export, import, and internal traffic complicated and vexatious, but, in the midst of so much wreck and ruin caused by the war, the laws referring to bankruptcy and the adjudication of bankrupt estates were ill understood, partial, and incongruous, and bore oppressively upon honest and legitimate commerce.

All this called for prudent and vigilant action, and into the mass of confusion the directors of the Chamber of Commerce threw their energies promptly and conscientiously. Mr. Campbell supported them with all the influence of his official position, and not without effect. Gradually unnecessary restrictions were modified or removed, laws governing commerce, manufactures, and shipping were simplified, and more equally applied ; and it is now matter of history that from the gentlemen who then constituted the directorate of the Chamber proceeded the organizing and fostering of the great cotton industry, the science of turkey red dyeing and calico printing, and the improvement and wonderful extension of chemical manufactures ; and subsequently, although less directly, perhaps, the business of shipbuilding and steam navigation, and the progress of the coal and iron trade. Indeed, the Chamber has watched with interest, and fostered with care, the share that Glasgow has taken in the various industries which have made Great Britain the leader in arts, science, and manufactures throughout the world.

Twenty-four years prior to the establishment of the Chamber of Commerce, Mr. Campbell had been a leading partner in the aristocratic Thistle Bank. This Bank, during a successful career of seventy years, maintained an honourable place among its rivals in the city and in the kingdom. Whatever opinion we may form regarding the expediency or the necessity of that movement which resulted in the various restrictions imposed upon the Scotch Banks by the Act of 1845, there can be no question, we believe, respecting the beneficial influence on the national industry, and especially on the prosperity and progress of our own city, of the simple banking system previously in operation.

The Thistle Bank, at its commencement, issued notes for one pound, five pounds, and ten pounds, under a proviso that they should be paid, at the option of the managers, either on presentation or at the termination of six months, with six months' interest at five per cent. To facilitate small exchanges, however, notes were in circulation for ten shillings, which were all payable on demand.

The original partners of the Bank were Sir Walter Maxwell of Pollok, James' Ritchie of Busby and Craigton, William Muir of Caldwell, John M'Call of Belvidere, Mr. Campbell, and the ubiquitous John Glassford of Dougalston.

The office of the Bank was on the east side of Virginia Street, and notwithstanding the high position held by the shareholders, the place is described as very quaint and unpretentious. It was reached from the street by a short double stair with iron railings, in the prevailing fashion of the time. On the landing was an iron-studded folding double door, which admitted the visitor into a square lobby, across which, and running parallel with the street, was a common counter, where a solitary teller sat with his back to the customers. At each end of this counter, partitioned off by green baize curtains, the little offices for the clerks were placed, while, in an inner apartment, whose only ornament was a small bouquet of flowers in a jug with a broken spout, sat the managers in all the dignity of wigs, knee buckles, ruffles, and high heeled shoes.

Mr. Campbell was the last survivor of the original co-partnery. His son, Mr. Campbell Colquhoun, assumed his father's place at his death, and on subsequent changes we find the names of James Ritchie of Craigton, James Rowan of Bellahouston, Robert Scott of Aitkenhead, Archibald Grahame, Writer, Mr. Hozier of Newlands, John and George Alston, Stephen Rowan, Richard Duncan, James Fyffe, and Charles Stirling,—all influential and well-known gentlemen in the city.

When the Thistle was incorporated with the Union Bank in 1830, the quaint old building was superseded by the handsome edifice erected by the partners of the unfortunate City of Glasgow Bank.

Mr. Campbell had married a daughter of Mr. Laurence Colquhoun of Killermont, and on the death of that gentleman he succeeded to the Killermont estate. As he had previously acquired the lands of Clathic, near Crieff, he took his title as a landed proprietor from that estate, on the death of his mother, Jean Campbell, who inherited the lands from John Campbell, her grandfather. He was owner of a considerable amount of property in the city, including the site of the ancient hospital of St. Nicolas, afterwards acquired by the first gaslight company, whose dingy buildings for many years were a prominent object in the upper part of High Street. He also purchased the estate of Ryding in Lanarkshire.

Dr. Strang, in his genial, gossiping history of the Glasgow Clubs, has given us a glimpse into some of the peculiarities of social life during the latter part of last century, which is extremely curious and interesting. Mr. Campbell, like most of his brother merchants in the city, was a member of one of these jolly old fraternities. The Hodge Podge Club, of which he was a leading member, was composed of gentlemen holding a high social position. They met in a tavern in Trongate, kept by one Cruikshanks. It was originally constituted with the object of assisting the members to form correct views upon matters of a literary, political, or philosophical nature, and also of improving them in the practice of public speaking. With these laudable objects the members met once a fortnight ; but, as might have been expected, the purposes of the club were found rather heavy and uninteresting, and it is wickedly reported that latterly its principal attractions consisted in a jolly Scotch dinner, where the dish from which the club took its name was an invariable accompaniment, the whole seasoned with wit and laughter, followed by profuse libations of the celebrated Glasgow Punch, in which the now forgotten beauties of that day were uproariously toasted. Dr. Moore, author of " Zeluco," and father of Sir John Moore, was, in the palmy days of the " Hodge Podge," the chief spirit of the club, and its poet laureate ; and at its anniversary dinners produced graphic sketches of the members after the manner of Goldsmith's " Retaliation," which kept the table in a roar, and many of which are still preserved. These imperfect and hastily drawn outlines are in many cases all that is now left to note the mental or physical peculiarities of men who were once the elite of the town, and to whom she is so much indebted—men whose names are fast falling into oblivion, and whose very graves are unknown. We wish that the following mere outline had been such

as would enable us to fill up a more definite picture of the old
worthy and honoured Glasgow merchant.

> " What whistling and singing now greeteth our ears?
> " By the music, 'tis Campbell of Clathic appears!
> "To do good he in will nor liberty fails,
> " I wish he'd leave whistling and mumping[1] his nails."

We would like, we hope fairly, to construe this little sketch into
an honest admiration of the will and ability to do good, so often
manifested in the experience of his brethren, notwithstanding the
occasional, perhaps the habitual, neglect of those conventional
amenities which are supposed to permeate what is called "polite
society." Mr. Campbell died in 1804. He left one son and four
daughters. His son, Archibald Campbell Colquhoun, Sheriff of
Perthshire, was promoted to the office of Lord Advocate for Scotland
in 1803, and Lord Clerk Register in 1816. He was Member of
Parliament for Elgin from 1807 to 1810, and for Dumbartonshire
from 1810 to 1820. He died in that year. The Sheriff's second
son, William Laurence Colquhoun, died at Malta, in 1861. His son,
William Campbell Colquhoun, now inherits Clathic. His sister was
the wife of our townsman, James Cleland Burns, who, with his
brother John, are now the head of the enterprising firm of shipowners, Messrs. G. & J. Burns.

[1] Biting.

JOHN ROBERTSON,

OF PLANTATION.

MR. ROBERTSON was a gentleman who exercised a marked influence on the prosperity of the city during the greater part of last century. Besides his large private business of West India merchant, he was a partner in the works commenced and carried on by George Macintosh and others for the manufacture of cudbear, cashier of the Glasgow Arms Bank, and principal proprietor of the firm designated the " Smithfield Nailree." Nor did he neglect his public duties, for we find him a Director of the first Board of the Chamber of Commerce, and Preceptor of Hutchesons' Hospital.

The Nailree was an old and very successful firm, instituted in 1737, for the manufacture of spades, hoes, axes, &c., for home use and exportation. Some of the old west-end inhabitants of Glasgow still remember the ranges of low-roofed buildings that formed the Nailree. Gibson, who wrote his history of the city in 1777, states that the export of iron goods from the town amounted annually to £23,000; and he urges a larger extension of the industry, on the ground that nearly the whole of the expense consisted in the price of workmanship, and that every article that could be made would meet with an immediate sale, even to the extent of £50,000 per annum. However insignificant such an output may appear at the present day, when the iron trade of Glasgow has attained such gigantic proportions, yet, keeping in view the fact mentioned by the same veracious historian, that the usual wages for an experienced workman seldom exceeded seven shillings weekly, the output of £23,000 represented a much larger amount of work than that sum could produce at the present day. We can see opportunity for many dainty pickings about this same Smithfield Nailree, especially when we know that the greater part of the Company's manufactures were exported to the American and West Indian Colonies, and that the profits upon the return products had already made many a handsome fortune. The Smithfield Company were, in fact, very prosperous. Their warehouse stood at the Broomielaw, near the foot of Robertson Street, so called after the brothers, James and John, who were the principal partners in the firm.

Mr. Robertson was also one of the principal partners and cashier of the Glasgow Arms Bank. In the early part of last century, shopkeepers and tradesmen—who had managed to scrape together any capital for which they had no immediate use—were in the habit of putting it into the hands of some successful merchant, whose position and character they esteemed a sufficient guarantee for its good use and safe repayment. The interest allowed was generally about five per cent. Country farmers found, as they supposed, a good investment, by placing their superfluous cash in the hands of the Bakers' Incorporation, or entrusting it to individual members of the trade,—those who received the funds taking great care to impress upon their creditors the extent of the obligation they conferred by the acceptance of the trust. Several heavy failures, however, among these trusted custodians demonstrated the necessity of a broader basis of security, and accordingly "The Ship Bank" and "The Glasgow Arms Bank" were both established in the same year, 1750.

The senior partners of "The Arms Bank" were Provost Cochran, whose cautious and wise policy in the memorable 1745 had won for him the respect and confidence of all classes of the community; and John Murdoch, who succeeded to the Provostship in 1746 and 1747, and who was also Provost in the year the Bank was opened. His town residence was the once spacious mansion, the pride of the city, which in later days did duty as the well-known Buck's Head Inn. In addition to these two gentlemen, twenty-seven of the most substantial Glasgow merchants became partners in the undertaking, one of whom, Mr. John Glassford, of Whitehill, was reputed, both as regards character and position, a tower of strength.

Both the "Ship" and "Glasgow Arms" commenced business in what was then the centre of city business life,—the "Ship," it is believed, in the crow stepped house, still standing on the south-east corner of the Bridgegate, now used as a coffin warehouse; and the "Arms" in Smith's land, nearly opposite to its rival. In 1759 the office of the "Arms" was removed to King Street, a few doors further south than its junction with Prince's Street, and finally, when Mr. Robertson became manager, the Bank office was in what was then esteemed a stately mansion, built for its reception by Deacon Ferrier, near the south-east corner of Miller Street. In the upper flats of this building Mr. Robertson lived in lordly style. His house was esteemed the wonder of the time, with its solid black mahogany balustrades, its polished oaken stairs, and its panelled walls ; while massive gates outside, and imposing offices, all testified to the grandeur and the stability of the establishment. In 1783 Mr. Robertson acquired the estate of Craigiehall, about fifty-two acres in extent, not far from the rural Clyde banks, at the junction of the Paisley Road with the quiet road leading to the ancient village of Govan. As the brothers Robertson owned extensive possessions in the West Indies, the small holding was called Plantation, a name which it still retains;[1] and here he resided till the change we are now about to relate took place.

No event in modern history has caused more disturbance than the French Revolution of 1789 and subsequent years, when all the evil passions of humanity sought to break bounds, and the very foundations of social order were shaken. Though the moral influence of that terrible time were but slightly felt in this country, yet, in the wild state of unrest, anxiety, and fear, to which they very naturally gave rise, trade and commerce of every kind were, for the time, fairly paralysed. In 1793 no fewer than 1956 bankruptcies passed through the *Gazette*, of which number 26 were banking companies. Three Glasgow banks were among the failures recorded, viz., the bank of Andrew, George, and Andrew Thomson, extensive private bankers; the Merchants' Bank, established by a number of substantial traders and merchants with the view of diminishing the power of its more aristocratic rivals; and lastly, the Glasgow Arms.

The official trustee for the creditors of this latter bank was Walter Ewing M'Lae, the well-known merchant and accountant. His son, James Ewing, subsequently better known in the city than even his father, was then a young man in his father's office; and it is recorded that the winding-up of the concern was conducted in a

---

[1] In 1830 the estate passed into the hands of Mr. William M'Lean, a well-known Glasgow merchant. From its vicinity to the Clyde it has become a very valuable possession.

manner which fully justified the confidence reposed on these gentlemen, and added not a little to their own prosperity and good name.
The "Arms," eventually, was enabled to meet all its liabilities, and
continue its business. It was incorporated with the Union Bank
in 1830. The experience of recent times forcibly suggests the
sacrifice of position and wealth, and even of life itself, by which this
settlement must have been attained. In the original list of the
members of the Chamber of Commerce, the date is recorded when
each gentleman, either by death or failure to contribute his annual
subscription, ceased to be acknowledged as a member, and the
number of names taken off the list about this time, for one or other
of the causes we have specified, is very striking. Mr. Robertson,
the subject of our sketch, disappears in 1794 ; his brother, who was
cashier in the Merchants' Bank, in 1792 ; Andrew Thomson, of
A. & G. Thomson, also in 1792 ; and three other gentlemen who
were known to be connected with the Glasgow Arms—viz., John
Bowman, Virginia merchant; Peter Murdoch, whose father was one
of the originators of the bank ; and Alexander Brown, ex-Dean of
Guild—are all struck off the list about the same time. Who can
estimate the depth and intensity of the misery these facts so forcibly
suggest ?

FAC-SIMILE

OF THE

ORIGINAL SUBSCRIPTION LIST

OF THE

GLASGOW CHAMBER OF COMMERCE,

1 7 8 3,

COMPRISING THE NAMES OF THE PRINCIPAL MERCHANTS, MANUFACTURERS, &c., IN
GLASGOW, PAISLEY, GREENOCK, AND PORT-GLASGOW IN THAT YEAR.

1 8 8 1.

SUBSCRIPTION LIST OF THE GLASGOW CHAMBER OF COMMERCE, 1783.

I. CAMPBELL & INGRAM'S LIST.

John Campbell jun.
Henry Riddell
John Robertson
Richard Marshall
Robert Dunmore
Wm. Ingram
Thomas Cornell
Jno. Wilson
Ro. Findlay
John Riddell
John Buchanan
Geo. Macintosh
Robt. Mackay
George Hamilton
Andw. Buchanan jr.
James Dennistoun
George Bogle
John Campbell
Alexr. Brown

Dugald Bannatine
John Laurie
Andrew Brown
John Campbell jun.
Archibald Graham
William French
Cunningm. Corbett
James Gordon
Alexr. Low
Daniel Russell
John Hamilton junr.
Joseph Scott
William Coats
Richd. Allan jun.
Watter Monteath
James Hopkirk
James McDowall
John Glassford
Alexr. Speirs
John Bowman

Thomas Donald
James McCall
Robert Bogle
W. Stirling
John Leitch
Andrew Thomson
James Somervell
John Gordon
James Oswald

Bruce Spiers
Alex Ritchie
Geo Crawford
Gilb: Hamilton
Alex McCaul
Alex Gordon
James Dennistoun junior
Walter Neilson
William Gray

Robt Dinwiddie
Archd Govan
Walter Colquhoun
George Buchanan Jun
Robert Dunlop
James Brown
John Craig
John Bogle
Peter Murdoch
Robert Buchanan
George Anderson
Arch Henderson
George Kippen
Robert McNair
John Maxwell
John Alston Jun
John Hay
David Watson

Rich'd Allan

David Black

John Christie

Jam'd. Wilson

Thomas Stenhouse

Rob't Houstoun

John Dunlop

John Lindsay

Geo: Miller Jun'r

John M'Donall

Thomas Bell

Walter Ewing

Robert Shung

William Smith

Thomas Buchanan

James Black

for W'm Cuninghame

James Blackie

James Wardrop

Rob't Bowen

William Robertson

George Brown

Ja' Stirling

Hugh Cross

Morehead Loudoun

John Shadden

Adam Lightbody

Alex'r Allan

Geo. Bogle for

Alex'r Cuninghame Craigends

A. MacAlpine

for

Hugh Colquhoun

William Riddle

Will'm Shaw

And'w Houstoun

John Orr

John Thomson Jun

David Dale
Thomas Meddon
Robert Thomson
James Mitchell
Mathew Wenston
Alexr Ure
Wm Finlay
Robt McMillan

Alexr Hendry
Willm Somervill
Wm Wardlaw
John Young
William Lang
John Auchincloss
Williams Carmichaele
Wm Risk

III. GLASGOW, PAISLEY, PORT-GLASGOW, &c.

Patk Colquhoun as provost
for the time of Glasgow
Patk Colquhoun.   Glasgow
James McGregor   Do
Robt Fulton   Paisley
Jas. Lownds   Do
Robt Corse   Do
John Wilson   Do
Claud Neilson   Do

Herbert Buchanan   Paisley
Thomas Stewart   Glasgow
John Black   Paisley
James Shittle   Do
Andr Sterling   Glasgow
Wm Gillespie   Andras
Humphry Barbour   Kilbarch
John Howe   Do

James Robertson *Glasgow*

William Carlile

Walter Stirling

George Thomson *Do*

Robt Dunlop *Do*

James Monteith *Jun Do*

Richard Collins *Dalnotter*

James Scott

James Wilsham

John Craig

William Shortridge

John Brown Jun *Do*

John Semple *Hamilton*

William Fleming

William Fleming } *Do*

Jno Macalpine

Darroch Toell *Do*

Alexr MacAlpine *Do*

James Finlay *Do*

John Austin *Do*

John Reid *Glasgow*

William Whyt *Do*

John Shiels *Do*

Andrew Sibbald *Do*

George Shunnibough *Do*

Robert Carrick *Do*

Jno Freeland *Do*

Johns Tennant *Do*

Robt Morrice *Do*

Andrew Miller *Do*

Henry Hardie *Do*

William Gardner *Do*

Donald Macbrayne *Do*

John Wilson *Anderston*

George Provan *Glasgow*

Walter Graham *Do*

Allan Arthur *Anderston*

John Rodger *Glasgow*

Hugh Niven *Anderston*

IV. MAGISTRATES OF GREENOCK.

V. MAGISTRATES OF PORT-GLASGOW.

James Paisley
John Bell
James Wilson
Gavin Maxwell
John Orr
Robert Hunter
Wm Stuart
Willm Wallace
Andr Brown

John Pollock
Wm Orr
John Cochran
William Orr Junr
John Chrystie
Robt Maxwell
Willm Wilson
John M'Kerrell

VII. NAMES NOT IN ORIGINAL LIST.

Chas Tennant
Charles Macintosh
Ja Ewing
Robert Dalglish
Henry Glassford

Alexr Crum
K Finlay
Henry Monteith
Rot Owen
Archd Smith

AT the termination of the war with America the commercial prospects of Glasgow were of the most gloomy kind. The great Virginia trade, which for a long series of years employed the largest share of the city capital, was now lost. Cotton spinning, with its accompanying industries, was yet unknown; in fact, except a growing traffic with the West Indies, and the manufacture of a few domestic fabrics, the trade of the town was extremely limited. It therefore became apparent that a means of combined action for opening up new sources of trade and commerce, and of organising a method whereby direct and efficient communication between the trade of the West and the Government and Legislature could be established was a pressing necessity. The result of much eager discussion was the formation of the Glasgow Chamber of Commerce in January, 1783, the first institution of its kind in the kingdom. The Edinburgh Chamber was not established till nearly three years later, namely, in December, 1785. The first meeting of the Chamber was held in the Town Hall on the 1st of January, 1783. The Chairman—Provost Patrick Colquhoun—submitted a plan of the proposed constitution, which provided that the Association should be established on the most liberal and equitable foundation, and should include in its membership the merchants of the principal towns in the West of Scotland. After providing for the election of office-bearers, arrangements for meetings, and other details, the Constitution proceeds to specify the outlines of the business committed to the charge of the Directors, namely :—

1. To consider of such plans and systems as shall contribute to the protection and improvement of those branches of Trade and Manufactures which are peculiar to this country, and which may be interesting to the members of the Chamber at large.

2. To regulate all matters respecting any branch of Trade or Manufacture which may be submitted to the Directors, for the purpose of establishing rules for the convenience and assistance either of Foreign Traders or Manufacturers.

3. To read and discuss all public and private memorials and representations of members of the Chamber, requesting the aid of the Directors in any matter regarding Trade or Manufactures.

4. To afford aid to members, whether as individuals or otherwise, who may apply for assistance, in negotiating any matter of business, whether local, or of a nature which requires the weight and influence of the Directors, in making application to the Board of Trustees, to the King's Ministers, or to Parliament.

5. To procure relief or redress on any grievance, hardship, oppression, or inconvenience, affecting any particular branch of Trade or Manufacture carried on by the members of this Society, by interposing the weight and influence of the Directors in any public negotiations that may be thought necessary to effect such relief.

6. To consider of all matters affecting the Corn Laws of this part of the United Kingdom in particular, as being of the utmost consequence to its Trade and Manufactures.

7. And, in general, to take cognisance of every matter and thing that shall be in the least degree connected with the interests of Commerce. To assist in pointing out new sources for promoting whatever may be useful and beneficial, and to attend to every application made to Parliament which may be thought injurious to the Trade and Manufactures of this Country. To support an intercourse and friendly correspondence with the Convention of Royal Burghs, and Board of Trustees for

Fisheries and Manufactures, for the purpose of communicating new and useful improvements to their attention.

The manner in which these objects was carried out are well illustrated by the following extracts from a letter written to the Chamber in 1836, fifty-three years after its establishment, by Mr. Dugald Bannatyne, on the resignation of his office as Secretary :—

"Having been a member of the Chamber since its origin, and having acted in "the capacity of its Secretary for 28 years, permit me to say a few words as to one "or two of the great principles which have all along guided its proceedings, and "with which it may be almost considered as identified.

"The first of these is Free Trade. The Chamber has been the invariable and "uncompromising advocate of this great principle, and has laboured zealously to "procure the speedy, though gradual removal, of all the shackles with which the "industry of the country was loaded.

"Another principle it has always strenuously supported is the necessity of a "uniform measure of value, an object to be secured only by a provision that our "paper currency shall be at all times immediately convertible into the precious "metals. During times of considerable difficulty in the financial history of the "country, it endeavoured constantly and anxiously to procure the adoption of this "principle; and since it has been adopted, the Chamber has been equally desirous "to discourage every attempt to depart from it.

" A third question in which the Chamber has always taken an active part is the "reform of Commercial Law. It has promoted every proposal which appeared "calculated to render this law more acceptable and sure, and its administration "more expeditious. Its exertions during the various discussions on the Bankrupt "Law have been known and estimated generally by the public throughout Scotland.

" I may add that the usefulness of the Chamber has been greatly increased by " its steadily and undeviatingly confining its attention to questions of a commercial "nature, excluding the consideration of other matter, which, however important or "interesting, would by their introduction have led to dissention, and have ultimately "prevented it from fulfilling its original and peculiar object—of representing the "matured opinions of this large and enlightened community on commercial subjects. "The weight of its representations has been also augmented by a rule of the

"Chamber—never to obtrude its opinions unnecessarily or officiously either on the
"Legislature or the Government, but to interfere only in those cases where there
"was an evident call on them to do so."

At the time this letter was written (1836) the membership
of the Chamber numbered 248.   Of the original members not one
then remained but Mr. Bannatyne himself; and of the list of
that year only three are now alive—namely, Walter Buchanan,
ex-M.P., the Vice-President of that year, and the oldest living
member of the Chamber; W. F. Burnley, now residing in Edinburgh; and William H. Dobbie, Fountainhall Road, Edinburgh.
Thirty years ago, when the writer of these sketches was
appointed to the office which he now holds in the Chamber,
the membership numbered 295.   Of these, the number who are
now engaged in the business and bustle of active city life, he
can nearly reckon upon his fingers; the rest have all retired
from business or are dead.   But the ancient institution still
remains in unabated vigour, the membership now numbering
upwards of 880, and its services are every year growing in importance.   That such is the case is manifested by the fact that there
are few towns throughout the kingdom enjoying the privilege of
extensive commerce or shipping, who have not also established a
Chamber of Commerce, and felt its advantages.   It is needless to
say that the same principles which guided the Chamber at its
formation are still carried out, so far as the altered circumstances of
the times admit.

The Chamber was incorporated by Royal Charter, dated 31st
July, 1783.   A new Charter was afterwards found necessary, in consequence of the increase of the city and great extension of trade and
manufactures, and was obtained on 28th July, 1860.   This Charter
now regulates the constitution and procedure of the Chamber.

ALEXANDER ALLAN was an enterprising and successful manufacturer and West India merchant. He built the well-known Newhall mansion, near the Clyde, at Rutherglen Bridge, from designs by Mr. Hamilton, architect. The mansion was superseded by the existing Newhall Terrace. Mr. Allan died in 1809. One of his sons, John Allan, was the principal originator and able secretary of the Royal Northern Yacht Club. The family is still represented by F. W. Allan, merchant, agent for the Union Steam-ship Company, Gordon Street.

RICHARD ALLAN, merchant, of Bardowie *(Tait's Directory,* 1783). RICHARD ALLAN, JUN., merchant, Jamaica Street *(Tait).*—These gentlemen, with Mr. Smellie, Virginia merchant, purchased two acres of ground at Dowhill, about the middle of last century, when the Gallowgate Port was removed. The price paid for the whole was £20 per acre, with a perpetual ground annual of £5 additional. This ground was advertised for feuing. The old advertisements describe the situation as very commodious, being readily accessible either by the Old Vennel, High Street, or by the Butts (the site of the Infantry Barracks). Moreover, one of the local attractions specified was the near access to the Burnside—the burn being the well-known, and now universally shunned, Molindinar.

JOHN ALSTON, Jun., merchant; counting-house, Exchange, 125.—Mr. Alston married a daughter of James Dennistoun of Colgrain. He inherited the estate of Westerton, bequeathed to him by his grandfather, John Miller, maltman, who projected Miller Street; and the property in which the old man held an interest there was also left to Mr. Alston. He died in 1835. The family of another race of Glasgow merchants—the Alstons of Muirburn—are collateral relations. John Patrick Alston, of Muirburn, is grandson of another John Alston, who had been for many years an American merchant, and was appointed manager of the Thistle Bank. His daughter, Anne Hay Alston, was the first wife of John Gordon of Aitkenhead.

GEORGE ANDERSON, rum merchant ; lodgings, third flat, first close south side of Argyle Street; cellar, east side Stockwell.— As a curious illustration of the advertising literature of the times, we find in the old periodicals Mr. Anderson's advertisements of " Five waters rum at £3 sterling per cask of 20 pints," signifying thus the amount of water required to produce the genuine Glasgow punch, the universal beverage. Mr. Anderson was the brother of James Anderson of the Field, a printwork now forming an adjunct to the extensive chemical works of St. Rollox. James was the grandfather of the late well-known James Andrew Anderson of Carlung, manager of the Union Bank, and brother of Alexander Dunlop Anderson, father of Professor M'Call Anderson.

ALLAN ARTHUR, an Anderston manufacturer. He married

the only daughter of James Monteith. Their daughter married Robert Hannan, an office-bearer with old James Monteith in the Anderston kirk, and was the mother of our well-known Glasgow citizen, James Hannan, of the renowned firm of Henry Monteith & Co. *(See Sketch of James Monteith.)*

DUGALD BANNATYNE.—In *Tait's Directory*, the address of the firm is given Johnston, Bannatine & Co., hoziers, Trongate; and in *Jones'*, Johnston, Bannatyne & Co., stocking manufacturers ; warehouse, north side Ingram Street. John Bannatyne, a brother of Dugald, was also a partner in the firm. A company was formed in the latter part of last century for the extension of Glasgow, of which Mr. Bannatyne was a principal partner and director. The company built the greater part of Brunswick Street, Hutcheson Street, John. Street, George Square, &c. Mr. Bannatyne was distinguished for his energy, probity, and intelligence. He was appointed postmaster in 1806 ; and on the death of Mr. Gilbert Hamilton he was unanimously elected secretary to the Chamber of Commerce, the duties of which office he discharged with great ability. Admirable portraits of Mr. Bannatyne and Mr. Hamilton, the property of the Chamber, are at present hung in the hall of the Merchants' House. Mr. Bannatyne died in 1842, having out-lived the first directors of the Chamber, and all its first members for many years.

HUMPHREY BARBOUR, of Bankhead, Kilbarchan, bleacher and linen thread maker, afterwards settled in Glasgow as a wine merchant. He married Elizabeth, daughter of John Freeland. *(See Sketch of John Freeland.)* Two of his sons were the founders of the well-known Manchester firm of Robert Barbour and Brothers.

Bleaching is still carried on in Kilbarchan, but in a very small way. Hand-loom weaving has been the principal industry of the place from the earliest times. At present it is estimated to employ about 1000 people. Kilbarchan was a considerable place during the latter part of last century and the first quarter of the present, and still retains many striking characteristics of the quaint old Scotch weaving village, to whose inhabitants Burns attributed the prayer—"Lord, send us a gude conceit o' oursel'." The prayer has been answered. The village is now little known except as the birth place of the renowned Habbie Simpson, whose statue graces the steeple attached to the old school-house.

JAMES BLACK of Craigmaddie. His town house was in that block of buildings still standing on the south-west corner of Miller Street. He was an extensive West India merchant, and came to Glasgow from Edinburgh. He was elected Dean of Guild in 1807–8, and Lord Provost in 1808–9; and his signature for Mr. Cuninghame of Lainshaw, in the original subscription list of the Chamber, is a sufficient indication of his social position. He married Hannah, daughter of Bailie John Shortridge, and was father-in-law to the well-known Dr. Muir of St. George's, Glasgow, and latterly of St. Stephen's, Edinburgh. Provost Black is not to be confounded with the Blacks of James Black & Co., calico printers, who were Glasgow people, nor with the Blacks of John Black & Co., printers, who were Paisley people.

GEORGE BOGLE, of Daldowie, was a Virginia merchant, a West India trader, and a most influential and respected citizen of Glasgow. He was an early partner in the Glasgow Tan Work, and in the Eastern Sugarhouse. He also assisted with other influential merchants to establish the Cudbear Work, managed by George Macintosh. The estate of Daldowie, which was acquired by the family of Bogles, had for nearly 200 years been in the possession of the Stewarts of Minto, an old Glasgow family, whose town residence was the " Duke's Lodgings," at the head of the Drygate, the site of which is now enclosed in the Northern Prison. The Mintos were ruined by the Darien scheme. Mr. Bogle's town house stood in the north-east end of the narrow wynd, known afterwards as Police Lane, which was then a *cul de sac*, closed at the end by a " heckler's shop." The house had a single outside stair fronting the present entry to the Bazaar. John Stirling, who lived next house to the Bogles, married Miss Bogle out of this house. Mr. Bogle died in 1784.

JOHN BOGLE, commonly known in his own day as " Wee Johnny Bogle," had been a resident merchant in Virginia for some years, and in the latter end of last century lived with his sister, widow of Dr. Thomas Brown of Langside. Their town residence was the first house built in George Street, which stood alone in the fields for years. Mrs. Brown feued part of what is now North Frederick Street for a vegetable garden. " Senex" says that these Daldowie Bogles were a sober, orderly race, who seldom entered into the gaieties of the city; but the Shettleston Bogles had the character of being quick, volatile, and fond of frolic. Mr. Bogle died about 1802.

ROBERT BOGLE, of Shettleston, was also largely engaged in the Virginia and West India trade. The firm of which he was the head was a very influential one, and comprised the names of Peter Murdoch, Richard Marshall, James M'Dowall, William

Clark, David Elliot, and John Dunlop.   Robert Bogle died about 1786.

WILLIAM BOGLE was a member of the Shettleston family. He was appointed Postmaster in the early part of this century.   He died in 1808, and was succeeded in office by Mr. Dugald Bannatyne.

JOHN BOWMAN, of Ashgrove, a Virginia merchant.—His father was Lord Provost of Glasgow in 1715, during the first rebellion, and in the following year. He was also a magistrate of the town at the negotiation of the terms of the Union in 1707, and was deputed to go to London to oppose the Union.   He died in 1723.   About the time that Virginia Street was projected, Mr. John Bowman, of Ashgrove, the son, purchased from Mr. Buchanan, of the Virginia mansion, the portion of ground upon which the Virginia Buildings now stand, and erected on it a splendid town house.   The garden which stood before his house was for years preserved, because of the pleasant prospect it afforded over the intervening gardens and orchards along to the Candleriggs, but subsequently Wilson Street was projected through it. Mr. Bowman, the younger, was a principal partner and director in the Glasgow Arms Bank.   John Bowman succeeded to his father's honours, being elected Lord Provost in 1764-65.   The Glasgow Arms Bank, of which Mr. Bowman was a partner, failed in 1793. *(See sketch of John Robertson.)*

ALEXANDER BROWN, son of John Brown, merchant and Provost of Glasgow in 1752-53.   To distinguish Alexander from John Brown of Lanfin, he was known as Dean of Guild Brown, he having been elected to that office.   He held office also as a

Magistrate and Councillor in 1779, under Provost French. In this year the celebrated Popish riot took place, when the mob broke into the house of Robert Bagnal, where the few Roman Catholics in the city (probably numbering not more than two dozen) were wont to meet for worship. The house was set on fire, and Mr. Bagnal's shop in King Street was also broken into, and his stoneware goods destroyed. Mr. Brown was the father of Mrs. Maclae of Cathkin. He died in 1794.

GEORGE BROWN, of Capelrig, was an extensive merchant and shipowner when the Chamber was instituted. He was of an old Glasgow family, his father having been a magistrate in 1768, and Dean of Guild at different times. George Brown married Mary Anderson, niece of Robert Barclay, of the firm of Barclay & Grahame, writers, Glasgow. Mr. Barclay, in 1765, bought the estate of Capelrig, in the parish of Mearns, which, at his death, he left to his niece, Miss Anderson, who thereupon took the family name of Barclay. Her daughter, Barclay Brown, married Peter Murdoch of Langbank, father of our townsman, J. Barclay Murdoch, and son of old Peter Murdoch, whose name appears in the list of subscribers to the Chamber. It will thus be seen that the gentleman named is grandson to two of the first of the city merchants, Peter Murdoch of the Glasgow Arms Bank, and George Brown of Capelrig. Miss Brown, daughter of the latter gentleman, still holds the estate of Capelrig, and resides in the old mansion, built by her granduncle, Robert Barclay, in 1769. Mr. George Brown died in 1831.

JAMES BROWN, insurance broker, son of William Brown, mentioned in John M'Ure's "List of Glasgow Shopkeepers" in

1736, and brother of William Brown, glover and skinner, foot of Havannah. James Brown's house was in Bell Street, and was subsequently occupied as the Buck's Head Tavern. In the same land Duncan Niven, the original of Smollett's Strap, had his shaving shop. Mr. Brown was one of the Glasgow merchants who were ruined by the American war. His daughter, Mrs. Agnes Baird, was the authoress of an exceedingly graphic and amusing book entitled "A Kick for a Bite," a book which is now very scarce. Mr. Brown, whose office was at the "back of the Exchange," was known as Broker Brown to distinguish him from another James Brown, whose place of business was across the way. This latter gentleman invented and sold those glass beads or bubbles, which, until the invention of more scientific apparatus, were universally used for testing the strength of spirits, and he was hence distinguished by the unfortunate name of "Bubbly Brown!" Sobriquets were very common in Old Glasgow. Indeed, "tae-names" of one sort or another were almost a necessity. The Browns, Reids, Campbells, and Buchanans were legion ; there was little choice of Christian names, and middle names were unknown. The "tae-names" were often significant enough ; but unfortunately they were not, as are those of the Banff fisher folk, officially used. One is confounded among the seniors, juniors, tertius, quartius, and maddened to find these titles constantly shifting on promotion by death vacancy. Even the simple Yankee expedient of an intermediate initial would have saved all trouble, and insured any number of James Browns (up to six and twenty) from the unsavoury cognomen of "Bubbly." Broker Brown died in 1803.

JOHN BROWN, Jun., of Lanfin, son of Nicol Brown, surgeon in Newmilns, Ayrshire, and brother of Dr. Thomas Brown of

Langside. Mr. Brown was a very influential and respected merchant. He was a member and principal partner of the firm of Brown, Carrick, & Co., bleachers, manufacturers, and general merchants, Bell's Wynd. He was also accountant and partner in the Ship Bank. Mr. Brown was highly prosperous in business, and became wealthy. He repurchased the property of Waterhaughs, which at one time belonged to his grandmother, Marion Campbell, but had passed out of the family ; and he added the estate to his own property in Ayrshire, upon which he built a mansion which he named Lawnfine, usually written and pronounced Lanfin. His town house stood in the narrow lane in which his bleaching warehouse was situated, overlooking on one side the Candleriggs bowling green, now the bazaar, and on the other the generally muddy lane. His son Nicol, at his father's death in 1802, succeeded to his estates, and, dying about four years after, left the property to his cousin, George Brown, eldest son of Dr. Thomas Brown of Langside. At the death of George Brown the next heir was his youngest brother Thomas. He got Daldowie through his mother and aunt, daughters of George Bogle. Langside was his father's property, and Lanfin the property of John Brown, jun., his uncle, and latterly of his brother George.

JOHN BUCHANAN of Carston.—James Buchanan of Carston, Killearn, was the father of seven sons, of whom four at least left their mark on the trade of this district. These were— John Buchanan of Carston, Archibald Buchanan, afterwards of Catrine, and James and George Buchanan, who appear in *Jones* (1789) as " English merchants and dealers in cotton yarn ; ware- " house, Oswald's Closs, Stockwell." John had his office beside them in Oswald's land. This stood where the eastern abutment of the Union Railway bridge now stands. John Buchanan was a great friend of Sir Richard Arkwright's, and was his first agent in Scotland. Archibald, his youngest brother, he sent as an apprentice to Arkwright's famous works at Cromford. Arkwright favoured the lad, taught him his business, and even had him to live in his house. Thus brought up, Archibald Buchanan took home an exceptional knowledge of cotton spinning, which his brothers and he soon turned to account. In these days, when steam was in its infancy, Scotland with her wealth of water-power bade fair to be the principal seat of manufacturing industry. Among the earliest of our streams which were turned to account for cotton spinning were the Teith, the Endrick, and the Ayr. The Buchanans had to do with all three. In 1785 they set down on the Teith a little factory, which has grown into the great Deanston works. In 1793 they sold this factory to a Yorkshire quaker, Benjamin Flounders, and moved to Balfron, on the water of Endrick, to a mill which Dunmore of Ballikinrain had built in 1789. This mill, improved and extended, forms the Ballindalloch Cotton Works, now possessed by Robert Jeffrey & Sons. In 1786 Claud Alexander of Ballochmyle, and the ubiquitous David Dale, set down on the Ayr a small spinning mill, which has grown into the great spinning, weaving, and bleaching works of Catrine. All these three works were bought by James Finlay & Co., of Glasgow—Ballindalloch, in 1793, from the Buchanans; Catrine, in 1801, from Ballochmyle and David Dale; and Deanston, in 1808, from friend Flounders. Archibald Buchanan, who had been managing first at Ballindalloch and then at Catrine, returned to his old quarters at Deanston. Eventually he handed over Deanston to his nephew, the well-known James Smith of Deanston, and once more took the management at Catrine. Beloved by his people, and respected by all, he died there in 1841, and was succeeded by his son, Archibald Buchanan, now of Catrine. The Finlays gave up Ballindalloch about 1845, but they still keep Deanston and Catrine, and are well known at both for making good wares and for being good masters. The relations between the Finlays and the Buchanans have been intimate. They both came from Killearn, and they were Highland cousins to begin with ; and Kirkman Finlay (long the head of James Finlay & Co.) and Archibald Buchanan married sisters, Janet and Hannah Struthers of Greenhead. Archibald Buchanan ; his son, Archibald Buchanan, now of Catrine; his nephew, James Buchanan, son of George Buchanan of Woodlands ; and his nephew, James Smith of Deanston, have all been partners of James Finlay & Co. There are no Finlays there now. John Finlay of Deanston was the last of them, and Archibald Buchanan is now the last of the old connection. Carston, which had long belonged to the Buchanans, was sold by James Buchanan, and now forms part of the Moss.

ROBERT BUCHANAN, GEORGE BUCHANAN, Jun., and ANDREW BUCHANAN, Jun.—Of these signatories, George and Andrew were sons of Andrew of Auchintorlie and Hillington. Robert's address is given in *Tait* with Andrew and George, east side of Jamaica Street. George was one of the earliest feuars in that street, and built the mansion which has been recently replaced by Arnott's warehouse. Andrew Buchanan, jun., lived to be the venerable Andrew of Ardenconnel, who died in 1835, aged 90. He married a daughter of James Dennistoun of Colgrain, and he and his father-in-law established the famous old business of Dennistoun, Buchanan & Co. We believe that Mr. Dennistoun and George Oswald of Scotstoun were partners in the still older firm of

Oswald, Dennistoun & Co. Ardenconnal's town house of 1800 is still standing at the south-west corner of Montrose Street. It has been occupied as a banking establishment, a School of Design, and is now the office of the sanitary staff.

THOMAS BUCHANAN, Ardoch, was a well-known and prosperous merchant. From his father he inherited Ardoch ; and from his father-in-law, John Gray, he bought Dalmarnock, and built thereon the existing mansion. When the original partners of the Ship Bank gave up, in 1775, Mr. Buchanan was one of the new copartnery, who, first as Moore, Carrick & Co., and subsequently as Carrick, Brown & Co., sailed the old ship with more than the old success. He also, with some of the influential city merchants as partners, entered upon a large " Hatt making " business, of which he latterly was sole proprietor, and carried it on with energy and success; and many a puncheon that fetched back rum or molasses from Jamaica or St. Kitts, had gone out filled with Ardoch's " Hatts." Mr. Buchanan had a large family. His eldest son, John Buchanan, was Member of Parliament for Dumbartonshire from 1821 to 1826, and succeeded his father in Ardoch, in Dalmarnock, and in the Ship Bank. John Buchanan seems to have had a perfect craze for stone and lime, for he built, and then sold, at a reckless rate, till the patrimonial estate was greatly impaired. Thomas, a second son of Ardoch, succeeded, through his mother, Jean Gray of Dalmarnock (the second wife of Mr. Buchanan), to the valuable properties of Eastfield and Stonelaw. He was the father of the late much esteemed Thomas Gray Buchanan, who added to his patrimony Wellshot, formerly the residence of Mr. John More of the Royal Bank.

JOHN CAMPBELL, Jun., was a member of the firm of Campbell & Ingram, merchants and insurance brokers; writing office, back of Exchange. He resided at the head of Jamaica Street, east side. His name stands first in the list of membership of the Chamber of Commerce; and, as that list shows, both he and his partner took great interest in the establishment of the Chamber. Mr. Campbell was one of the first Board of Directors. He was an influential member of the community, and was chosen Lord Provost of the city in 1788 and 1789.

JOHN CAMPBELL, Sen.—This gentleman, along with numerous descendants and kinsfolks, were leading representatives of the great West India interests in Glasgow—an extensive and lucrative business which followed on the breaking up of the Virginia trade. The firm enjoyed a high degree of prosperity in the palmy days of the trade in sugar and rum. Its members having the same Christian names were so numerous that it was found convenient to confer on each a distinctive appellation, which was generally derived from some peculiarity in appearance or habits—such as " Black Mungo" and "White Mungo," "Sandy Doune" and " Business Sandy," "Dignity," &c. All these gentlemen took much interest in the affairs of the city, and Mungo Nuter Campbell was elected Lord Provost of Glasgow in 1824 and 1825. Latterly, through causes which are well understood, the West India trade fell into a languishing condition. In 1866 the last representative of the numerous partners in the firm, "White Mungo," died, and the once prosperous house of John Campbell, sen., & Co., ceased to exist. Alexander, the eldest son of John Campbell, sen., the founder of the firm, was a distinguished officer in the army. He died in 1849.

ROBERT CARRICK, manager, Ship Bank.—In our sketch of the Virginia merchants we gave some account of this bustling merchant and banker, one of the most widely known business men of his day. His father, as we have mentioned, was a tutor in the family of Provost Buchanan of Drumpellier; and in 1750, when the Ship Bank was established, under the name of Dunlop, Houston & Co., Robin, the astute son of the former tutor to the Buchanan family, was engaged as a junior clerk in the bank. At its formation the bank had six partners, viz.—Colonel Macdowall of Castle Semple, Provost Andrew Buchanan of Drumpellier, Robert Dunlop of Houschill, Allan Dreghorn of Ruchill, Provost Colin Dunlop, and Alexander Houston, Virginia merchant. The "Ship" continued to transact its business in the Bridgegate establishment for 26 years. By that time many of the original partners had retired or were dead. The partnership was changed, and the establishment was removed to the west wing of the Shawfield Mansion, in 1776. In 1760 two wings had been erected by Mr. Macdowall, which projected on each side of the great house in a line with the Westergate and Trongate—a very common form of architectural decoration at the time. The eastern wing is still preserved, and forms the south-east corner of Glassford Street and Trongate. The western wing was sold to the new partners of the bank. The firm appointed Mr. Carrick as manager and cashier of the establishment. The principal partners were—George and James Moore, John Brown of Lanfin, his brother, Dr. Thomas Brown, of Langside, Thomas Buchanan of Ardoch, and the manager himself. The title of the firm was changed to Moore, Carrick & Co. In 1783, further changes in the partnership having taken place, the firm was finally changed to Carrick, Brown & Co., by which designation the bank was known during Mr. Carrick's life. The two wings of the Shawfield Mansion were precisely similar in their details, and a glance at the eastern wing may enable us at the present day to form a correct idea of the appearance which the bank presented upwards of a century ago, if in addition we fill all the squat windows with strong, rusty iron bars like a country jail. The inside of the bank was also very quaint. The public were admitted into a rather dark lobby, which led from the Argyle Street entrance. The business rooms were carefully defended from the public by a high wooden railing, with a narrow shelf on the top. There was no table or counter of any kind upon which notes or change could be handled except the shelf mentioned. The lobby was very small, and it was no easy task to count the cash, especially when a crowd of eager customers were jostled together in the narrow space, each bawling his orders over the high rail to the cautious cashier, who slowly and deliberately counted a handful of notes over and over again, altogether unmindful of the hubbub surrounding him. This functionary presided over a small desk—affirmed to be an old tea-chest fixed on supports, and covered with black leather. A dive was made into this receptacle, and a handful of notes fished out and counted, while the lid rested upon the cashier's head. When the proper summation was effected, slowly the lid was lowered and locked, and the transaction duly recorded in a parcel of detached papers, which he invariably carried in his hand, and called his "blotter." This process was repeated over and over again daily during the business hours. Mr. Carrick was also a partner in the firms of Henry Hardie & Co., wholesale linen drapers; and Brown, Carrick & Co., extensive muslin manufacturers, bleachers, and general merchants. The bank was closed for an hour daily, and during this time Mr. Carrick took the opportunity of visiting the establishments mentioned, which were situated in Bell's

Wynd. His dwelling house was in the upper flat of the bank buildings ; and his domestic establishment was superintended by an elderly lady, a relation of his own, with the utmost regard to strict economy. He had also a country house at Mount Vernon. Mr. Carrick was elected a bailie in 1796, Dean of Guild in 1802 and 1803, and a director of the Glasgow Chamber of Commerce. He died in 1821.

WILLIAM COATS was the son of Archibald Coats, who, as we have noticed elsewhere, was carried off, along with Bailie Carmichael in 1745, as an hostage that the town of Glasgow would be true to its engagement with the rebels. The firm of which William Coats was one of the principal partners was a very prosperous one. His name appears in *Jones' Directory*, 1789, under various denominations—general merchant, wholesale hardware merchant, wholesale linen merchant, &c. He also appears in the list of Virginia merchants. Mr. Coats took a great interest in the affairs of the town, was Dean of Guild in 1787–88, and one of the first Directors of the Chamber of Commerce. Like his brother, John Coats Campbell of Clathic, he was also a member of that jovial fraternity, the Hodge Podge Club ; and he is described by the club poet, Dr. Moore, thus :—

Honest Will Coats,
Not a kindlier heart betwixt this and John Groats !

RICHARD COLLINS.—The firm of Edward & Richard Collins, paper makers and bleachers, Dalmuir, of which Richard Collins was a member, is noticed in *Tait's Directory*. Richard was the father of Edward Collins, bookseller and publisher, who is well remembered in Glasgow, and whose sons have prosecuted the same business with much success.

PATRICK COLQUHOUN, Provost of Glasgow in 1783; lodgings, north side of Argyle Street (*Jones*).—Mr. Colquhoun was one of the most talented and most respected of the early Glasgow merchants. He was a descendant of an ancient family, the Colquhouns of Luss, and was born in Dumbarton in the year of the Rebellion, 1745. His father was a schoolfellow of the celebrated novelist, Tobias Smollet. As Mr. Colquhoun was left an orphan at an early age, his relations sent him to try his fortune in America, where he acquired such a ripe experience of the Virginia trade, then in the heyday of its prosperity, that he came back to Glasgow in 1766, when he was only twenty-one years of age, and began business as a merchant on his own account. About this time, he married a relation of his own, a daughter of James Colquhoun, Provost of Dumbarton. He was very prosperous in business. In 1782 he was elected Lord Provost of the city. He was also the principal promoter of the Glasgow Chamber of Commerce, and was its first chairman. About this date he purchased part of the estate of Woodcroft, on which he built a luxurious country house, and also planted and ornamented the grounds. His portion of the estate, which he called Kelvingrove, now forms the greater part of our spacious West End Park. Provost Colquhoun's splendid mansion is now the Kelvingrove Museum. Mr. Colquhoun was a voluminous writer. In his literary career he published twenty-seven treatises on various subjects; amongst others, on "The Resources of the British Empire," "Education," "The Poor Law," "Police," &c. His intimate and varied knowledge of the subjects which he discussed brought him under the notice of the Corporation of London, and he was prevailed upon to go to the metropolis, for the purpose of organising the system of police, especially the river police, which, it was reputed, had fallen into disorder.   Under Mr. Colquhoun's careful supervision a great improvement was effected.   He continued to labour at this task till the end of his long and useful life.   The University, in 1797, conferred on him the degree of LL.D.   He died in 1820.

THOMAS CONNELL, a partner in the famous old firm latterly known as Stirling, Gordon & Co.   It was founded about the middle of last century, by Provost Arthur Connell and James Somervill of Hamilton Farm, under the title of Somervill, Connell & Co. In the list of Virginia merchants of 1774, we find the firm of Bogle, Somervill & Co. ; but the operations of Somervill, Connell & Co. were chiefly confined to the West India traffic, especially after 1780, when Mr. Stirling, a West India merchant, was assumed as a partner, and the firm was changed to Somervill, Gordon & Co. In 1790 the name of the firm was again changed to Stirling, Gordon & Co.   The chief partners at that time were the well-known John Gordon of Aikenhead, his brother, Alexander, and John Stirling of Kippendavie, whose father was an extensive Jamaica merchant, and left his son a large fortune.   The firm was very prosperous, and consisted of gentlemen whose names in the latter part of last century were as household words, and who are yet known as the chief of the old Glasgow aristocracy.   Few who know anything of the history of Glasgow progress have not heard of the following gentlemen, all partners at some time of the firm, viz :— Charles Stirling of Cadder, who from the circumstance of his having a cork leg was known as "Cork Stirling," James Fyfe, Neil Malcolm of Poltalloch, James Murdoch Wallace, son of the eccentric John Wallace of Kelly and Whitehill ; William and Charles Stirling of Kippendavie, and William Leckie Ewing of Arngomery, father-in-law to the present worthy chairman of the school board, Mr. Michael

Connal.   Latterly, Graham Somervill of Sorn Castle, and William Stirling, jun., of Tarduf, were the sole partners of the firm, and in 1864 it ceased to exist, being wound up in that year.   Mr. Connell died in 1784.

CUNNINGHAM CORBETT, of Tollcross, West India merchant and rum importer.   The family of Corbetts held the estate of Tollcross for upwards of 500 years.   Mr. Corbett was distinguished in Glasgow for his services in organizing the Glasgow Armed Association, composed chiefly of the shopkeeper class, and popularly known as the "Sugarallie Corps," whose aims and aspirations found description in the strains of Blind Alick, the street poet of the period, thus—

> " We are the Glasgow Volunteers,
>   And we do receive no pay;
>   Colonel Corbett's our Commander,
>   And with him we'll fight our way.
>   Here's a health to Colonel Corbett,
>   And likewise to all his riflemen ;
>   For when they do lay down the sword,
>   Then every one takes up a pen !"

Mr. Corbett was Bailie of Gorbals in 1784, and Chairman of the Glasgow Chamber of Commerce in 1802 and 1803, of which body he was long an efficient director.   He died in 1829.   On the death of himself and his brother James of Porterfield, who died in 1825, the family on the male side became extinct.   The estate was sold to James Dunlop of Garnkirk, and is now the property of his grandson, Mr. James Dunlop.

ROBERT COWAN.—In *Tait's Directory,* 1783, Mr. Cowan

is designated dealer in victual, Grahamston. He was an extensive grain dealer, and the large brewery at Grahamston belonged to him. He also owned the property upon which the brewery was situated as far west as Hope Street ; and he acquired the estate of Nethercroy, in Dumbartonshire, which was his country residence. Mr. Cowan was of an old Glasgow family. He was born in 1735. In 1763 he married Lillias, daughter of Dr. Alexander Horsburgh, Glasgow, and had a numerous family. His son, John, was a partner in the great Brewery Company of Anderston. His fourth son, Robert Cowan, surgeon, married, in 1795, Helen, daughter of the Rev. John M'Caul, D.D., Tron Church, Glasgow. The eldest son of the family—Robert Cowan, M.D., born 1796—was Professor of Medical Jurisprudence in the University of Glasgow, and was the author of " Vital Statistics of Glasgow." He died in 1841. His only surviving son, and the only member of the Cowan family connected with Glasgow, is John B. Cowan, M.D., LL.D., Emeritus Professor of Materia Medica in the University of Glasgow, who now resides at Helensburgh. Robert Cowan was one of the first Board of Directors of the Chamber of Commerce, and took much interest in the institution. He was also a member of the Merchants' House and a director of the Town's Hospital. He died at Nethercroy in 1813.

WILLIAM CRAIG, of the Waterport, a timber merchant.— He built a spacious dwelling-house in Clyde Street, which stood till 1829, immediately east of the house occupied by the celebrated Robert Dreghorn of Ruchill (" Bob Dragon "). Until a very recent period a cart road led down to the Clyde, before Mr. Craig's house, and in the beginning of this century the river was fordable here at low water. A little island stood at this ford in the centre of the river, which, we are informed by Mr. Reid ("Senex"),was the arena where many a stone battle was fought between the lads of Glasgow and the Gorbals weavers. On this island Mr. Craig for many years stored his timber. Mr. Craig was a promoter and partner of the Ship Bank, a magistrate in 1769, President of the Chamber of Commerce 1803–1804, and for twenty-two years he held the office of Preceptor of the Town Hospital in Clyde Street, where a tablet, erected by his fellow-citizens, long recorded his services. He died in 1804.

GEORGE CRAWFORD, writer, was the son of Francis Crawford, merchant, Glasgow. In 1772 Mr. Crawford was apprenticed for three years to Messrs. Barclay and Roberton, writers, Glasgow. He was admitted burgess, Guild brother, and member of the Merchants' House in 1780, and in the same year married Janet, daughter of Robert M'Lintock, one of the prime movers in the establishment of the Merchants' Bank, instituted by a number of substantial merchants with the view of breaking the supposed monopoly enjoyed by the Ship and Thistle Banks. Mr. Crawford was clerk to the Incorporation of Wrights from 1784 till the time of his death, in 1822.

THOMAS CRAWFORD.—In the list of the old Virginia firms we find among the principal Dinwiddie & Crawford, and Thomas Crawford & Co. Mr. Crawford built a land of houses in Bell's Wynd. He resided there, as we find by *Jones' Directory*, in 1789. Some of the first families in the town resided in the Wynd; among the rest, James Finlay and his son Kirkman Finlay.

WILLIAM CUNINGHAME, of Lainshaw, one of the best

known and most prosperous of the Virginia merchants.—The firm with which he was connected held a large stock of tobacco at the outbreak of the war with America. During the progress of the war the market gradually rose, till the original price had exactly doubled itself, when a meeting of the partners was called to consider the propriety of disposing of their stock on such favourable terms. It is a curious proof of the confidence which the Virginia merchants entertained in the potency of British valour—a confidence which was largely shared by the community in general—that, at the meeting alluded to, it was agreed to sell the whole stock. Mr. Cuninghame became the purchaser, and as the prospects of a settlement of the contest favourable to the mother country became more gloomy, and the likelihood of a peaceful solution of the quarrel became hopeless, tobacco rose to an extravagant price, and Mr. Cuninghame, by his lucky speculation, made a great fortune. Like his brother merchants in similar circumstances, he too would distinguish himself by building a town mansion. At this time the Cow Lone, now Queen Street, was a narrow and muddy country road, running northward from the Westergate between two ragged hedges, till it communicated with another country road leading to the Cowcaddens, which was then the common meadow where the cows of the town were driven each morning. On the north-west corner of the Cow Lone there stood, about 1778, a lowly-thatched farm steading or cowfeeder's cottage, the site of which was the property of John Neilson, who is described in the titles as "land labourer in Garioch," a little place near Maryhill. The plot upon which this unpretentious establishment stood was purchased by Mr. Cuninghame, and he built thereon one of the finest houses in the west of Scotland, said to have cost £10,000, a very large sum considering the price of labour. This house, which still graces the town, has undergone many romantic changes. At Mr. Cuninghame's death it was purchased by the old firm of William Stirling & Sons. One of the wings was used as the office of the firm, and for twenty-eight years the mansion-house was occupied by members of the family. In 1817 the house was purchased by the Royal Bank. A handsome double stair was erected in front of the house, in the then prevailing style, which reached up to the front drawing-room windows. The space in front was covered by shrubbery. The banking business of the firm was conducted in Mr. Cuninghame's mansion for ten years, till, in 1827, an association of merchants was formed—the chairman of which was James Ewing of Strathleven—to provide a new west-end Exchange, the old coffee room at the Cross being found insufficient for the increasing numbers who frequented it, and too far removed from the centre of city traffic. The bank buildings were purchased by the association, and, under the superintendence of Mr. Hamilton, architect, great additions and alterations were made, and the old mansion house was transformed into the present Royal Exchange. The original house forms the front part of the building facing Queen Street. Its curious nests of little apartments, now mostly transformed into shipbroking and insurance offices, yet indicate the extent of the original establishment, and are well worth visiting for the sake of the old associations by which they are surrounded. Mr. Cuninghame died in 1789. His descendents still hold Lainshaw.

JAMES DENNISTOUN of Colgrain.—Mr. Dennistoun was the descendant of an old Dumbartonshire family that occupied Colgrain as far back as 1377. He was largely engaged in the Virginia trade, and always took an interest in municipal affairs. His town house was situated in the second flat, first close west of

Miller Street.   Mr. Dennistoun was a young man during the rebellion of 1745, and it is said would willingly have taken part in the contest on behalf of Prince Charles, but was prevented by his father.   He, therefore, retired to England till the contest was over; and in 1746 came back to Glasgow, and took the oath of allegiance with his brother merchants.   In 1750 a movement was instituted for building an Episcopal place of worship in Glasgow.   Among the principal promoters of the scheme were Mr. Dennistoun and Mr. Alexander Oswald of Auchencruive.   These gentlemen, with some others, purchased a piece of land, forming part of Willow Acre, occupied by a family of gardeners named Moody; and in 1751 the Greenside Church, erected upon this patch of ground, was opened for public worship.   A violent prejudice existed in Glasgow against the Episcopal form of worship, and the "whistlin' kirk," as it was called, came in for a large share of the public antipathy.   Andrew Hunter, a douce mason, and a member of the Shuttle Street Secession Church, was severely reprimanded for the "sin and scandal" of being engaged in the work of raising this "temple of error," and being found obdurate and intractable, was forthwith excommunicated.   Nay, a zealous old wife of the same communion was said to have declared—" That passing the " building one morning 'afore folk was up,' she saw, with her own " eyes, a muckle mason, girded with an apron, who was doing the " work of 'ten men,' and, therefore, could be none else than 'Auld " Sawney' himsel'."   Amongst the managers of the church were some of the first families in the town—the M'Dowalls, the Oswalds, the Spiers, the Colquhouns, and many of the landed aristocracy. Duncan Niven, the prototype of Smollett's "Strap," was the first treasurer of the church, and Mr. Alexander Oswald its first preses. Mr. Dennistoun's name holds a prominent place among the first directors of the Chamber of Commerce. He died 1796, leaving Colgrain to his eldest surviving son, James, also a member of the first Chamber.

ROBERT DINWIDDIE of Germiston.—Some years before the Union opened up the colonial trade to the merchants of Glasgow, two Dumfriesshire families came to reside in the town, who in after years became the most enterprising Virginia merchants. These were the families of Coulter and Dinwiddie. John Coulter, early in the last century, purchased from the noble family of Hamilton the small estate of Whistleberry—now better known as Auchinraith—upon which he built a substantial country house. John was an active citizen of Glasgow, and became Lord Provost of the city in 1736 and 1737. His son, Lawrence, commonly called "Lowrie Cooter," was one of the most notable, although one of the most eccentric, men of his time. His intensely earnest face and curiously shambling gesture have been preserved in the well-known print of "The Morning Walk," by Kay, in his "Edinburgh Portraits," first published in 1796. Like many other impulsive men, Lowrie cherished an overweening sense of his own wisdom. In the middle of last century part of the old wall surrounding the Bishop's palace—which stood on the site of our Royal Infirmary—still remained. An old prophet had predicted that this ruin would some day tumble, and in its fall overwhelm and smother "the wisest man in Glasgow!" This wall, therefore, became an object of terror to the eccentric merchant, and no inducement could prevail upon him to venture near it while it stood, lest his own foolhardiness should hasten the literal fulfilment of the dreaded prediction. Although Whistleberry was then and is still one of the most pleasing country seats around Glasgow, Lowrie preferred, till his death, a residence in his town house, situated in the fragrant precincts of the Briggate.   The last of the family was Margaret, a maiden lady, who, at her death, left the property to her 'cousin, Robert Dinwiddie, of Germiston, the subject of the present sketch. Mr. Dinwiddie's father, Lawrence, was also elected Lord Provost of Glasgow in 1742 and 1743.   Robert Dinwiddie was for many years a resident merchant in Virginia.   He died in 1790.   The families of Coulter and Dinwiddie were both generous benefactors to the Merchants' House.   The last of the Dinwiddie family was Robert, who died a young man at Rome in 1819.   William Lockhart, M.P., of Milton-Lockhart, became next heir to the family inheritance.   He was cousin-german to the Dinwiddies, who have now all passed away.

THOMAS DONALD of Geilston, in the parish of Cardross, and county of Dumbarton, a Virginia merchant, and head of an old and successful firm of tobacco importers.—His father, James Donald, was engaged in the same business from a very early date. James took much interest in the affairs of Glasgow, and was a bailie of Glasgow in 1749 and 1753.   He died about 1760.   He had a brother, Robert Donald of Mountblow, who was Lord Provost in the disastrous years 1776 and 1777, when the revolt of the American colonies brought so much misery and ruin on the trade of Glasgow.   By the promptitude and forethought of the worthy Provost and his associates in office, much was done to alleviate the general distress.   He was unwearied in his endeavours at this time to procure some mitigation of the crisis, the pressure of which was greatly intensified by the restrictions of the Corn Laws. We append a curious document, the copy of a tavern bill charged against the Provost and a few friends during a conference and anti-Corn Law demonstration held at Edinburgh in the latter end of the year 1777. The result of the conference was that no arrangement could be effected between the Glasgow deputation and the representatives of the landed interest in Edinburgh, and it was resolved that Glasgow should oppose the Corn Law Bill in Parliament. The document also gives a curious picture of the convivial habits of that time. It is preserved among the papers of the Chamber. We think there may have been some difficulty about its final settlement :—

POOLE'S COFFEE HOUSE, PRINCES STREET, EDINBURGH.

	£	s	d
Dec. 12.—To supper, oisters, &c., -	£0	6	0
To sherry, - - - - -	0	2	6
To punch, - - - -	0	6	0
To brandy, - - - - -	0	0	6
To porter, - - - -	0	1	4
To bread and beer, - - - -	0	0	9
To tea for one, - - - - -	0	0	8
To cadie and paper, - - - -	0	2	6
Dec. 13.—To dinner in No. 11, - - -	1	10	0
To 12 B claret, at 4s. 6d., - - -	2	14	0
To 2 do. Meadaria, - - - -	0	8	0
To 1 do. port, - - - - -	0	2	0
To 4 do. porter, - - - -	0	1	4
To bread and beer, - - - -	0	2	0
To biscuits, - - - - -	0	0	2
To punch, - - - -	0	3	9
To paper and cadie, - - - -	0	0	8
To glass brock, - - - - -	0	0	8
Dec. 14.—To breakfast for 4, at 10d., -	0	3	4
To dinner for 2 in No. 10, - - -	0	2	0
To port, - - - - - -	0	2	0
To bread and beer, - - - -	0	0	4
Carry forward, - £6	10	6	

	Brought forward,	-	£6	10	6
Dec. 14.—To tea for 3, at 8*d.*,	-	- - -	0	2	0
To paper,	- - - - -	-	0	0	2
Dec. 15.—To dinner in No. 9,	- - -	-	1	0	0
To 4 B claret,	- - - -	-	0	18	0
To 1 do. Meadaria,	- - -	-	0	4	0
To 3 do. port,	- - - -	-	0	6	0
To 7 do. porter,	- -	-	0	2	4
To punch,	- - - -	-	0	2	3
To bread and beer,	- - -	-	0	1	4
To biscuits,	- - - -	-	0	0	6
To cadie and paper to Mr. Fairley, &c.,			0	1	6
To oisters, &c.,	- - - -	-	0	1	6
To punch,	- - -	-	0	3	0
To paid for a man,	- -	-	0	0	4
Dec. 16.—To breakfast for 7, at 10*d.*,	-	-	0	5	10
To 3 jelies in coffee room,	-	-	0	0	9
To cadie on Sunday and to-day,	-		0	2	0
To soop,	- - - - -	-	0	0	3
			£10	2	3
Oysters,	- - - -	-	0	2	0
			£10	4	3
Servants,	- - -	-	0	5	9
			£10	10	0

Received of Robert Dunlop Eleven pounds Strl. in full of the above on Dec. 16, /77.

Ten guneas,   Mattw. Poole.

Thomas Donald, the subject of this sketch, married, in 1773, Jane, daughter of Provost Colin Dunlop of Carmyle. His second son, Colin Dunlop Donald, writer, Glasgow, a gentleman well known and highly respected, was commissary clerk of Glasgow 1817 to 1824, and Lanarkshire 1824 to 1858. He married Marianne Stirling, daughter of John Stirling, of Wm. Stirling & Sons of

Cordale and Dalquhurn, the oldest existing commercial name in Glasgow. Janet, their daughter, was the first wife of James Dunlop of Tollcross, great-grandson of Provost Colin Dunlop. Thomas Donald's grandson, Thomas Donald of Bournemouth, son of Captain James Donald, is the lineal representative of this honoured and successful family. Colin Dunlop Donald's eldest son, called Thomas for his grandfather, after the good old Scotch fashion, succeeded his father as commissary clerk in 1858, and still holds the office. Another grandson, Colin Dunlop Donald, is a member of M'Grigor, Donald & Co., writers, as also a great-grandson, another Colin Dunlop Donald. Thomas Donald died in 1798.

JOHN DUNLOP of Rosebank.—Mr. Dunlop was the youngest son of Provost Colin Dunlop of Carmyle, and was himself Provost of Glasgow in 1794. Early in the last century Rosebank was the property of Provost Murdoch, and through his daughter, Margaret, it became the property of her son-in-law, John Dunlop. His town residence was on the east side of Queen Street. Mr. Dunlop planted and beautified Rosebank till it became the most pleasant country residence around Glasgow. In 1801 Rosebank was sold to David Dale, and it was occupied by that good man till his death. The society of Mr. Dunlop was much prized. He was an accomplished gentleman; he sang beautifully, and was himself a pleasant song writer. Two of his songs have come down to the present day—they do honour to his head and heart—" O dinna ask me gin I lo'e ye," and " Here's to the year that's awa'." Dr. Moore, the poet-laureate of the Hodge Podge Club, thus sketches Mr. Dunlop, who was one of the most esteemed members of that social brotherhood :—

> " A hogshead rolls forward the worthies among—
> What grumbling and growling it makes at the bung ;
> 'Tis as jolly a cask as ere loaded the ground—
> 'Tis plump John Dunlop with his belly so round."

Mr. Dunlop was appointed Commissioner of Customs at Bo'ness. He was afterward removed to Greenock, where he died in 1820.

ROBERT DUNLOP, of Drumhead, was the second son of Robert Dunlop of Househill, a well-known Glasgow merchant. He and his brother, Provost Colin Dunlop, were among the original founders of the Ship Bank in 1750. His son, Robert, inherited the estate of Drumhead from his mother, Mr. Dunlop's second wife, a daughter of Archibald Buchanan. As his elder half-brother, James, died without male heirs, the estate of Houschill fell into the family of Robert; and his great-grandson, Robert Buchanan Dunlop, is present proprietor of Drumhead and Househill. Dorothy, the daughter of Robert Dunlop, of Househill, married Robert Findlay of Easterhill, and her grandson, Colonel John Findlay, now holds the estate.

ROBERT DUNLOP, of Clober, inherited the estate and works from his uncle, James M'Gregor, first Vice-President of the Chamber of Commerce. He carried on business in Glasgow under the firm of Dunlop, Hamilton & Co. His grandson now holds the estate.

ROBERT DUNMORE of Kelvinside and Ballikinrain.— The Dunmores were esteemed the very chief of the old tobacco lords, Bailie Thomas Dunmore, Robert's father, being among the first in Glasgow who, after the Union, prosecuted the great

Virginia trade. In 1749 Thomas bought Bankhead, then a portion of the Ruchill estate, upon which he built the picturesque mansion of Kelvinside, which he made over to his son, Robert, in 1776. Robert—having married the only daughter of his partner, John Napier of Ballikinrain—obtained possession of that estate on his father-in-law's death. When the cotton trade had obtained a footing in Scotland, Robert built a small mill at Balfron, on the Endrick, which was purchased by the Buchanans of Carston, and, under their fostering care and that of the Findlays, the little factory was enlarged and extended till it became the famous Ballindalloch works. *(See sketch of the Buchanans of Carston.)*

ROBERT EUING, baker and victualler, Trongate *(Tait)*.— This occupation he combined with an extensive grain trade, inherited from his father, Bailie William Euing, an excellent public-spirited citizen, originally from the parish of Drymen. Mr. Euing's sister, Isabel, married Archibald Smith of Jordanhill, West India merchant, of Leitch & Smith. She died in 1855, aged 101. Her nephew was the well-remembered citizen, William Euing, of the firm of William Euing & Co., underwriters, Exchange, who died recently at an advanced age. Robert Euing died in 1786.

WALTER EWING, merchant, Trongate *(Tait)*, afterwards WALTER EWING MACLAE of Cathkin.—The Ewings were an ancient Dumbartonshire family. The estate of Cathkin was acquired in 1730 by John Maclae of Cardross, who left it to his son, Walter, who, dying childless, was succeeded by his nephew, Walter Ewing. He assumed the name of Maclae, and is the subject of this sketch. From the esteem and confidence in which this gentleman was held, he was entrusted frequently as an arbitrator, and employed to wind up some of the largest and most important of those bankruptcies which occurred in the unfortunate year of the revolt of the North American colonies in 1777; and such was his reputation that (1793), on the failure of the Glasgow Arms Bank, he was appointed judicial factor, a duty which he performed to the entire satisfaction of all concerned. Mr. Ewing Maclae married Miss Margaret Fisher, daughter of the Rev. James Fisher, and grand-daughter of the Rev. Ebenezer Erskine, two of the four ministers who first seceded from the Church of Scotland, and who founded the Secession Church, now an important and numerous body. Latterly Mr. Ewing Maclae resided constantly at his estate of Cathkin. He left a family of two sons and three daughters. The eldest, Humphrey Ewing Maclae, married Jane Brown, daughter of Mr. Alexander Brown, Dean of Guild, in 1784, who was a man of culture and a good classical scholar. James Ewing, the second son, was perhaps the best known public man in Glasgow in the middle of the century. He held the important offices of Lord Provost and Dean of Guild, and was the first Member of Parliament for the city under the Reform Bill. He published his views on the East India monopoly and on the Test and Corporation Acts, and was the author of a pamphlet on the interesting subject of Pauperism. He purchased the estate of Strathleven in Dumbartonshire. At his death he left munificent sums to the Merchants' House, Royal Infirmary, and other benevolent and religious institutions. The eldest daughter of Mr. Ewing Maclae was married to Mr. Alexander Crum of Thornliebank, and left a family. John Crum, the eldest, succeeded to Cathkin, which, at his death, became the property of his eldest son, Alexander Crum Maclae. The second son, Walter Crum of Thornliebank, was a calico printer, an F.R.S., and a man of great scientific acquirements.   The third son, being left the estate of Strathleven by his uncle, assumed the name of Ewing, and is now Humphrey Ewing Crum Ewing, the head of the eminent firm of James Ewing & Co., one of the few remaining ancient West India houses.   He represented the burgh of Paisley in Parliament upwards of seventeen years, and, on the death of Sir James Colquhoun of Luss, was appointed Lord-Lieutenant of the county of Dumbarton.   Alexander Crum, son of Walter, of Thornliebank, is now Member of Parliament for Renfrewshire.

ROBERT FINDLAY of Easterhill (Findlay, Hopkirk & Co.)—Mr. Findlay was an eminent merchant and tobacco importer. His father, Dr. Robert Findlay, was admitted Professor of Divinity in the College and University of Glasgow in 1783, which office he held till his death in 1814.   Dr. Strang, describing the old gentleman, says :—" A figure, never very large, but shrunk and attenuated " by age, was surmounted by a full bottomed wig and cocked hat, " under the weight of which he seemed to totter.   But his mild eye " and benevolent expression of countenance secured the deference " of the citizens and the affections of his students ; while his learning " and liberality, and his courteous and kind demeanour, inspired the " latter at once with reverence and gratitude."   Dr. Findlay was translated from the Low Church, Paisley, to the Ramshorn Church, Glasgow, in 1756, having held, before his ordination in Paisley, charges in Stevenston and Galston.   He outlived his son twelve years.   Robert Findlay, in 1784, bought from his partner, James Hopkirk, the estate of Easterhill, being part of the ancient lands of Dalbeth.   He married a daughter of Robert Dunlop of Househill, and purchased the house No. 42 Miller Street for his town residence, where his son Robert, who succeeded him, was born.   The counting-house was situated at the back of Mr. Findlay's residence. Mr. Findlay was elected Dean of Guild in 1796 and 1797, a Magistrate in 1783, one of the first Board of Directors of the Chamber of Commerce, and Chairman of the Chamber in 1789, 1794, and 1795.   He died in 1802, and was succeeded by his son Robert, father of Colonel John Findlay, and our fellow-citizen Thomas Dunlop Findlay, the former of whom represents the old family, and holds the estate.   Under the name of Findlay, Duff & Co., Robert carried on an extensive business as a general merchant. The firm, about 1814, opened Virginia Buildings, between Virginia and Miller Streets, an arrangement which has been found of great service to the merchants in both streets and to the general public. Mr. Findlay, like his father, was an active member and director of the Chamber of Commerce, and chairman in 1836 and 1837.   He died in 1852.

JAMES FINLAY, merchant and manufacturer; lodgings, Crawford's Land, Bell's Wynd (*Jones*), founder of James Finlay & Co.—This famous firm, now in its second century, still flourishes with the vigour of youth.   Its story from the time when James Finlay wove his first webs or shipped his earliest ventures cannot be told here—it would be an epitome of our industrial and mercantile history since Glasgow took a new departure after the Virginia collapse.   Some account of the firm's connection with the cotton trade will be found under *John Buchanan;* and some idea of its present importance was given in a recent lawsuit, when it was proved to have cleared £1,000,000 within twenty years.   James Finlay was one of the Finlays of the Moss, Killearn.   These Finlays sprang from a Walter Finlay who came south from Inverness about 1600, and became tacksman of Spittal of Killearn.   His descendant, John Finlay of the Moss, had four sons, of whom James, the founder, born 1727, was the youngest; the other three were William of the Moss, John of Carston, and Edward of James Finlay & Co. These three have no male representatives. James Finlay married Abigail Whirry, and had two sons. The elder, Major John Finlay, married Helen, daughter of George Thomson, banker in Glasgow, and had an only child, George Finlay of Athens, the historian of Greece, an ardent Philhellene in his younger days, and to the last, in spite of disappointment and disillusion, the firm friend and wise adviser of his adopted country. By his wife, a Greek, George Finlay had an only daughter, who died before him.

James Finlay's second son was KIRKMAN FINLAY of Castle Toward,[1] long the head of James Finlay & Co. His name deserves a place with the four young Virginians on the roll of those who have notably helped to make Glasgow. It was his rare case to lend an impetus to both her manufactures and her commerce. Finlay's cottons gave her a name for both make and finish, and if she has more than her own share of the great trade to the East, she may thank Kirkman Finlay for it. He had been one of the keenest and ablest opponents of John Company's monopoly, and as soon as the India trade was thrown open he pushed in and led the way to others. The first ship direct from the Clyde to India, the van of a vast fleet, was freighted by him—the " Buckinghamshire," of 600 tons, for Calcutta direct. Napoleon's Berlin Decrees gave him a still rarer chance to show his powers. The despot's attempt

---

[1] This name is said to have been taken by James Finlay from Alderman Kirkman of London, a business connection for whom he had a high esteem. It has become naturalised in the Finlays, and from them transplanted into the well-known mercantile family of the Hodgsons, with whom the Finlays have had intimate relations.

to starve us out Kirkman Finlay met by organizing a complete system of running the Continental blockade with depots outside and agencies inside the lines.   It was a bold game and the stakes were high, but he played for both patriotism and profit, and he scored both honours and tricks.[1]   Kirkman Finlay was more than a mere man of business—he was a man of broad views in all matters; he had read and thought, and his opinions, especially on mercantile questions, were listened to when he was in the House of Commons, and quoted there when he had left it; always a busy man, he still found time for much public and charitable work—he was a liberal and a kindly man, and his word was as good as his bond.   To do Glasgow justice, she gave him all the honours she had to give. He was Governor of the Forth and Clyde Navigation, President of the Glasgow Chamber of Commerce eight times, Dean of Guild, Lord Provost, Member of Parliament, Dean of Faculty, and Lord Rector of the University.   Even a statue has been raised to his memory; it has a fitting place in the vestibule of the Merchants' House.   Of all who troop past it we wonder how many, now-a-days, think how much the Glasgow that they·live by owes to Kirkman Finlay.   The day of his election was a great day in Glasgow.   He was well known and well liked, and had done the town good service; he was a citizen, and no citizen had been M.P. since Neil Buchanan in 1741; he was Provost, and no Provost had been M.P. since Robert Rodger in 1708, and the good people "tint their reason a' thegither;" he was franked of all expenses; medals were struck inscribed "Faith, Honour, Industry, Independence.—Finlay, 1812;" there was cheering and toasting and chinking of glasses in front of

---

[1] The partners of James Finlay & Co. at this time were very numerous; they held stated Meetings and kept regular Minutes.   If these Minutes exist, they would throw some light on the operations of the time.

the Town Hall; finally, his constituents seized their Member's carriage and dragged him along Trongate to his house in Queen Street. This was on 30th October, 1812. They paid his house a second visit on 7th March, 1815. They found him not at home, and they broke all his windows and then went away. He had been voting for "Prosperity Robinson's" Corn Bill, and they were not pleased.[1] By his wife, Janet Struthers of Greenhead, Kirkman Finlay had three sons—James Finlay and John Finlay, both partners in the old house, and Alexander Struthers Finlay of Castle Toward, formerly of Ritchie, Stewart & Co., of Bombay, and then M.P. for Argyllshire. Kirkman Finlay of Dunlossit, eldest son of James Finlay, is now the male representative both of the founder of James Finlay & Co., and of his far-back forebear, the tacksman of Spittal of Killearn.

JOHN FREELAND, merchant in Glasgow, born 1758.—This old and much-respected family long traded under the firm of John Freeland & Co. as yarn merchants in Glasgow, and cotton spinners at Bridge-of-Weir, in Renfrewshire, and was well known in the cotton yarn trade. Cotton spinning was introduced into the county of Renfrew about 100 years ago. Wherever sufficient water-power could be obtained cotton spinning mills were erected, and the process carried on. The Calder at Lochwinnoch, the Black Cart at Johnstone, the Levern in Neilston parish, and the White Cart at Paisley, had all mills driven by these streams. This was during the ten years between 1780 and 1790, and, in course,

---

[1] It was a stirring week in other places as well as Glasgow. While her fellow-citizens were breaking Kirkman Finlay's windows, the Londoners were wrecking the houses of Prosperity Robinson and his friends. That same day the Parisians read in the *Moniteur* that Bonaparte had escaped from Elba; and next morning the *London Gazette* announced our defeat at New Orleans.

villages soon arose around the mills for the accommodation of the workers. But it was not till the year 1793 that the large mill on the Gryffe, at Bridge-of-Weir, was built. It was at first one of the largest cotton factories within the county. The members of the firm originally were Messrs. Freeland of Glasgow, and Mr. Hastie from Paisley. But even prior to the era of spinning by water-power there were mills on the principle of "hand jennies," which were turned by the hand only. Some others were driven by oxen. Mr. Hastie was proprietor of one of the former of those early mills at Paisley, along with his partner, Mr. Davidson. Mr. Hastie was father of the late Archibald Hastie, M.P. for Paisley. Messrs. Freeland and Hastie, it appears, composed the firm when the Gryffe mill was erected in 1793. Latterly, however, John Freeland & Company gave the name to the firm for a long series of years. John and Robert Freeland were in the company apparently from the beginning. As the old partners died out their places were taken by successors of the same name and family. Robert appears to have lived a bachelor, but John married Catherine Scott, daughter of John Scott of Orbiston, and they had issue, of whom three sons and one daughter lived to a good old age. The eldest was John Freeland, who became a West India merchant. He was long resident in one of the islands in company with Mr. Young, under the firm of Young & Freeland. This generation only knew him by his munificent donations, which every now and again he sent from his retirement at Nice to this or that good object in his native city. The great addition which has just completed the Western Infirmary of Glasgow has been built from a sum of £40,000 bequeathed by him. His brother, Robert Freeland, of Gryffe Castle, was a manufacturer of cotton goods in Glasgow, and also became a member of the firm of John Freeland & Company at

Bridge-of-Weir. At one time he gave work to the numerous cotton cloth weavers in Girvan, Ayrshire. At that time his town residence was in Fyfe Place, West George Street, and his warehouse in same street, on the opposite side, but farther up. In course of time he removed, and joined his brother, George Scott Freeland, in the warehouse at 56 Wilson Street, a very popular resort for many years for the merchants of Glasgow who dealt in cotton and cotton yarn. The yarn produced at the factory in Bridge-of-Weir by Messrs. John Freeland & Company generally obtained a good price in the market. Robert Freeland also acquired several lands, by purchase, adjacent to Bridge-of-Weir, thereby enrolling himself as a landed proprietor in the county. These were the lands of Gryffe Castle, and the corn mill and mill lands of the "Mill o' Gryffe," within the old parish of Kilellan, now joined to Houston; also the farms of Lintwhite, Coalbog, and Lochermill, in the parish of Kilbarchan. He built a mansion house at Gryffe Castle in 1843, which became his country residence, while his town house was at 5 Albany Place in the city. He took great interest in everything connected with Bridge-of-Weir—the cotton works, the church, education, the poor of the village—and bestowed much care on the improvement of his estate. He was a J. P. of Renfrewshire, and held other public appointments. At the Disruption in 1843 he joined the Free Church, and was one of its warmest supporters, giving largely to many of its schemes. The present Free Church in the village at one time belonged to the "Old Light Burgher body," but being for sale in the year 1844, Robert Freeland purchased both the church and manse, and gave them over as a donation to the newly-formed denomination. In the year 1838 Messrs. John Freeland & Company (Robert and his younger brother, George Scott Freeland,) built and endowed the seminary at Bridge-of-Weir, which continued under their trusteeship till 1873, when it was given over by Robert, then the only surviving trustee, to the School Board of Houston and Kilellan. He was, at the same time, the sole surviving partner of the "old firm of John Freeland & Company." He died at Gryffe Castle on 29th March, 1874, in the 80th year of his age. Under his will legacies to public institutions—but chiefly to the Free Church of Scotland—were left to the amount of £27,000. He was buried in the family "lair" in the High Church yard, Glasgow.

GEORGE SCOTT FREELAND, his younger brother, and junior partner of the firm, predeceased Robert by about seventeen years. He died suddenly at 5 Albany Place, Glasgow, in March, 1857, aged 62 years. He also lies in the Freeland burial place in the "auld kirk yard." He was long the active managing partner of the firm both at Bridge-of-Weir and 56 Wilson Street. Under his management the mill at Bridge-of-Weir was largely extended and improved. In 1856, the year before he died, he was negotiating for the purchase of an extensive range of buildings in St. Andrew's Square, Glasgow, with the view of founding and endowing an educational institution and a home for poor children. This was not, however, at the time carried out, and he died early in the next year. But George Scott Freeland is not without a very fitting memorial. His sister, the late Mrs. Janet Freeland or Barclay, widow of Dr. Matthew Barclay, late minister of Old Kilpatrick, founded, in 1875, two scholarships in the Free Church College, Glasgow, of £30 annual value, to be awarded to students in the third year of their theological course, and to be held for two years. The old established firm of John Freeland & Co. is now extinct. It continued for about eighty years. Robert was the last of the firm. The works at Bridge-of-Weir were kept going for about two years after his death, but in 1876 they were discontinued, and advertised for sale. No purchaser appearing, they were entirely gutted, the machinery sold piecemeal last year (1880), and nothing now remains but the empty walls, with two water wheels and two steam engines, without a single spindle to turn.

WILLIAM FRENCH.—Mr. French is believed to have begun life in Glasgow as a clerk with Mr. Cuninghame of Lainshaw, and was afterwards his partner. The warehouse and stores were situated in that old-fashioned land still standing on the south-west corner of Virginia Street—built by Deacon John Robertson—and now a clothing establishment. Subsequently Mr. French entered into partnership with George Crawford, under the firm of French, Crawford & Co. He was also a partner with Alexander Speirs & Co. Like his former partner, Mr. French appears to have passed through the severe crisis of 1777 without ruinous loss, for in 1778 and 1779, before the first effect of the general stagnation had time to expend itself, he was elected Lord Provost of the city. Two notable events occurred in the last year of his provostship, which must have added much to the onerous duties of the office. These were the Bagnal riot—where the house of a Roman Catholic was sacked by the populace—and the turmoil known as the Cambric riot—the latter an event which places in a curious light the popular opinions of that time with respect to freedom of trade. A heavy duty was then imposed upon all cambrics of French manufacture imported into Britain. This was some time before the invention of cotton spinning, and the weaving of cambrics from French and Flemish yarns constituted a large proportion of the manufacturing industry of the city. In 1779 a bill was introduced into Parliament for the abolition of the duty on French cambrics. When the news of this movement reached Glasgow the weavers became alarmed. The measure was represented as having for its object the destruction of an important native industry for the benefit of the French, our natural enemies. A violent tumult was raised, the mob marching in procession through the town with an effigy on horseback of the minister who had introduced the bill, carrying in one hand a copy of the document, and in the other a piece of French cambric. This image was carried to the place of execution, and, with loud execrations, publicly hanged, and afterwards blown to pieces. Mr. French was successful in keeping the rioters under control, and the obnoxious measure was afterwards withdrawn. Provost French was one of the most active promoters of the Chamber of Commerce, and his name stands third in the list of its first directors. One of his daughters was married to Mr. Robert M'Nair, grandson of the eccentric Robert M'Nair of Janefield, the most successful shopkeeper ever Glasgow produced. Another daughter was married to Mr. Glen, merchant, who bought the house which stood at the foot of Queen Street, commonly called M'Call's blackhouse. Mr. French built that range of houses still standing on the south-side of Ingram Street, between the Union Bank and Glassford Street. He died in 1802.

WILLIAM GILLESPIE, linen and calico printer and cotton yarn merchant, Anderston *(Jones).*—Like his friend, Mr. Monteith, he was a bleacher and "wee cork," whose energies were devoted to the prosperity and growth of the village. About 1796 Mr. Gillespie established a spinning factory at Woodside, being the first of its kind near Glasgow. Henry Houldsworth, who had come from England about the time that the cotton manufacture was begun in Scotland, was a principal partner in the adventure, which was highly successful. The spinning factory stood at the junction of the Pinkston Burn and the Kelvin, then a pure crystal stream, celebrated in song, and very unlike the stagnant nuisance it has since become. William Street and Richard Street, called after the father and son, mark the situation of their bleaching and printing works. Mr. Gillespie had a country house at Bishopton, now on the Caledonian branch of the Greenock line of railway. His town house was in North Street. His son, Colin, owned and occupied the old romantic North Woodside House, so well remembered by those who loved an evening stroll to the "pear tree well." Dr. John Mitchell, the Anderston Secession minister, married a daughter of Mr. Gillespie. Their sons, until very recently, had a large spinning factory in the east end of the city. Dr. James Mitchell, late Dean of Faculty, is a member of this family. Mr. Gillespie was one of the kirk session with his friend James Monteith, and, like him too, he sleeps in the old Anderston kirkyard. His grandson, William Honeyman Gillespie, was owner of Torbanhill, with its rich stores of the famous "gas mineral." Mr. Gillespie died in 1807.

JOHN GLASSFORD, of Dougalston and Whitehill.—Mr. Glassford was a native of Paisley ; his father, James Glassford, was a merchant and magistrate in that town. John Glassford early in the last century entered into the Virginia trade, and rose rapidly till he became one of the foremost amongst the merchant princes of Glasgow. At that time the Virginia trade took up the greater share of the capital of the city. Mr. Glassford was owner of twenty-five ships, and it was believed that he passed money through his hands yearly to the extent of half a million sterling. His commercial transactions were not confined to the Virginia trade, but almost all the principal manufacturing establishments in the town had his support. He was a leading partner in the Glasgow Arms and Thistle banks. He held shares in the Glasgow Tanwork Co., and also in the Dyeing and Calico Printing Co. established at Pollokshaws by Provost Ingram, one of the oldest and most prosperous businesses of its kind in Scotland; and he was one of the principal promoters of the Cudbear manufacture conducted by George Macintosh & Co. He built, in the eastern suburb of the city, the spacious mansion of Whitehill, which, with its thirty acres of garden and pleasure ground, he surrounded by a high wall. He drove daily to this residence in a coach and four. He purchased the estate of Dougalston, from which he took his title; and he had for his town residence the Shawfield mansion, with its splendid garden, where Glassford Street now stands. In this house he dispensed princely hospitality, and there he died in 1783. The able authors of that valuable volume, "The Country Houses of the Old Glasgow Gentry," say:—"Mr. Glassford lived high, and he married high—a "baronet's daughter, and then an earl's. He bought more land, he "entailed, and he died, having done his best to found a family that "should keep his name alive; but it all came to nothing. The "Cuninghames, the Speirs, and the Ritchies, are still conspicuous "among our landed gentry. The Glassfords are gone. Their "heirs are seeking to found a fortune on the other side of the globe, "and Dougalston has passed to a merchant of our own day, en-"riched by trade to distant markets that John Glassford probably "never heard of, but yet helped to open up." In glancing over the memorial tablets which record the names of those who are laid in the old Ramshorn kirk yard, there are none of them so suggestive of mutation as one standing in the south-west corner, which tells the family history of John Glassford, at one time the very prince of Glasgow merchants, and now almost forgotten, the very stone which tells his story displaying an embodiment of neglect, decay, and desolation.

ALEXANDER GORDON, a member of the firm of Stirling, Gordon & Co., and oldest son of Alexander Gordon, and brother of John, of Aikenhead.—About 1804 he built a spacious house on the site now occupied by Royal Bank Place. To preserve the pleasant view over the gardens and meadows westwards, he acquired the ground now forming the site of Gordon Street, which he laid out with much care. He was a gentleman of refined and artistic taste, which he cultivated by the collection of rare and valuable paintings and drawings. His collection was said to be worth £30,000, and was highly prized by Mr. Gordon himself. From this peculiarity, which his brother merchants esteemed a sort of craze which they could neither understand nor sympathise with, he was usually called "Picture Gordon." Another peculiarity of Mr. Gordon, which called forth vigorous remonstrances from many of his friends, was exhibited in his fitting up part of his stables into a neat little theatre, and here his family and their young friends spent many a happy evening in amateur theatrical representations, none enjoying more heartily nor applauding more vigorously the juvenile performances than the kindly and liberal-minded gentleman himself. Mr. Gordon died in Canada, in 1849, in the 95th year of his age.

JAMES GORDON, a Virginia merchant, trained in the establishment of Mr. John Glassford. He subsequently became son-in-law to that gentleman, and died in 1803.

JOHN GORDON, of Aikenhead.—Mr. Gordon was a principal partner in the extensive West India firm of Somervell, Gordon & Co., afterwards Stirling, Gordon & Co.   His father, Alexander Gordon, by his wife, Isabel Fleming, daughter of John Fleming, a prosperous maltman, acquired a considerable section of land on the banks of St. Enoch's Burn, then a pure trouting stream, running through St. Enoch's Square, and emptying itself into the Clyde, near the bridge.   Here he built a handsome and substantial house on the north side of the old Westergate, in which he and his family resided for many years.   In fact, the old house is still standing, being included in the extensive range of warehouses occupied at present by the firm of Stewart & M'Donald.   About the time the American colonies rebelled, Mr. Gordon's neighbouring laird, Andrew Buchanan, son of Maltman George, who died in 1737, laid out in the Lang Croft several steadings for feuing, running north from Mr. Gordon's house, now known as Buchanan Street.   On one of these feus James Johnston, a Glasgow merchant, built an elegant house (see map of 1783), a short way north of our present Arcade.   The failure of so many of the Virginia merchants during the progress of the war put a complete stop to building operations for a time, and Mr. Johnston's house stood alone among the vacant feus for many years, its garden occupying the site of Prince's Court.   This house and garden were bought by John Gordon, and occupied by him as his town house till his death.   He also purchased the estate of Aikenhead from Robert Scot, of the Thistle Bank, on which he built a spacious country house in 1806.   Many of the older Glasgow merchants remember Mr. Gordon well.   At the time when political feeling ran high, he and his partner, Charles Stirling, were esteemed the leaders of the Tory party in Glasgow.   Mr. Gordon has been described as a stately, well-made gentleman, of somewhat lofty bearing, enhanced by his style of dress ; for notwithstanding the varied changes of fashion and custom, he kept to the last by the knee breeches, ruffles, and powdered hair. He was greatly respected by his brother traders and by the public, as an upright and honourable merchant, a good citizen, and a benevolent and hospitable gentleman. He was appointed chairman of the Chamber of Commerce in 1804 and 1805. He was twice married—first to a daughter of John Alston, merchant and banker, Glasgow. Their only child married Mungo Campbell, of John Campbell, sen., & Co. ("Black Mungo"). On the death of his first wife, Mr. Gordon married a daughter of Gilbert Hamilton, Lord Provost in 1792–93, and first secretary of the Chamber of Commerce. John Gordon of Aikenhead, their only son, now occupies the estate, and represents the honoured name. Mr. Gordon died in 1828.

ARCHIBALD GRAHAME.—Archibald Grahame was originally a writer in Glasgow. On the failure of the firm of Matthew and John Orr, who were ruined by working coal on their estates of Camlachie and Gateside, these properties, along with Barrowfield, were sold to Robert Scot of Aikenhead, and James Dunlop of Garnkirk. The latter gentleman was also unfortunate, and the shares of the estates belonging to him passed into the hands of Mr. Grahame, who also purchased besides, from John Buchanan, M.P., son of Thomas Buchanan of Ardoch, the estate of Dalmarnock. Archibald Grahame was for many years cashier of the Thistle Bank, established in 1761. He was a member of the first Board of Directors of the Chamber of Commerce, and Chairman in 1790–91–98–99. He is represented in Glasgow by his grandson, James Grahame, C.A. While we write, the death is announced of Thomas Grahame, W.S., in the 89th year of his age,

He was the father of the gentleman last named, and the eldest and last surviving son of the old banker, Grahame.

WALTER GRAHAM, rum merchant ; cellar, Wallace Court, south side of Bell's Wynd. Mr. Graham was one of the best known and most popular citizens of Glasgow in the beginning of this century. Of polished manners and ready conversational powers, his society was eagerly sought after to grace all social parties making any pretension to good fellowship as it was then practised. He was the best judge of the celebrated Glasgow rum punch in the city, and his great skill in the manufacture of this compound — which was then esteemed one of the fine arts — was much prized. On the death or retirement of Mr. Richard Marshall, first superintendent of police in the city, Mr. Graham was appointed to that office. He held it only from 1803 to 1805, as he positively refused to undertake the drudgery connected with night watching. He was esteemed one of the leaders of the Tory party in politics ; and on the arrival of the London mail with news respecting the progress of the continental wars in the beginning of this century, Mr. Graham always undertook the duty of reading the despatches in the Tontine Reading Rooms, and invariably diversified the performance with remarks of his own, more characteristic than polite. He died in 1833.

GILBERT HAMILTON, Carron warehouse, Queen Street *(Tait)*.—Mr. Hamilton was a highly-respected and successful Glasgow merchant. He was the son of Archibald Hamilton, also a Glasgow merchant. His grandfather was the Rev. Archibald Hamilton, minister of Cambuslang in 1688. Gilbert Hamilton was the first bill collector of the Bank of Scotland in Glasgow. He was frequently chosen trustee on bankrupt estates, and conducted the business entrusted to him with much prudence and care. He was elected Lord Provost of Glasgow in 1792 and 1793. This latter year witnessed the outbreak of the French Revolution, and proved a most disastrous year to Glasgow, being marked with many failures and great commercial distress. Mr. Hamilton was the most active of those benevolent gentlemen in Glasgow who distinguished themselves by the measures then originated to afford relief. Mr. Hamilton bought the estate of Glenarbuck in Dumbartonshire, where he resided till his death. He was appointed the first secretary of the Chamber of Commerce, and discharged the duties of that office with great satisfaction to his brother directors and to the Chamber. He died in 1808.

JOHN HAMILTON, of Northpark, an extensive West India merchant.—His father, Dr. John Hamilton, was minister of the Inner High Church from 1749 till 1780. His grandfather, also a Dr. John Hamilton, was minister of the Blackfriars' or College Church, from 1713 till 1742, and his great-grandfather, Rev. John Hamilton, was minister of Carmichael in 1650. When Episcopacy came into Royal favour, this latter gentleman was displaced for refusing to conform to this mode of worship; but in 1672 he received the benefit of "indulgence," and was reseated in the parish by the Privy Council. John Hamilton was a much respected and highly influential member of the community. He was a Merchant Bailie in 1793, Dean of Guild in 1809 and 1810, and Lord Provost in 1801, 1802, 1803, 1810, and 1811. He died in 1829, aged 73. Several of his sons were West India merchants, and resided abroad. Perhaps the best known of this family was William of Northpark, who was Lord Provost of Glasgow in 1829, and an active and respected citizen. His daughter, Mary Anne, was married to John Patrick Alston of Muirburn, head of the existing firm of Campbell, Rivers & Co. The Hamiltons have numerous relations alive, the lineal representative of the family being George William Hamilton, son of Archibald of Woodside, the second son of John of Northpark.

HENRY HARDIE.—Henry Hardie & Co., wholesale linen drapers, Wallace Court, south-side Bell's Wynd. The firm comprised in its membership Robert Carrick, John Brown of Lanfin, the brothers M'Alpine, and William Fleming. It was known afterwards as Brown, Carrick & Co.

ARCHIBALD HENDERSON was a well-known Virginia merchant, and chairman of the Chamber of Commerce in 1787. His firm of Archibald Henderson & Co. were among the leading tobacco importers when the Chamber was founded. As a member of the Hodge Podge Club he has a stanza in Dr. Moore's famous song of the Club. It speaks of him as—" Begot, born, and bred in " John Calvin's meek faith." He was a son of the Rev. Archibald Henderson of Blantyre. What the father's views had been, may be gathered from his having been one of the few ministers who gave a hand to Whitfield in the " Cambuslang wark." What the son's views were may be gathered from Dr. Moore's verses. Archibald Henderson has descendants through a son who settled in Virginia, but he has no representatives in this country. His son was Richard Henderson, Town-Clerk of Glasgow, who lived, as his father before him had done, in the tenement still standing at the south-west corner of Virginia Street.

JAMES HOPKIRK was the son of Thomas Hopkirk, an extensive and successful Virginia merchant, and a partner in the firm of M'Caul, Smellie & Co., Virginia merchants. About 1754 Thomas Hopkirk acquired the lands of Dalbeth from Henry Wardrop, and at his death, in 1781, left the estate to his wife, Elizabeth Smellie, sister of his former partner. He was succeeded in business by his son James, who married a daughter of John Glassford of Dougalston. James wrought extensively the coal on his estate. He was a partner in the firm of Findlay, Hopkirk & Co., extensive merchants in Glasgow, and sold Easterhill, part of his Dalbeth estate, to his partner, Robert Findlay. Mr. Hopkirk was chairman of the Chamber of Commerce in 1808 and 1809. He died at an advanced age in 1835. Part of the lands of Dalbeth is now used as a cemetery in connection with the Roman Catholic body, who have also established a convent and reformatory on the grounds.

ANDREW HOUSTON, ROBERT HOUSTON or HOUSTON-RAE, sons of Alexander Houston, founder of the famous West India house of Alexander Houston & Co., and one of the six founders of the old Ship Bank (or Dunlop Houston & Co.) The country house of the Houstons was Jordanhill. Their town house was the stately mansion on the south side of Argyle Street, facing Queen Street, which is delineated in Stuart. Their counting-house long adjoined. Alexander Houston married the daughter of Colin Rae of Little Govan, and left three sons, Andrew, who succeeded through his father to Jordanhill, Robert, who succeeded through his mother to Little Govan, and Alexander of Rosehaugh. Andrew and Robert were partners in Alexander Houston & Co.; so were William MacDowall of Garthland and Castle Sempill, Lord Lieutenant and

M.P. for Renfrewshire, and his brother, Provost James MacDowall. These two were sons of William MacDowall, one of the six original partners of Dunlop Houston & Co. In 1795 the town was startled by the failure of the great house of Houston. So great a failure Glasgow had never seen, not even in the crash of the American war. Indeed, to this day Glasgow has seen no such failure, except only in connection with the City Bank disaster. It was a tangled hank, too, and many years passed before the liquidation was closed;[1] but in the end the surviving partners had a satisfaction that few bankrupts have. Stocks and monies, stores and plantations abroad, houses and lands at home, were gone; but every one had been paid principal and interest. There was even some small reversion, and the MacDowalls were able to make a fresh start with a modest estate. They have called it Garthland, after the ancient patrimony they had lost. Their partners were less fortunate. The Houstons of Jordanhill and the Raes of Little Govan have ceased out of the land. The case of the Raes was peculiarly hard. Had they been able to hold on by their lands, they would have been one of the richest families in the kingdom. Little Govan itself has been a mine of wealth, above ground and below, to the Dixons. But the Rae estate also included Aikenhead and other valuable properties. The whole fetched £70,000. They must now be worth much

---

[1] There were innumerable creditors, the Crown heading the list with a quarter of a million. There were all sorts of trust deeds and securities; there were claims and counter claims, suits and cross suits, inhibitions, arrestments, and multiplepoindings beyond count or reckoning, and matters were in a hopeless deadlock. Out of this they were only relieved by a special Act of Parliament. Under it Charles Selkrig, accountant, Edinbrurgh, was named trustee, with special powers. There were also English trustees for the English assets. The trustees had immense labour, but they had a good estate to work upon. From an interim report by Mr. Selkrig at a time when the trust was not yet fully realised, it appears that up to that time he had received £629,866 1s. 9d., while £157,597 1s. 1d. had passed through the hands of the English trustees. Who would have thought that any Glasgow house of last century could have been on the scale which these figures indicate?

more than £70,000 a year. The Raes, whose candle was thus abruptly put out, had long been settled in these parts.[1] They were Raes of Tannochside, now St. Enoch's, before they crossed the water to Little Govan. Robert Rae, of Tannochside, married his cousin, Elizabeth Dunlop, of Garnkirk, and was great-grandfather of his unlucky namesake and heir, Robert Houston Rae. The Houstons of Jordanhill were of a very old Galloway family, the Houstons of Busbie, now represented by Sir George Houston Boswell. Andrew Houston, of Jordanhill, married Margaret Wallace, sister of John Wallace of Kelly, and left a son, Sir Robert Houston, whose grandson, Captain J. F. Houston, R.A., now represents the Houstons of Jordanhill. Neither Houston-Rae nor Alexander Houston of Rosehaugh have any living representatives.

WILLIAM INGRAM.—Messrs. Campbell & Ingram, merchants and insurance brokers, Exchange. He and his partner, John Campbell, jun., took much interest in the establishment of the Chamber in 1783, and through their exertions a number of the most influential merchants in the city were induced to become members of the institution, as our *fac-simile* list testifies.

GEORGE KIPPEN, tobacco merchant.—His warehouse was in the short street leading from the east side of Saltmarket to St. Andrew's Church, known as the Baxter's or Baker's Wynd. He acquired the Busby estate. His son, William Kippen, was son-in-law to John Alston, jun., from whom he inherited property in

---

[1] Robert Rae, merchant, burgess of Glasgow, with Halbert Gladstone, merchant in Edinburgh, and others, owned the frigate "George," of 60 tons, a privateer, with letters of marque against the Dutch in the war in 1665. In 1730 James Rae, merchant, bought from the Town Council, for something under £300, sixty acres of the Wester Common—a bad sale for the common good.

Miller Street, and succeeded to the estates of Busby and Westerton. The family is now represented by Durham Kippen of Busby.

JOHN LAURIE, merchant, Greenhead; counting-house, High Street, above No. 10.—In the beginning of this century two brothers, James and David Laurie, feued land on the south bank of the Clyde from Hutchesons' Hospital, and built thereon a range of buildings, of which Carlton Place forms a part. The district, which was said to be a model specimen of street architecture, was named after its founders, and still bears the name—Laurieston. John Laurie was a relative—uncle, it is said—to the builders of Laurieston, and the prime agent in the speculation. Mr. Laurie was one of the first directors of the Chamber of Commerce, and through life took an active interest in all its transactions. He was a magistrate in 1784 and 1787. He died in 1811.

JOHN LEITCH, of Kilmardinny, of Leitch & Smith, West India merchants.—Mr. Leitch's town address was Spreull's Land, Trongate. About the beginning of this century Mr. Leitch purchased Kilmardinny from the widow of William Colquhoun of Garscadden, and resided there till his death. In 1833 the estate was purchased by our respected townsman, William Brown, the descendant of an old Glasgow family. In 1846 it was again sold to a Gibraltar merchant, William Whyte, who, before his death, sold it to the late Robert Dalglish, long M.P. for the city. Mr. Dalglish's representatives have now sold it to Mr. Thomas Reid.

ALEXANDER LOW, merchant, Robertson's Court, South side Argyle Street *(Jones).*—Mr. Low was a magistrate of the city when the Chamber of Commerce was instituted, and was one of its first Board of Directors.   He was appointed Dean of Guild in 1789 and 1790, and died in the latter year.

ALEXANDER M'ALPINE, of M'Alpine, Fleming & Co., calico and linen printers, Bell's Wynd.—He was also a member of the firm of Brown, Carrick & Co.   Their bleaching grounds were on the south side of St. Enoch's gate, where M'Alpine Street, Brown Street, and Carrick Street, named after the principal members of these firms, now stand.   Mr. M'Alpine was an excellent accountant, and served in that capacity in the Ship Bank.   He was one of the first Board of Directors, and an active promoter of the Chamber of Commerce.   After his death his family went to London.   His grand-daughter was said to be the celebrated actress and singer, known as Miss Ellen Tree, and afterwards Mrs. Charles Kean.

DONALD MACBRAYNE.—Like many active and energetic merchants in the city, Mr. MacBrayne came from the Highlands early last century to push his fortune in Glasgow.   He was of an ancient Highland family, and the representative of the Macnaughtans of Macnaughtan.   He was a partner in the firm of Adam Good & Co., calico and linen printers, Currie's Closs, High Street, afterwards changed to MacBrayne, Stenhouse & Co.   Donald's son, David, married a daughter of the Rev. Dr. Burns of the Barony Church. Among other children, David had three sons, J. Burns MacBrayne, insurance broker, David MacBrayne, the well-known shipowner, and Robert MacBrayne, a member of the old Glasgow firm of Black & Wingate, at present all worthy citizens of Glasgow.   George Burns of Wemyss House, uncle of these gentlemen, and the last survivor of Dr. Burns' family, established the great shipping firm of

George and James Burns. He was one of the founders of the
renowned Cunard Line; and the splendid line of steamers, which
opened up the attractive route to Iona and the Western Isles, was
established, and for many years managed, by him and his nephew,
David MacBrayne, who is now proprietor of the Line.

JAMES M'CALL, of Braehead, was a well-known merchant in
Glasgow. His office was on the east side of Miller Street. His
father, Samuel M'Call, a member of an old Dumfriesshire family,
came early to Glasgow, and was a successful merchant there in
1723. Samuel M'Call was twice married, and had a large family,
the most notable of whom were—John of Belvidere, a leading
Glasgow merchant; James of Braehead, whose name stands in our
lithographed list; and George, of George M'Call & Co., and
M'Call, Smellie & Co., Virginia merchants. James was a Virginia
merchant, whose connection with the leading Glasgow families past
and present is somewhat noticeable. His sons were Samuel of
Brachead and Glynton, county Cork, Thomas of Craighead; James
of Daldowie, and his twin brother, John of Ibroxhill, founder
of the firm of John M'Call & Co. The family of Braehead has
been intimately mixed up with Glasgow society. His daughter,
Elizabeth, married David Russell, and by their son, James,
she became grandmother to General Sir David Russell, K.C.B.;
Admiral John Russell, and Graham Russell, now Graham
Somervell, of Sorn Castle, Ayrshire. The only daughter of
Elizabeth, Sarah, by her marriage with James Crawford, became
the mother of Jane Tucker Crawford, wife of James Ewing of
Strathleven, M.P. The second daughter of Braehead's family,
Helen, married Henry Wallis of Maryborough, county Cork.
Their daughter, Sarah, became the wife of the late William

Smith of Carbeth Guthrie. Another daughter married George Dennistoun, and became mother of James W. Dennistoun, now of Dennistoun. George, of M'Call, Smellie & Co., married Mary Smellie, a sister of his partner. Samuel M'Call, wine merchant, Glasgow, is the direct lineal representative of the first Samuel M'Call, the founder of the family.

ALEXANDER M'CAUL, son of the Rev. John M'Caul of Whithorn, and chaplain to James, Earl of Galloway.—Alexander was a partner in the firms of Henderson, M'Caul & Co., and Somervill, Bogle & Co. His brother John was minister of the parish of Symington in 1751, and was translated to the Tron Church, Glasgow, in 1782. *(See sketch of Robert Cowan.)*

JAMES M'DOWALL, of Garthland. *(See sketch of the Houstons.)*

JAMES M'GREGOR, wholesale linen merchant, east side of Candleriggs.—Mr. M'Gregor was owner of the extensive bleaching works at Clober, near Milngavie. About 1773 he built the mansion house, which, with subsequent additions and improvements, is still standing there. One of his daughters married the world-renowned James Watt, who fitted up the works at Clober with machinery, which at the time was the theme of universal admiration. Mr. M'Gregor was Dean of Guild when the Chamber of Commerce was established, and was elected first deputy-chairman of the Chamber. He was succeeded in his business by his nephew, Robert Dunlop, of Dunlop, Hamilton & Co., whose grandson now inherits the property.

JAMES MACILWHAM.—In the latter part of last century Mr. Macilwham, who was a small Anderston manufacturer, had no place of business in the city. Like his friends, James Monteith, Allan Arthur, and others in the same line of business, he transacted his usual affairs in Pinkerton's small public-house, opposite the Tron Steeple, a practice which the custom of the time sanctioned. When the muslin trade was fairly begun, however, he, along with his brother John, established the firm of James and John Meikleham—so the original name was modified. The concern was highly successful. Their warehouse stood. on the east side of Glassford Street. One of the early partners in the business was the late well known James Davidson of Ruchill, who, on the death of the brothers Meikleham, commenced business as a manufacturer on his own account, and, like his partners, he too was very successful. The original firm was carried on for many years by a nephew of the brothers Meikleham, Mr. Darnley. It is worth notice that William James Davidson—the present possessor of Ruchill, and son of James Davidson—has been a member of the Chamber of Commerce for the long period of forty-one years, during the greater part of which time he has also been an esteemed director.

ROBERT MACKAY, West India merchant and rum importer. After the American war, and till the cotton trade obtained a permanent footing, the importation and sale of West India produce formed the most important and profitable part of the business of the city. The counting-house of the firm was in Dunlop Street. Mr. Mackay was associated with his friends, George Macintosh and David Dale, in the unfortunate speculation of these gentlemen and others to establish a cotton spinning factory at Dornoch, in Sutherlandshire.   Mr. Mackay died in 1802.   *(See sketch of George Macintosh.)*

ROBERT M‘NAIR, senior partner in the firm of Robert M‘Nair & Son, of the Gallowgate Sugar Works.   After the death of the first Robert M‘Nair of Jeanfield, which took place in 1787, the business was carried on by his sons, Robert and James, of Calderbank, the former of whom had been a partner in the original firm.   In the end of last century, Robert and James M‘Nair built a large sugar refinery in the Back Cow Lone, now Ingram Street, at its junction with Queen Street, where the extensive warehouses of Arthur & Company (Limited) now stand.

RICHARD MARSHALL.—Marshall, M‘Dowall & Co., west side of Queen Street, rum importers and West India merchants. The stores of the company were situated in Madeira Court.   Mr. Marshall was also a member of the firm of Robert Bogle & Co.   He was a magistrate in 1778, and a very energetic and active citizen. When the Act was passed for embodying the police force in Glasgow in the beginning of this century, Mr. Marshall was appointed their first superintendent.

JOHN MAXWELL of Dargarvel, Renfrewshire, a merchant in Glasgow.   He died in 1790.   His son William, who was also a well-known Glasgow citizen, resided in the house situated at the corner of Gordon and Buchanan Streets, now included in the premises of Frazer & Green.   A grand-daughter of John Maxwell is the wife of Thomas Donald, commissary clerk of Lanarkshire. The family is now represented by William Hall Maxwell of Dargarvel.

PETER MURDOCH, merchant and sugar refiner, one of the old aristocratic race whom Glasgow delighted to honour. His grandfather, Peter Murdoch, was Provost in 1730-31. His uncle, John Murdoch, was Provost in 1746-47-50-57-58-59, and his aunt was the wife of Andrew Cochrane of Brighouse, Provost in the eventful '45. His father, Peter Murdoch, was a city merchant, and his mother a daughter of Sir Archibald Stewart of Blackhall. He himself was a member of the influential firm of Robert Bogle & Co., and a principal shareholder and partner with Messrs. Spiers, Glassford, and others in the Glasgow Arms Bank. Mr. Murdoch died at Auldhouse in 1817, in the eighty-third year of his age. For upwards of fifty years he had been a member, and latterly the father of the Hodge Podge Club, who presented him with a portrait of himself, now in the possession of his great-grandson, J. B. Murdoch.[1]

WALTER NEILSON, merchant, west side of Candleriggs, was the son of John Neilson, described as "Land labourer, Garioch." John seems to have been a market gardener and cow-feeder, and, as his circumstances improved, a maltman. He purchased several riggs of land adjoining the old Cow Lone, which became valuable property when Queen Street was built, and the old market gardener's son inherited a good patrimony.

JOHN ORR of Barrowfield, advocate and town-clerk.—Mr. Orr, in 1775, inherited from his father, William Orr, the valuable properties of Camlachie, Gateside, and Barrowfield. On succeeding

---

[1] In our sketch of George Brown, of Capelrig, we inadvertently stated that Peter Murdoch, of Langbank, father of the gentleman named, was a son of this Peter Murdoch; he was a grandson.

to these estates, he formed a partnership with his brother for working the coal on the estates. The enterprise, however, was unfortunate, and ended in the sequestration of the company in 1791. Ten years before this time Mr. Orr had been appointed town-clerk for Glasgow, which office he retained till his death in 1803.

JAMES OSWALD, merchant, was the youngest brother of George Oswald of Scotstoun, and Alexander Oswald of Shieldhall. He died in 1785, aged 43. James Oswald, a younger member of the same influential family, served in the first Reform Parliament, and in four others, as member for Glasgow. A statue has been erected to his memory, which now stands in George Square. He died in 1853.

MATHEW PERSTON, of Mathew & John Perston, lawn and cambric manufacturers.—He had his warehouse at 165 Saltmarket, and his house in Campbell Street, Dovehill. The Perstons have since owned the fine residences of Thornwood, Partick, and Brooksby, Largs. Mathew Perston was elected chairman of the Chamber of Commerce in 1802, on the death of Mr. Henry Riddell. He married Elizabeth Reid, daughter of John Reid and Elizabeth Reid, sister of "Senex," and was father of the late Mathew Perston of Brooksby. He died in 1833.

GEORGE PROVAN, drysalter; Shop, west side of High Street.—This well-known and unpretentious little shop, which is situated a few doors north of the Cross Steeple, in High Street, has a romantic interest in the history of the progress of Glasgow. George Provan, an enterprising Glasgow merchant in the end of last century, here carried on business for the sale of paints, oils, and general drysaltery goods, under the firm of Provan & Coats. Robert Henderson, the original and senior partner in the firm, afterwards known as Robert and John Henderson, entered the establishment as a junior partner. He had previously been a clerk in the employment of the eccentric Mrs. Brown, cotton merchant. *(See sketch of David Dale.)* As the young man was found to be faithful and capable he rose rapidly, and in the end of last century he assumed full charge of the business. His brother John, latterly of Park, was following out the business of a wright in Bo'ness, where the Henderson family long resided, and he was persuaded to join his brother in the High Street. It is said that John did not take kindly to the change, from the healthy air of his native town to the duties of his new occupation, with its irksome confinement and disagreeable smells. The business under the charge of the brothers, however, rapidly extended, and an establishment was opened by them in London which expanded into a large East India trade, and soon became one of the most extensive in the kingdom, and so prosperous that both brothers became wealthy. John is well remembered for the numerous and munificent sums which he bestowed upon various religious and benevolent associations, (said to be about £40,000 annually during the last twenty years of his life), and the great legacies he left in aid of church extension and similar objects at his death. John died in 1867. Robert was accidentally drowned crossing the Clyde in a ferry-boat near his own house in 1842. Their nephew, Mr. William M'Ewen, is at present (1881) President of the Glasgow Chamber of Commerce, an honour which was also conferred some years ago on his elder brother John. William has also taken a prominent part in the public business of the city, having been Dean of Guild in 1868 ; and, like his uncles, has been a generous patron and steady friend to the numerous charitable and useful institutions of the city.

JOHN RIDDELL, of M'Call & Riddell, Virginia merchants and extensive West India traders. Mr. Riddell was a Magistrate when the Chamber of Commerce was instituted, a merchant Councillor, and President of the West India Association in 1789, and Lord Provost in 1786 and 1787. He died in 1794.

WILLIAM RISK, thread manufacturer and bleacher, head of the Green. Risk Street, Calton, still points out the locality, we believe, where the bleaching and manufacturing operations of Mr. Risk were carried on.

ALEXANDER RITCHIE, merchant, Horn's Land, Argyle Street. *(Tait.)*

JAMES and WILLIAM ROBERTSON were brothers of John Robertson of Plantation, manager of the Glasgow Arms Bank. James was cashier and partner in the Merchants' Bank, and William was manager of the old and successful Smithfield Iron Work, of which the three brothers were the principal partners.

DAVID RUSSELL, merchant, east side of Queen Street, member of the firm of Stirling, Gordon & Co.—*(See sketch of James M'Call.)*

JAMES SCOTT, and JOSEPH SCOTT, merchants, father and son. Their counting-house was long on the east side of Virginia Street, afterwards the Excise Office.

JOHN SEMPLE, a successful bleacher and manufacturer in Finnieston.   In 1770 a portion of the lands of Stobcross, consisting of upwards of 20 acres, was set apart for feuing.   Mr. Semple acquired the greater part of this property.   He died in 1810.

THOMAS SHEDDEN, of Thomas and Robert Shedden, muslin manufacturers, High Street.—There were several of these Sheddens here, off-shoots of the Sheddens of Beith.   The last of the Glasgow Sheddens was the late William Shedden, muslin manufacturer, whom some may remember as blind.   He had over-strained his eyes in connection with his manufacture.   He left an only child, Thomas Shedden, late of Ardmay, Loch Long.

WILLIAM SHORTRIDGE, of Todd, Shortridge & Co.— *(See David Todd.)*   He lived " 4 flat, Shortridge's Land, south " side Argyle Street " (June, 1787).   Shortridge's Land was the tall tenement which stood at the west corner of Dunlop Street, opposite the Buck's Head.   It was removed a few years ago in widening the entry to Dunlop Street.   It had been built by William's father, Bailie John Shortridge, a tough, old worthy, who fought the rebels at Falkirk, and lived to fight his neighbours in the Law Courts.   He had a right to be tough, for his mother was a Spreull of the tough and worthy stock, that produced old " Bass John " and other like-minded Spreull's.   " Bass John " was tried for treason and rebellion and fighting on the side of the Covenanters at Bothwell Bridge.   Though acquitted on a verdict of " not proven," the Government, to prevent his treason in the future, if they could not punish him for anything in the past, detained him, and he was for six years kept a prisoner in the Bass Rock.   William Shortridge, by his wife, Elizabeth

Yuille, had a numerous family; but none of these left descendants except Margaret, wife of James Burns of Kilmahew. Their only child, John William Burns, is sole representative of William Shortridge. William Shortridge's brother, James, under the will of his cousin, Janet Spreull, " Bass John's " daughter, succeeded to Spreull's Land in the Trongate—the only entail within the burgh—and took the name of Spreull. He married Margaret M'Call of Belvidere, and was father of John Spreull, late City Chamberlain. James Black of Craigmaddie, another original subscriber to the Chamber, married William Shortridge's sister. Another sister married John Smith of Craigend.

ARCHIBALD SMITH, of the firm of Leitch & Smith, West India proprietors, was a younger son of James Smith of Craigend, Strathblane. Early in life he went to Virginia, but on the breaking out of the War of Independence he took the King's side, and, losing his property, returned home, and joining Mr. Leitch, founded the old Glasgow firm that bore their names. In 1799 he was Dean of Guild, and Chairman of the Chamber of Commerce in 1815. In 1800 he bought Jordanhill, a property now in possession of his great-grandson. His wife was Isobel, daughter of Bailie William Euing, and aunt of the late William Euing of the Royal Exchange, whose fine literary and artistic tastes and numerous charities are still fresh in the memory of his fellow-citizens. Archibald Smith died in 1821, and his widow in 1855, aged 101. Archibald Smith's sons were well-known citizens of Glasgow. The eldest, James, who succeeded to Jordanhill, was senior partner of James and Archibald Smith & Co., West India proprietors, the successors of Leitch & Smith. He never, however, took any active part in its management, leaving that to his youngest brother Archibald, who still survives, in his 86th year, and is one of the oldest Members of the Chamber of Commerce. James Smith's tastes were of a scientific and literary nature; and while his publications on geology and conchology have been of much value, his most important work is his book on the " Voyage and Shipwreck of St. Paul." He was a Fellow of the Royal Societies of London and Edinburgh, and many other learned bodies. He died in 1867. He was succeeded in Jordanhill by his son Archibald, an eminent English lawyer, and a celebrated mathematician. He was the first Scotch Senior Wrangler at Cambridge.[1] He died some years ago, and his son, James Parker Smith, is now the proprietor of Jordanhill. He intends to join the Bar, and so far he has already followed his father's footsteps, having taken, like him, very high honours at Cambridge. Archibald Smith's second son was the late William Smith of Carbeth Guthrie. He was Dean of Guild in 1821, and Lord Provost in 1822. Like his father he was a West India proprietor, and, in partnership with his cousin, Robert Brown, carried on business under the firm of Smith & Brown. Two of his sons, Cuningham Smith and John Guthrie Smith, of William Euing & Co., grandsons of the subject of this notice, are citizens of Glasgow, and members of the Chamber of Commerce.

WILLIAM SMITH.—William Smith, of Muirbank, was a Bailie in 1801. His daughter, Margaret, was the first wife of the late James Burns of Kilmahew, and his daughter, Agnes, was the wife of the late John Robertson Reid of Gallowflat, and mother of Francis Robertson Reid, now of Gallowflat.

JAMES SOMERVILL, of Hamilton Farm, one of the

---

[1] See " The Old Country Houses of the Old Glasgow Gentry," Second Edition, p. 142, for notice of Archibald Smith.

original partners of Somervell, Gordon & Co., afterwards Stirling, Gordon & Co.   He died in 1791.

PETER SPIERS, of Culcreuch, a younger son of Alexander Spiers of Elderslie.   He sold the Virginia mansion, his father's town residence, with the consent of his mother, who held it in life rent, to the Dunlops of Carmyle.   He carried on a large spinning factory at Culcreuch, in Stirlingshire, and died a rich man in 1831.

THOMAS STEWART, of the Field, bleacher, St Rollox.— His daughter, a celebrated beauty of that day, was married to Thomas Campbell Haggart of Bantaskine.   Their daughter, Eliza, who was also esteemed a great beauty, was the wife of Alexander Spiers, M.P. for Richmond, grandson of Alexander Spiers of Elderslie.   She became the mother of the late Alexander Spiers, M.P. for Renfrewshire.   After the death of her first husband, Mr. Spiers, which took place in 1844, she married Edward Ellice, M.P., and died quite recently.   Thomas Stewart died in 1825.

WALTER STIRLING, merchant, Miller Street, cousin-german to William Stirling, being son of his uncle, William Stirling, surgeon in Glasgow, by his wife, Elizabeth Murdoch. He was deformed, and was known as "Humphy Watty." He died unmarried in 1791, and left his books and his house and a sum of money to found Stirling's Library, the first free public library in Scotland.

JOHN TENNENT, one of the two founders of "John and "Robert Tennent, brewers and maltmen, Drygate," the only firm that appears absolutely without change in the first Glasgow

Directory and in to-day's.[1] John and Robert Tennent were sons of Hugh Tennent, Deacon of the Gardeners in 1746. He had a market garden where St. Rollox Chemical Works now stand. He ultimately owned the ground, and his son sold it for £5000 to Charles Tennant, founder of Charles Tennant & Co. The two families are noways connected. Hugh Tennent came from Cumbernauld, Charles Tennant from Ayrshire. John Tennent has now no male descendants. His representative is his grand-daughter, Barbara Tennent, wife of Edmond Ronalds, late Professor of Chemistry in Queen's College, Galway. Her father was Hugh Tennent, who married Barbara Grahame of Mugdock. Andrew Tennent, John's younger son, banker and bill broker in Glasgow, married Margaret, daughter of John Young II. *(see John Young)*, but left no family. Robert Tennent, the younger of the two founders, has numerous descendants in both male and female line. His eldest son was the late well-known Hugh Tennent of Wellpark. —he it was who made the business what it is; yet he had not been bred a brewer. Till he was in middle life he was in the West India firm of Middleton & Tennent, and he only left this in 1835, when the brewery business was in sore need of help. His partner in his former business was William Middleton, through whose good firm of William Middleton & Co. many a barrel of Wellpark beer in after days found its way to the West Indies and the Spanish main. By his wife, Christian Rainey, sister of the late respected Professor Harry Rainey, Hugh Tennant had, with other children, William (whose son is Hugh Tennent of Wellshot Brewery), and Charles Stuart Parker (whose children now represent the Tennent interest in Wellpark, and whose widow is now wife of R. F. F.

---

[1] William Stirling & Sons also appear in *Tait*, 1783, but by a misprint as William Stirling & Co. Several other existing firms appear, but not identically.

Campbell of Craigie, M.P.)   The solum of the great brewery is a feu off the Wester Craigs, an ancient possession of the Merchants' House.   Edwin and Robert Donaldson (from whom John and Robert Tennent acquired it) feued it from the House in 1757 for a feu-duty of £9 10*s.*, with a grassum every twenty-seventh year. The ground (described as the "Wellpark," and including "Bog-acre,") extended to five Scotch acres, and the feu-right included a power to the feuars "to collect the springs, with open or close "drains, from the other lands of the Wester Craigs to the said "Wellpark or five acre parke, without molestation or hindrance for "ever."   Wester Craigs has grown into the suburb of Dennistoun; and we do not know that the Tennents still supply their vats from it "either by open or by close drains."   Their "five acre parke" cannot, however, be dear at the £9 10*s.* of feu-duty, even with the grassum every twenty-seventh year.

ANDREW THOMSON, of Faskine, a member of the firm of M'Call, Smellie & Co., Virginia merchants.—The family began banking operations in 1785, under the firm of Andrew, George, and Andrew Thomson.   In the disastrous year, 1793, they were unfortunate, and failed.

ROBERT THOMSON, a successful Anderston manufacturer. He was the grandfather of the late well-known Neil Thomson of Camphill.   He died in 1790.

DAVID TODD, third flat Reid's new land, south side Argyle Street, and of Todd, Shortridge & Co., linen printers; wareroom, east side High Street, near the Cross. *(Jones' Directory.)* This well-known firm had their works at Levenbank on the Leven, now owned by Archibald Orr Ewing & Co.[1] The Shortridge was William Shortridge *(see Notice of him)*. David Todd was also a partner in the cotton spinning firm of Todd & Stevenson, with mills at Crosslee, near Bridge-of-Weir, and at Springfield, near Glasgow. Springfield is said to have been the first cotton mill built in these parts to be entirely worked by steam. On David Todd's death the mills were divided, the Stevensons taking Crosslee, and the Todds Springfield. David Todd's sons, John and Charles, were well-known citizens. John Todd carried on the printing on the Leven, and had as his partner Alexander Fletcher (afterwards of Alexander Fletcher & Co., the business with which George Anderson, M.P., was connected). John Todd latterly resided at his estate of Finnick-Malise, near Drymen, and died there unmarried in 1872, aged 85, the last of the Todds. Charles Todd carried on the Springfield business. There he had as his partner Samuel Higginbotham, who has just died at the good old age of 83. Under his energetic management the business developed into the well-known firm of Charles Todd & Higginbotham, whose great works opposite the Green are an epitome of the cotton industry from the original bale to the printed calico. In these works and in the warehouse at Springfield Court the name of David Todd's old place is preserved ; but the original Springfield has vanished. It stood on the south-side of the Clyde below Windmillcroft, and close by the Fisherman's Hut. The Clyde Trust, after a memorable jury trial, acquired it for harbour extension ; and the largest vessels now float in the reeking pool which now covers the very site of the old mill.

---

[1] Levenbank, the nearest to Lochlomond of the many works on the Leven, was founded in 1784, and was bought by A. Orr Ewing & Co. in 1845.

WILLIAM WARDLAW, father of the venerable Dr. Ralph Wardlaw, and himself a much esteemed citizen ; bailie in 1796, and again in 1800 ; merchant and manufacturer, of the firm of Smith & Wardlaw.   His house was in Charlotte Street, east side ; his warehouse was on the south side of Smith's Court, off Candleriggs.[1] Wardlaw is an east country name.   William Wardlaw, of a family originally from Fife, came here from Dalkeith, where Dr. Wardlaw was born.   He had married Anne Fisher, daughter of the Rev. James Fisher, and grand-daughter of Ebenezer Erskine, father of the Secession.   Anne Fisher's sister, Margaret, was wife of Walter Ewing MacLae of Cathkin, and mother of the late Humphrey Ewing MacLae of Cathkin, James Ewing of Strathleven, M.P., and Mrs. Crum of Thornliebank.   William Wardlaw and Ewing MacLae followed the Erskines and Fishers in Church matters ; and Ralph Wardlaw, though so well known as an Independent, was brought up a Burgher Seceder.

JAMES WARDROP, of Springbank House, near the Clyde Iron Works.—The property, which consisted of about twenty acres, formed part of Wester Dalbeth, belonging to an ancient family—the Grays of Dalmarnock.   His father purchased the estate about 1780, and laid it out with great taste ; and on his death, it passed into the hands of James.   He and his brother John established a business as American merchants and importers of tobacco. The firm, however, was unfortunate, and the estate was sold to their sister, Miss Isabella Wardrop ; and was again sold by her in 1806

---

[1] In premises vacated by James Finlay & Co. "Smith's Court" was so named because owned by Archibald Smith of Jordanhill. On the north side of the court was a calender, in which he was a partner There is a calender there now.

to a Glasgow merchant, Mr. Taylor, whose descendants, we believe, still retain the property.

DAVID WATSON, merchant and banker in Glasgow.—Here is his advertisement from the *Glasgow Journal* of 1767 :—" David " Watson, merchant in Glasgow, takes in Ayr, Dumfries, Perth, " and British Linen Bank notes at a discount of one penny a pound, " or if there is a hundred pounds of one kind, at a discount of a " quarter per cent., and pays the value in Edinburgh or Glasgow " notes." A handsome commission, but the turn-over was, no doubt, small. Mr. Watson died in 1783. His sons, James Watson and Robert Watson of Linthouse, were private bankers, under the firm of J. & R. Watson, of which a third brother, Gilbert Watson, W.S., was afterwards a partner. J. & R. Watson long carried on a large business, but were eventually wound up in 1832. Their office, which had first been in Trongate, was latterly in Virginia Street, near the bottom on the west side. It was bought by the Glasgow Union Bank (now the Union Bank of Scotland), which had till then been up a stair in Old Post Office Court. A daughter of Mr. Watson married Alexander Smith, banker in Edinburgh, and had, with other children, Donald Smith, of the Western Bank, and a daughter, wife of the late J. G. Kinnear, secretary of the Chamber of Commerce, and mother of A. S. Kinnear, advocate, Dean of Faculty. David Watson owned Stob-cross. He had bought it in 1776 from Matthew Orr, 60 Scotch acres mansion house and all, for £3000. After his death his executors sold it to John Phillips, merchant in Glasgow, for £3750. Phillips's executors resold it to a syndicate in 1844 for £58,246. And the syndicate up to 1870 had realised a quarter of a million from three-fourths of the whole, and from the enormous rise since

1870 will probably realise quite as much for the remaining one-fourth. Indeed, sales have been made at from £3 to £5 per square yard.

WILLIAM WHYT, a partner of Lothian, Wardrope & Co., "silk manufacturers and merchants; warehouse, first close below "the well, High Street." *(Tait, 1789.)* This well was known as the Cross Well—it was at the end of the Old Vennel. Vennel and well have now alike disappeared.

JOHN YOUNG, merchant in Glasgow.—The Youngs are an old race of Glasgow merchants, whose name has only last year disappeared from our Directory. A window on the south side of Blackadder's Aisle bears this inscription :—" 1863. George, Hew, " William, and James Young, in memory of their brother, their " father, their grandfather, and their great-grandfather, all named " John Young, all merchants in Glasgow, and all buried in the " churchyard nearly opposite this window." The family is now represented by a fifth John Young, son of the above George. John Young I., born 1707, died 1777. He came here from Eaglesham, and was originally a manufacturer. Afterwards he was a partner in the Virginia and West India firm of Young & Bogle, and in the "Cumberland Weaving Factory," on the south side of Gallowgate. At one time, for the sale of his manufactures, he had lived much at Carlisle, and stood so well there that the Corporation, on his leaving, gave him a silver tankard, now in the possession of his great-great-grandson, John V. John I. married Margaret Kirkpatrick, daughter of John Kirkpatrick, from the neighbourhood of Closeburn, and had John Young II., born 1759, died 1795. He appears among the original subscribers to the Chamber, alongside of

John Auchincloss and William Lang.   These three were partners
of " Young, Auchincloss, Lang & Co., manufacturers ; warehouse,
" south side, head of Gallowgate." *(Directory, 1789.)*   They
appear in " David Dale's List," which consists mostly of manufacturers, doubtless David's customers for yarn.   John Young II.
married Anne Brown, daughter of George Brown (who was twice
Dean of Guild—1763 and 1771—and was worthy of the honour),
and had John Young III., born 1788, died 1855, of Young &
Freeland, West India merchants. *(See John Freeland.)*   He long
lived in No. 1 Blythswood Square, and his family were known from
others of the name as " the Youngs in the Square."   He married
Agnes Tennent of Wellpark, and had, with other children, John
Young IV., merchant in Glasgow ; George and Hew, twins, merchants in Glasgow, both dead ; William, now of Lloyd's, London ;
and a daughter, Janet, whose husband was John Buchanan, of the
old firm of Dennistoun, Buchanan & Co., and one of whose sons is
Thomas R. Buchanan, Fellow of All Soul's, Oxford, late candidate
for Haddingtonshire.   John Young IV. died of cholera in the
visitation of 1849.   He left no children ; and the representative of
this old race of Glasgow merchants is John Young V., son of
George Young, and grandson of John Young III.   John II. had a
posthumous son, George Kirkpatrick Young of Glendoune, merchant in Glasgow, who married Isabella Murdoch, and had a son,
J. G. K. Young, now of Glendoune.

MAGISTRATES

AND

MERCHANTS OF GREENOCK.

ARCHIBALD CAMPBELL, wine merchant, of the firm of Campbell, Anderson & Co.   He resided at Finlayston, where he died.   He is represented by his grandson, Mr. Campbell of Auchendarroch, Argyllshire.

JOHN DUNLOP, writer, father of the temperance movement in Scotland.   His portrait—a very fine one—is to be seen in the Temperance Institute, Greenock.   He died in London.   He was the grandfather of the late M.P. for Greenock.

WILLIAM FULLARTON, grain merchant ; residence, Galley's Green, now George Square.   The U.P. Church is built on its site.   His son died lately in Ayrshire, possessed of considerable landed estates.   Another son was editor of *Bengal Hurkaru*, and founder of female education in India.

JAMES GAMMELL, shipowner and founder of the Greenock Bank, of Garvel Park, Greenock, now called Gammell's Point (site of new docks).   Representatives—his grandsons, Captain Gammell of Drumtochty, Kincardineshire, Major Gammell of Ardiffery and

Countesswells, Aberdeenshire, and their sister, Mrs. Stewart, Liberton Manse, Edinburgh.

JOHN HAMILTON, a leading merchant. He built a mansion house at the head of what is now called East Blackhall Street. It was acquired by the Caledonian Railway, along with the adjoining mansion and grounds, called "Virginia House," belonging to Roger Stewart. Mr. Hamilton's sons and grandsons are extensive merchants in London.

WILLIAM HAMILTON, son of John Hamilton.—He removed to Liverpool, and, along with William Laird and John Forsyth—all clever men—acquired a sandy district on the banks of the Mersey for a few hundred pounds, now called Birkenhead. He wrote letters in the *Liverpool Albion*, proposing to construct docks, to be entered by a ship canal from the mouth of the Dee, and thus avoid the banks at the mouth of the Mersey. The Liverpool Corporation became alarmed, and at once offered £20,000 for part of the foreshores. Hamilton Square, Birkenhead, was built by and called after himself. Laird's grandson, John, a grand nephew of Hamilton, built the famous "Alabama" Confederate cruiser. John Laird was then M.P. for Birkenhead.

JOHN KIPPEN, wine merchant.—One of his daughters married Mr. Crooks, of Leitch & Smith, Glasgow; and another married a Mr. Watson, of Greenock, afterwards a manufacturer in Glasgow.

HUGH MOODY, merchant, residing in Cathcart Street. His house is now taken down, and a branch of the Royal Bank built on its site.   He is represented by his great-grandson, Archibald Robertson, cashier, Royal Bank, Glasgow.

WALTER RITCHIE, an enterprising merchant.—Carried on, by several clippers, a contraband trade in dry goods from the South Pacific with the Spanish colonies, bartering goods for gold and silver plate.   He had also a large mahogany cutting establishment in Honduras.   He is represented by Major Ritchie of the Indian service.

JAMES SCOTT, wine merchant.—He removed to London, where he died without issue.

ROGER STEWART, proprietor of Ronachan, Argyllshire.— A leading and enterprising merchant and shipowner; Virginia House, Greenock.   He was chief magistrate of Greenock in 1795–97. To his indefatigable exertions was due the restoration of " Fort Jervis," skirting the " Bay of St. Lawrence "—where the east harbour of Greenock now stands.   This was a formidable fort in those days, mounting twelve 24-pounders.   It was about this time the people of Greenock and on the Clyde were in a state of wild alarm through the French squadron, under Thurot, burning ships off Ailsa Craig.   Mr. Stewart lent to the British Government during the American war his crack ship " Defiance," originally fitted out by Captain H. Dundas Beatson, Naval Service, as a " Letter of Marque," mounting 32 guns.   On the second day after leaving the Clyde as convoy to a fleet of merchant ships, she fell in with and engaged, off the coast of Ireland, the United States frigate "Wasp," 72 guns.   After a gallant fight the " Defiance " struck, being " on fire fore and aft."   The "Wasp" was disabled from pursuit of the merchant fleet, and was easily captured next day by a British frigate of the same calibre from Cork. Mr. Stewart's son, who died last year, father of the Church of Scotland, at Liberton, Edinburgh, was a youth in the "Defiance" when captured, and delighted to tell how the gallant Captain Athole fought his ship against such heavy odds. Mr. Stewart's representatives are his grandsons, Roger and James Stewart, merchants, Mobile, General Roger Stewart Beatson, R.E., Rotherwood, Bedford, and his brother, G. B. M. Beatson, manager of the Royal Exchange, Glasgow.

GABRIEL WOOD, father of the Admiral Wood who gave the money to build and endow the Sailor's Home at Greenock.

MAGISTRATES

AND

MERCHANTS OF PAISLEY.

JOHN BELL, merchant, Saccel.

ANDREW BROWN, merchant, New Street, commenced business in 1753. He married Mary, daughter of Nathaniel Forrester of Arngibbon, in Stirlingshire, and dyer in Paisley, and had a daughter, Jean, who married William Sharp. Mr. Brown assumed Mr. Sharp as his partner, and the firm in Paisley was then Brown & Sharp, gauze weavers. They had also a house in London; and Mr. Semple, in his interesting work "St. Mirren" (Paisley, 1872, p. 97), says of them :—" This is the oldest manufacturing firm " in Paisley; is still carrying on business, and had weathered all the " fluctuations that have occurred during the last 118 years."

JOHN CHRISTIE belonged to an Aberdeenshire family. Early in life he settled in Paisley, and was the founder of the firm of Christie, Corse & Co., leading merchants there in the Russian and Baltic trades. He introduced the manufacture of soap into Paisley in 1764, and he was one of the original partners in the Paisley Union Bank, and in every way a man of energy and public spirit.   He is well represented in Glasgow and the West of Scotland by his grandson, Thomas Craig Christie of Bedlay, &c.

ROBERT CORSE, of Greenlaw, Paisley, was a representative of the old family of Cross or Corse of Crossmill, in Renfrewshire. He was in partnership with John Christie, under the firm of Christie, Corse & Co., and was also a partner in the Paisley Union Bank.   He erected and resided in the fine suburban mansion of Greenlaw.   His sister married Mr. Kibble of Whiteford, near Paisley, and her family succeeded to Greenlaw, and were well-known calico printers in Glasgow some years ago.

ROBERT HUNTER, merchant, Causewayside.

GAVIN MAXWELL, of Westbrae, merchant, Townhead.

JOHN M'KERRELL was a member of an old Ayrshire family. He was some time partner with Humphray Fulton, whose daughter he married.   They had a son, Fulton M'Kerrell, who was a very well-known Paisley man fifty years ago.   He married Mary, daughter of James M'Call of Braehead, but left no male issue.

JOHN ORR, silk manufacturer, Great George Street.

WILLIAM ORR and WILLIAM ORR, Jun.—The Orrs were a very important family in Paisley last century, and a branch of them are represented in Glasgow by John and Robert Orr, the Orr Ewings, and others.

JAMES PAISLEY was a merchant near the Cross.

WILLIAM STUART, of Gryffe Castle, merchant in Paisley, was also a partner of Stuart, Locke & Co., cotton spinners, Arthurlie, a firm which came to a close in 1811. His grandson, Colonel William Stuart Beatson, fell at Lucknow, while serving as Adjutant to Havelock. His great-grandson, Colonel William Stuart Beatson, is an officer in the army, and at present in India.

WILLIAM WALLACE, silk manufacturer, New Sneddon.

JAMES WILSON, merchant, near the Cross.

JOHN WILSON, manufacturer in Paisley, married Margaret, daughter of Andrew Sym, merchant in Glasgow, and Grizel, eldest daughter of James Dunlop, fourth of Garnkirk. John Wilson had a large family, of whom the eldest was the late Professor John Wilson of Edinburgh—the "Christopher North" of *Blackwood's Magazine*.

NAMES OF SUBSCRIBERS.

No. OF COPIES.

a Alexander Allan, shipowner, 2 Park Gardens, ... 1

Mathew Anderson, secy., Chamber of Commerce, Ashbourne, Milliken Park, 1

William Rae Arthur, 1 Crown Gardens, Dowanhill, ... 1

William Auld, 4 Park Terrace, ... 1

James Aitken, Burton Hill, Helensburgh, . 1

John Affleck, Union Bank, ... 1

John Anderson, jun., 2 Park Circus, . 1

George Alexander, Dowanhill Gardens, . . . 1

William Boyd Anderson, 4 Grosvenor Crescent, . 1

John Alexander, Menstrie Bank, Dowanhill, . . 1

Edward Alexander, 13 Claremont Gardens, 1

M. C. Alston, Craighead, Bothwell, . . 1

Walter Alexander, 4 Burnbank Gardens, . 1

Cauvin S. Alston, Governor, Dundee Prison, . 1

F. W. Allan, The Manse, Cathcart, . . . 1

a Hugh Brown, 9 Claremont Gardens, . . 1

a Robert Balloch, Eamont Lodge, Dowanhill, . . . 1

a J. C. Bolton, M.P., of Carbrook, . . . 1

J. C. Bunten, 24 Park Circus, . 1

A. S. Baird, 26 Sardinia Terrace, . . . 1

George Brown, 149 West George Street, 1

Hugh Barnett, Elmwood, Crosshill, . . 1

Howard Bowser, 13 Royal Crescent, West, 1

George Breen, Italian Consul, ... 1

George Burns, Wemyss House, Wemyss Bay, 1

John Burnet, St. Kilda, Dowanhill Gardens, . . 1

		No. of Copies.
Robert Boyd, jun., 5 Hamilton Drive,		1
J. W. Burns, of Kilmahew, .		1
J. C. Burns, 1 Park Gardens,		1
James Bain, Bank of Scotland, ...		1
Colonel David Carrick Robert Carrick Buchanan, of Drumpellier,		1
Moses Buchanan, 5 Berlin Place, Pollokshields, ...		1
James Black, of Auchentoshen, ...		1
John Burns, surgeon, 15 Fitzroy Place, . . .		1
Thomas D. Buchanan, M.D., 24 Westminster Terrace,		1
J. Ritchie Brown, M.D., Saltcoats, . . .		1
Robert Binning, 8 Bowmont Gardens, W., .		1
a Michael Connal, Parkhall, Killermont, .		1
a James Campbell, of Tillichewan, .		1
a William Clark, Mile-End Factory,		1
a D. S. Cargill, 9 Park Terrace, . .		1
Peter Clouston, 1 Park Terrace, . .		1
J. A. Campbell, LL.D., M.P., of Stracathro,		2
William Connal, 19 Park Circus, . . .		1
Stewart Clark, Kilnside, Paisley, . .		1
A. P. Coubrough, Blancfield, Strathblane,		1
Thomas Craig Christie, of Bedlay, . .		1
Robert Carruth, Clydesdale Bank,		1
James Caldwell, 130 Elliot Street, . . .		1
J. M. Cunningham, 3 Crown Circus, Dowanhill,		1
David Croll, 114 Broomielaw, ...		1
W. B. Craig, 1 Westbourne Terrace, . .		1
John G. Couper, Holly Bush Villa, Langside, .		1
John Campbell, 14 Kelburn Terrace, . .		1
James Currie, 31 George IV. Bridge, Edinburgh,		2
J. N. Cuthbertson, 29 Bath Street, . .		1
James Clarkson, 55 Roselea Drive, Dennistoun,		1
James Cowan, 124 Renfield Street, . .		1
William Cairney, 11 Derby Terrace, ...		1
a W. J. Davidson, 32 Drumsheugh Gardens, Edinburgh, .		2
a James Dunlop, of Tollcross, ...		1
Wm. Denny, Bellfield, Dumbarton,		1

No. of Copies.

Andrew Dougans, Almond Bank, Bridge of Allan,	1
R. H. Dunn, 4 Bellmont Crescent,	1
George Duncan, 223 West George Street,	1
N. Dunlop, 1 Montgomerie Terrace, Kelvinside,	1
J. M. Dawson, Elcho House, Balfron,	1
Colin R. Dunlop, of Garnkirk,	1
Wm. Duncan, Coltness Iron Co.,	1
C. D. Donald, jun., 172 St. Vincent Street,	1
Franc G. Dougall, 10 Broompark Terrace,	1
Thomas Donald, 196 Bath Street,	1
Walter Easton, 32 Royal Exchange Square,	1
J. S. Fleming, 16 Grosvenor Crescent, Edinburgh,	1
Robert Fraser, 2 Crown Gardens, Dowanhill,	1
Daniel Frazer, 17 Grosvenor Terrace, Kelvinside,	2
John Fyfe, 9 do. do.	1
Matthew Fairley, 10 Woodlands Terrace,	1
James Fleming, 7 Fitzroy Place,	1
T. D. Findlay, of Easterhill,	1
a Charles Gairdner, Union Bank,	1
a Leonard Gow, Hayston, Kirkintilloch,	1
a J. H. N. Graham, Drums House, Langbank,	1
a David Guthrie, 9 Park Circus Place,	1
Bailie Goldie, Airdrie Cotton Works,	1
J. Wylie Guild, 17 Park Terrace,	1
Robert Gourlay, Bank of Scotland,	1
Thomas Grieve, 3 Kew Terrace,	1
James Galbraith, Beach House, Wemyss Bay,	1
Wm. Galbraith, 3 Blythswood Square,	1
Robert Gourlay, 1 Kirklee Avenue,	1
Wm. Geddes, Battlefield House, Langside,	1
Arch. Galbraith, Johnston Castle,	1
Allan Gilmour, 4 Park Gardens,	1
William Graham, Lambhill,	1
William Gardner, Anderston Grain Mills,	1
Gavin Greenlees, 25 Iona Place, Mount Florida,	1
William Gourlay, York House, Bridge-of-Allan,	1

No. of Copies.

a Anthony Hannay, 10 Claremont Gardens, .   .   1
a James Hannan, 17 Woodside Terrace, .   .   2
a Thomas Henderson, Minard Castle, .   .   2
A. F. Hamilton, 21 Lansdowne Crescent,   1
John Hunter, Burnfoot, Ayr,   .   .   .   1
W. H. Hill, Barlanark, . • .   .   .   1
Alex. Harvie, 16 Elmbank Crescent, .   1
Robert Hogg, 15 Cadogan Street,   1
D. G. Howat, Springfield Court,   .   1
James Heathcrill, Marylea, Bearsden, .   1
Robert Hutcheson, 21 Burnbank Gardens, .   1
G. W. Hill, Union Bank, ...   1
Albert Harvey, 16 Westbourne Gardens, .   1
James Hume, A. Paul & Co., Bridgeton,   1
John Ingram, 63 Ingram Street,   .   1
John Inglis, 115 Cannon Street, London,   1
Anthony Inglis, Broomhill, Partick, .   .   .   1
a J. L. K. Jamieson, 9 Crown Terrace, Dowanhill, .   .   .   1
Thomas Johnstone, The Crescent, Leslie Road, Pollokshields, .   1
Robert Jackson, 16 Royal Crescent, Crosshill,   .   .   .   1
John Jeffrey, Largo House, Largo,   .   .   1
a James King, Campsie, ...   5
G. M. Kerr, Clunaline, Lenzie, .   .   .   1
Charles M. King, Antrimony House, Campsie,   1
W. S. Kennedy, Allanbank, Crosshill,   .   1
John Kidston, Nym Park, Barnet, Hertz,   1
James Kirkland, Rosebank House, Lenzie,   1
Robert Ker, Dougalston,   .   .   .   1
William Ker, 1 Windsor Terrace,   1
Robert King, Levernholm,   .   .   1
Andrew King, Provost, Rutherglen, .   1
David Laidlaw, Chasely, Skelmorlie,   .   1
David W. Lindsay, Saracen Foundry, .   1
James Low, Lilly Bank, Lenzie, .   .   .   1
William Lyle, 3 Roslea Drive, Dennistoun,   1
a Stephen Mason, 24 Belhaven Terrace, .   1

a John M'Gavin, 19 Elmbank Place,   .   . 2
a A. H. Maclean, 13 Grosvenor Terrace,   .   1
a W. H. Minnoch, 6 Woodside Crescent, .   2
a John M'Laren, 5 Belhaven Terrace, ... 1
a William M'Ewen, 11 Park Terrace, president of Chamber of Commerce,   1
   James Miller, 21 Woodside Place, ... 1
   Alex. Moffatt, Henderson Brothers, "Anchor Line,"   1
   John M'Lennan, Parliamentary Sale Office, London, .   1
   P. C. Macgregor, Breadiland, Paisley, .   .   .   1
   A. B. M'Grigor, LL.D., 19 Woodside Terrace, .   1
   G. B. Motherwell, Arranview, Airdrie, .   .   1
   William Mitchell, 18 Kew Terrace, .   1
   John Miller, Northbank, Dowanhill, .   .   1
   M. M. Moore, 10 Bothwell Street, .   1
   R. C. Maclaurin, Dunedin Lodge, Lenzie, .   1
   George Munsie, 1 St. John Terrace, Hillhead, .   1
   Francis Murray, Monkland House, .   .   . 1
   D. T. Maclay, 3 Woodlands Terrace, .   .   1
   David M'Brayne, jun., Lilly Bank House, Hillhead, .   . 1
   George M'Callum, Rosebank, Cambuslang, .   1
   Walter M'Farlane, Saracen Foundry, .   .   . 1
   T. A. Matheson, 3 Grosvenor Terrace, .   .   1
   Robert M'Brayne, 4 Lilly Bank Terrace, Hillhead,   . 1
   Kenneth M'K. M'Leod, Sanitary Chambers, .   1
   James Miller, Port-Dundas Pottery, .   . 1
   James Maclehose, 61 St. Vincent Street, .   2
   William Murdoch, 9 Newton Place, .   2
   John M'Ewen, Glenlora, Lochwinnoch,   1
   James M'Tear, 16 Burnbank Gardens, ...   2
   Thomas Marr, Scottish Amicable Life Assurance Society, .   1
   John Matheson, East Field, Rutherglen, .   .   .   1
   A. Maxwell, 8 St. James' Terrace, .   .   1
   Andrew M'Clelland, 4 Crown Gardens, .   1
   James Morton, ex-Provost, Greenock,   1
   Mitchell Library, Ingram Street, .   .   1
   John Moncur, 9 Bellgrove Street, .   1

No. of Copies

	No. of Copies
David Murray, Moore Park, Cardross, .	1
J. O. Mitchell, 7 Huntly Gardens, .	1
Archibald Melville, Grahamston, Falkirk,	1
John M'Lellan, 12 Newton Place, . .	1
Robert Murdoch, 23 Robertson Street, .	1
David M'Cowan, 7 Lynedoch Crescent, .	1
J. B. Murdoch, Hamilton Place, Langside,	1
Donald Matheson, Park Terrace, . .	1
James M'Call, wine merchant, . . .	1
Walter Neilson, Kenmuir House, Bishopbriggs, .	1
William Nowery, 64 Warroch Street, Anderston, . . .	1
J. Stewart Nairn, M.D., Crosshill, ...	1
Richard Owen, Parliamentary Sale Office, 13 Gt. Queen Street, London,	1
W. E. Outram, 16 Grosvenor Terrace, Hillhead, ...	1
Robert Orr, Wallside, Falkirk, . . .	1
Mrs. Patrick Playfair, 12 Woodside Place, . .	1
James Paterson, 307 Broad Street, Mile-End, ·	1
James Park, 14 South Park Terrace, Hillhead, .	1
Robert Pirrie, 9 Buckingham Terrace, . . .	1
Robert M. Proctor, 34 Hamilton Street, Greenock,	1
Walter O. Pagan, Birnam Terrace, Crosshill, .	1
Walter Paterson, 8 Claremont Gardens, . . .	1
P. Sandeman Peat, 8 Kelvin Drive, Kelvinside,	1
a M. E. Robinow, 6 Park Circus, ...	3
a John Ramsay, M.P., of Kildalton, .	1
James Roberton, LL.D., 1 Park Terrace, . .	1
Robert Raphael, 26 St. James' Terrace, Hillhead, .	1
Jacques Van Raalte, Netherlands Consul, . .	1
John Roxburgh, 15 Lynedoch Crescent, .	1
J. G. Rodger, 1 College Lawn, Cheltenham, .	1
Thomas Reid, Kilmardinny, . .	1
George Readman, Clydesdale Bank, . .	1
James Robertson, Northwood, Helensburgh, .	1
David Ritchie, Hopeville, Dowanhill Gardens, .	1
G. F. Ross, 29 Huntly Gardens, ...	1
W. A. Robertson, Dunard House, Dowanhill,	2

No. of Copies.

		No. of Copies.
	Andrew Rintoul, Burnbank, Helensburgh, .	1
	A. D. Rutherfurd, 9 Princes Terrace, Dowanhill,	1
	Alex. Ralston, Rockford, Illinois, U.S., . .	1
a	David Sandeman, Woodlands, Lenzie, .	1
	A. Sutherland, Cleddans House, by Airdrie, .	2
	Boswell Sandeman, Ferndean, Lenzie, .	1
	James Hay Stuart, Commercial Bank, .	1
	Richard Sandeman, Blair Cottage, Lenzie, .	1
	Hugh Steven, Milton Iron Works, . . .	1
	James Stirling, Rockend House, Helensburgh, .	1
	Robert Smith, Brentham Park, Stirling, . .	1
	John Speirs, 1 Royal Exchange Buildings, .	1
	J. Guthrie Smith, Mugdock Castle, .	1
	J. B. Sheriff, Carronvale, Larbert,	1
	Moses Smith, 49 Cochrane Street, .	1
	A. M. Scott, Kerland, Crosshill,	1
	James Stewart, 41 Oswald Street, . . .	1
	Alexander Sinclair, Ajmere Lodge, Langside,	1
	J. R. Stewart, 19 Park Terrace, . . .	1
	Archibald Sandeman, 7 Queen's Crescent, .	1
	James Salmon, 197 St. Vincent Street, . .	1
	Thomas Stout, 178 St. Vincent Street, . . .	1
	David Sinclair, Brachead, Nithsdale Road, Pollokshields,	1
	J. G. Sandeman, Ardmay House, Arrochar, . .	1
a	Charles Tennant, M.P., of the Glen, ...	5
	James Tennant, St. Nicholas Buildings, Newcastle-on-Tyne,	1
	James Templeton, 7 Woodside Crescent, . . .	1
	John Turnbull, Place of Bonhill, Renton, .	1
	William Tennant, 9 Mincing Lane, London, .	1
	Henry Todd, Stapleford, Pollokshields, .	2
	George Thomson, 18 Woodlands Terrace,	1
	Hugh Turner, Hazlewood, Bridge-of-Weir, . .	1
	James Templeton, jun., 7 Woodside Crescent,	1
	J. S. Templeton, 1 Park Circus, . .	1
	John Ure, Lord Provost of Glasgow,	1
	William Ure, 21 Whitevale Street,	1

No. of Copies.

a James White, of Overtoun, Dumbarton, .   1
a Sir James Watson, 9 Woodside Terrace, .   1
   J. A. Wenley, Drumsheugh Gardens, Edinburgh, .   1
   John Wilkie, 2 Lynedoch Place, . . .   1
   Alex. Whitelaw, Drumhead, Cardross, . .   1
   W. B. Watson, Bernard Street Mills, . . .   1
   J. B. Wingate, 7 Crown Terrace, Dowanhill, .   1
   Hugh Wright, 6 Grafton Place, . . .   2
   T. Williamson, 4 Woodlands Terrace, . . .   1
   William Wilson, 9 Kelvin Drive Terrace, Hillhead, .   1
   John Wilson, Aucheneck, by Drymen, . . .   1
   Alex. Waddel, 37 Monteith Row, .   1
   Alex. Wylie, Dalquhurn, Renton, .   1
   John Wordie, 49 West Nile Street, . .   1
   R. B. Watson, 48 Castle Street, Liverpool, .   1
   George Williamson, 2 Bank Street, Greenock, .   1
   Robert Wylie, 45 Buchanan Street, . .   2
   W. W. Watson, City Chamberlain, . .   1
a Robert Young, 11 Great Western Terrace,   1
a George Younger, 10 Lynedoch Crescent, .   1
   James Young, 11 Newton Terrace, ...   1
   John Young, M.D., Professor of Natural History, Glasgow University,   1

INDEX.

ERRATA.

Page 21, Line 12.—For " Dugaldson," *read* " Dougalston."

" 144, " 5.— " " liberty," *read* " ability."

" 188, " 27.—Delete " bookseller and publisher."

" 193, " 10.—For " Crawford," *read* " Crauford."

" 193, " 21.— " " Crawford," *read* " Craufurd."

" 196, " 9.— " " Auchincruive," *read* " Scotstoun."

" 202, " 6.— " " Greenock," *read* " Port-Glasgow."

" 239, " 16.— " " and died," *read* " who died."

" 256, " 12.— " " Parkhall, Killermont," *read* " Parkhall, Killearn."

No. of Copies.

a James White, of Overtoun, Dumbarton, .   1

a Sir James Watson, 9 Woodside Terrace,   1

J. A. Wenley, Drumsheugh Gardens, Edinburgh, .   1

John Wilkie, 2 Lynedoch Place,   1

Alex. Whitelaw, Drumhead, Cardross, .   1

W. B. Watson, Bernard Street Mills, .   1

J. B. Wingate, 7 Crown Terrace, Dowanhill, .   1

Hugh Wright, 6 Grafton Place, .   2

T. Williamson, 4 Woodlands Terrace, .   1

William Wilson, 9 Kelvin Drive Terrace, Hillhead, .   1

John Wilson, Aucheneck, by Drymen, .   1

INDEX.